TEA-TOTALLY DEAD

Jaqueline Girdner

BERKLEY PRIME CRIME, NEW YORK

TEA-TOTALLY DEAD

A Berkley Prime Crime Book / published by arrangement with the author

PRINTING HISTORY
Berkley Prime Crime edition / April 1994

ISBN: 0-425-14210-8

Berkley Prime Crime Books
are published by The Berkley Publishing Group,
200 Madison Avenue, New York, New York 10016.
The name BERKLEY PRIME CRIME and the BERKLEY PRIME CRIME
design are trademarks belonging to Berkley Publishing Corporation.

PRINTED IN THE UNITED STATES OF AMERICA

10 9 8 7 6 5 4 3

MORE MYSTERIES FROM THE
BERKLEY PUBLISHING GROUP...

JENNY McKAY MYSTERIES: This TV reporter finds out where, when, why...*and* whodunit. "A more streetwise version of television's 'Murphy Brown.'" —*Booklist*

by Dick Belsky
BROADCAST CLUES   LIVE FROM NEW YORK
THE MOURNING SHOW

CAT CALIBAN MYSTERIES: She was married for thirty-eight years. Raised three kids. Compared to that, tracking down killers is easy...

by D.B. Borton
ONE FOR THE MONEY   TWO POINTS FOR MURDER

KATE JASPER MYSTERIES: Even in sunny California, there are cold-blooded killers..."This series is a treasure!" —Carolyn G. Hart

by Jaqueline Girdner
ADJUSTED TO DEATH   MURDER MOST MELLOW
THE LAST RESORT   FAT-FREE AND FATAL
TEA-TOTALLY DEAD

FREDDIE O'NEAL, P.I., MYSTERIES: You can bet that this appealing Reno P.I. will get her man... "A winner." —Linda Grant

by Catherine Dain
LAY IT ON THE LINE   SING A SONG OF DEATH
WALK A CROOKED MILE

CALEY BURKE, P.I., MYSTERIES: This California private investigator has a brand-new license, a gun in her purse, and a knack for solving even the trickiest cases!

by Bridget McKenna
MURDER BEACH   DEAD AHEAD

CHINA BAYLES MYSTERIES: She left the big city to run an herb shop in Pecan Springs, Texas. But murder can happen anywhere... "A wonderful character!" —*Mostly Murder*

by Susan Wittig Albert
THYME OF DEATH

LIZ WAREHAM MYSTERIES: In the world of public relations, crime can be a real career-killer... "Readers will enjoy feisty Liz!"
—*Publishers Weekly*

by Carol Brennan
HEADHUNT

For my mother-in-law,
Eileen Booi,
who I am happy to say
bears no resemblance to Vesta Caruso.

ACKNOWLEDGMENT

I'd like to thank Gary Erickson of the Marin County Coroner's Office for his good-natured answers to my gruesome questions. Any gruesome mistakes, however, are strictly my own.

CAST OF CHARACTERS

KATE JASPER: Marin County's own, organically grown, accidental sleuth. She owns Jest Gifts, a gag gift company.

WAYNE CARUSO: Kate's lover. The shy restaurateur is a former bodyguard, but can he guard his own heart from his mother's merciless jabs?

VESTA CARUSO: Wayne's mother. After more than twenty years of incarceration and over-medication, she was released from Shady Willows Mental Health Facility. Now she's high on accumulated rage.

HARMONY FITCH: Vesta's new friend. She's moved out of her car and into Vesta's condo, where it's safe. The aliens can't get her there.

ACE SKERITT: Vesta's little brother, a former professional wrestler. Are his warm and winning ways as phony as his trick falls?

ERIC SKERITT: Ace's grandson. He's thirteen and he knows *everything*. But does he know who the murderer is?

TRENT SKERITT: Older brother to Ace and Vesta. He's the respected dean of Fulton College. And he's as cool as Ace is warm, at least on the surface.

INGRID SKERITT: Trent's wife. She looks like Barbara Bush, but the former First Lady never cried this much.

LORI OLIVER: Trent and Ingrid's daughter, a masseuse with long, red fingernails and a penchant for New Age seminars.

MANDY OLIVER: Lori's daughter, a twelve-year-old artist and vegetarian. Does she like animals better than people?

DRUSILLA NORTON: Just call her Dru. The youngest of the Skeritt elders, her bubbly personality seems to be going flat.

GAIL NORTON: Dru's daughter, a morose psychotherapist. Her father committed suicide.

BILL NORTON: Dru's second husband and stepfather to Gail, a quiet man . . . far too quiet.

CLARA KUSHIYAMA: Vesta Caruso's part-time nurse. She survived an internment camp in World War II, but may not survive her involvement with Vesta.

PAUL PAULSON: Vesta's nosy neighbor. He'd love to sell you some predeveloped real estate.

DETECTIVE SERGEANT UPTON, DETECTIVE AMADOR, OFFICERS YODER, ZAPPETINI AND LEE: Members of the La Risa Police Department.

JENNY QUINTARA: Investigator for the Marin County Coroner's Office.

JUDY MULLIGAN: Kate's warehousewoman. She has a problem.

BARBARA CHU: Kate's best friend. Barbara is a psychic, but is she intuitive enough to spot a murderer?

FELIX BYRNE: Barbara's lover, a newspaper reporter and major pest.

Assorted Police Personnel, Waitresses, Waiters and Mourners.

– One –

"You just don't understand," Wayne told me.

He kept his hands clamped on the wheel of his Jaguar and his eyes clamped on the road ahead of him, the road that was taking us north to La Risa, where Wayne's mother was living in the condo he had bought for her. We whizzed by a Safeway truck.

"But—" I tried.

"You can't understand," he explained impatiently. "It's not just Mom. It's her *and* her whole family. *My* whole family! They're not like normal families—"

"Are you scared?" I interrupted.

He turned to me, quiet for a moment. I looked into his face, a battered face dominated by a large, cauliflower nose and heavy brows that were presently lowered like curtains to shield his vulnerable brown eyes. God, I had learned to love that face.

"Scared to death," he answered softly, then turned his half-hidden eyes back to the road.

I should have figured it out sooner. Wayne was babbling. And Wayne had never babbled. Not in all the time I'd known him. When I'd first met him four years ago, he'd been shy and silent. Then he'd progressed to monosyllables. And eventually to actual speech. But never babbling. On the other hand, he hadn't faced the third day running of his family reunion before either.

"It won't be that bad," I told him. I reached a hand over to squeeze his well-muscled thigh. I wished I could give him a good hug, maybe hold him in my arms, but that wasn't a good idea while he was switching lanes. And babbling.

"It *is* that bad, Kate," he insisted, his usual baritone growl thinned by tension into an unnatural soprano. "You haven't been there. . . ."

I squirmed guiltily inside my seat belt as Wayne went on. I had excused myself from the first two days of the reunion on the grounds of work. I really did have work to do. It was October, time for Jest Gifts to gear up for Christmas. Past time. I had designed new ornaments for all the legal specialties this year. So, while I had pored over mail orders, inventory lists and production schedules for items like Santas in gilded cages (for the criminal attorneys) and red-nosed reindeer in leg casts (for the personal injury specialists), Wayne had spent the last two days with his family, neglecting his own duties as owner and manager of a string of restaurants and art galleries that he had inherited from a man whose body he used to guard.

Now it was Friday evening. It was my turn to meet the Skeritt clan for a buffet dinner at Vesta's. At least they weren't coming to our house.

". . . not to mention Uncle Trent's wife and daughter and granddaughter," Wayne was saying. "And Uncle Ace's grandson. And Aunt Dru and her daughter and husband—"

"I'm sorry. I missed some of that last bit," I said. "So tell me again," I prodded. "These are all your mother's side of the family—"

"I don't have a father's side of the family," he interrupted gloomily, then pressed his lips back together. His face in profile was unmoving, carved rock. But the tendons in his neck were alive and bulging with feeling. Even the veins in his arms seemed to throb.

And that was the second time Wayne had interrupted me. He didn't usually do that either. Or indulge in blatant self-pity. Guilt yes, self-pity no. Until now. Not that I blamed him. He was right, he didn't have a father's side of the family. He was an illegitimate child. His mother had been born Vesta Skeritt. She had only been a teenager some forty-three years ago when she gave birth to Wayne, listing the long-dead Enrico Caruso as the father of her baby and calling herself Mrs. Caruso. Wayne's real father had never been mentioned.

I squeezed his thigh again sympathetically. Even his thigh muscles were tensed to rock hardness.

"So, your mother has a sister and two brothers?" I prompted in a voice of forced cheer, hoping to jump-start Wayne again. Watching his veins throb in silence was even worse than listening to him babble.

"She has three sisters," Wayne answered dully. "Aunt Dru, she's the one you'll be meeting tonight. Then there's Aunt Nola, the one who couldn't come to the reunion because she's at a halfway house. She's an alcoholic." He let out a long sigh that ended in a high, keening note. Did he even know he had made the sound? "And Aunt Camille. She's the well-adjusted one. But of course, *she's* not coming."

I nodded. He swiveled his head around on his shoulders as he zoomed past a gold BMW. The exercise did nothing to loosen the bulging tendons in his neck. Maybe I could talk him into a professional massage after dinner tonight.

"Two brothers," he continued. "Uncle Trent, he's the dean of Fulton College now. He helped us out financially when I was growing up. But I just never could bring myself to . . . to . . ."

"To like him?" I guessed. I was good at charades too.

"Yeah, that's right. Now with Uncle Ace, it's always been different," Wayne's face softened for a moment. "He was as close to a father as I had growing up. He took me camping, took me to the park and the zoo. Got me interested in weight-lifting. All kinds of stuff. And Aunt Ellen, his wife. She was a sweet-natured woman. She died about fifteen years back, some kind of cancer. It was real hard on Uncle Ace." The softness had left Wayne's face. It was carved in rock again.

I wondered what was in his mind. Was he mourning for his Aunt Ellen? Or was he remembering his childhood days when Ace hadn't been there, Vesta's "bad days" when she had beat and humiliated Wayne for a series of transgressions he had never understood?

"Ace was a professional wrestler, you know," Wayne added in a monotone.

I knew. Wayne had told me no less than four times in the

last half hour. He really was rattled. What was going on at this reunion, anyway?

"Wayne?" I said tentatively.

I wasn't sure if he heard me. He let out another sigh. This one ended in a groan.

"Sweetie, what's wrong?" I asked finally.

Wayne was silent for a few heartbeats. When he answered, it was in a whisper.

"Mom's pretty angry about Shady Willows," he said. Then he rolled his shoulders a couple of times and stepped down on the gas to pull around a Volkswagen Rabbit.

"Oh," I said softly.

Now that I knew what was bothering him, I wasn't sure what I could say to him to make it better. What can you say about a mistake that was made over twenty years ago? If indeed it had been a mistake. All I knew was what Wayne had told me, his evidence dredged from his own guilt-tinged memories. That Vesta hadn't been able to cope when Wayne had left home for college at eighteen. That she had made a series of frantic phone calls, twice swallowed too many sleeping pills and finally, just about the time that Wayne was sitting down to his first midterm exam, she had gone in early to the bar where she waited tables and very calmly slit her wrists. After that, Vesta Caruso had been declared incompetent and had been committed to the Shady Willows Mental Health Facility, where she had sat drooling in front of the TV in the day room for the next twenty years or so.

Wayne's mother might still have been at Shady Willows, but a year or two ago a nosy social worker had figured out that Vesta was over-medicated. Relying on the social worker's recommendation, the hospital staff had reluctantly cut Vesta's daily dose of downers in half. Bingo! Vesta wasn't drooling anymore. She was talking. And she was angry. And Wayne felt guiltier than ever, blaming himself for not realizing that Vesta's condition had been caused by her medication. Not that there was any way he could have known.

The brief three months Vesta had subsequently spent living with Wayne and me must have been a relatively minor version of hell for us compared to what Vesta had endured at

Shady Willows, but I still don't care to repeat the experience. Ever. My own neck was tense now. My whole body was tense. I took a deep breath. She wasn't living with us anymore, I reminded myself. She had her own condo, paid for by her loving son. I took another breath.

"Don't let her manipulate you too much," I said gently into the silence.

Wayne sighed once more. "I know my mother manipulates me," he replied impatiently. Then he softened his tone. "I know it intellectually, but emotionally . . ." He shook his head. "I just want to make her happy, Kate. At least for a couple more days. It's her birthday tomorrow."

"You already got her the present she wanted," I grumbled. Was it jealousy that ignited my outrage over the poor little minks who had given their lives so that Vesta could have a fur coat? It was certainly too late for the minks' sakes. The coat was already sitting in a box in our living room, tied up in a great big pink bow.

"I can't expect you to like Mom, not after what she did to you," Wayne commented quietly. "After she tried so hard to split us up." He turned to me, and I glimpsed a plea in what I could see of his eyes. "But just for a few days, Kate, could you . . . well, pretend?"

I gulped down my own sigh. I was a big girl, more than forty years old now. I ought to be able to handle the assignment.

"I'll do my best," I said brightly.

Five long, silent minutes later, Wayne pulled his Jaguar up to the curb in front of La Risa Green, the condominium complex where Vesta lived. *And*, I suddenly remembered, where Vesta's new friend and whipping girl, Harmony Fitch, lived. Harmony was a leftover from the sixties who was currently "crashing" in Vesta's spare room. She and Vesta had a lot in common, including large, unhealthy doses of paranoia and a fondness for smoking dope and plotting revenge.

As we walked up the well-groomed path to Vesta's ground-floor unit, I asked Wayne if Harmony was going to be there.

"Yeah, she is," he replied grimly. The muscles in his jaw

tightened visibly. I could just imagine how the Skeritts were getting along with Harmony. I wondered if she had told them about the UFO's yet.

Wayne gave me one last chance at Vesta's front door.

"Don't have to come in if you don't want to," he offered brusquely.

"I wouldn't miss it for all the Perrier in Marin County," I replied, and pasted on what I hoped looked like a cheery smile.

"Thank you," he whispered. He bent down and kissed my smiling lips gently. I pulled him closer and the kiss heated up, melting all the resentment in my body to a small pool of lust. "I love you, Kate," he growled.

"I know," I told him huskily. "I just remembered."

Then I turned and rang the doorbell before I could change my mind and run home.

Somehow, I hadn't expected a pair of white-faced clowns to open the door. Especially clowns with weapons. The first clown had huge, sad eyes and carried an upraised, wooden baseball bat. The second one had a large red happy smile and held what looked like a space gun, or maybe a space Uzi. The gun's arm-length barrel was opaque white plastic, its trigger and butt a transparent fluorescent yellow, and on top of the whole thing was a foot and a half long, lime-green object shaped like a plump hot dog.

"Stick 'em up," the happy clown said and raised the space gun to aim the white plastic barrel at the center of my forehead.

- Two -

I STIFFENED, THEN relaxed. The white clown faces were only painted masks. And I knew who the two clowns were that wore them. I recognized the happy one by the cackles coming from behind her mask and the black, Addams family–style dress that clothed her skinny body. That had to be Vesta. The sad clown to her right was wearing a leather jacket with handfuls of tiny crystals and crosses woven into the fringe. I would have known this was Harmony even if I hadn't spotted the jacket she always had on. Her scent, made up of leather, perspiration, patchouli oil and dope, was unmistakable.

"All right, you guys—" I began.

The happy clown pulled the trigger on the space gun.

A shock of cold water hit my face. I raised my hand to block the spray just as it dribbled to an end.

"Mom, stop that!" Wayne ordered as I sputtered. He snatched the space gun from Vesta's hand before I had a chance to. Unfortunately, he didn't squirt her back. I took a deep breath, trying to slow my racing pulse.

The sad clown put down her baseball bat and handed me a towel that had been tucked into the pocket of her leather jacket. I wiped my face, glad I hadn't had time to put on makeup this evening, glad that my short dark curls were waterproof by nature. But my ears were still ringing with the adrenaline the spray of cold water had called up.

"Trick or treat!" Vesta and Harmony called in unison as they pulled off their masks. They should have left them on, I thought peevishly.

Vesta was a tall, bone-thin woman with long, dyed black hair and a pair of navy blue eyes set under low, heavy brows not unlike Wayne's. Only the brows looked better on him. Of course, I might have been the tiniest bit prejudiced. I glared at Vesta without speaking.

She drew her thin lips back from her teeth in a malevolent smile. Somehow I didn't think I was going to learn to appreciate Wayne's mother. Not in this lifetime anyway. Pretend, I reminded myself. Pretend this was just a friendly little prank.

I took one last swipe at my face and handed the damp towel back to Harmony. I still couldn't trust myself to speak.

"That was really cool!" Harmony shrilled. Then she laughed.

A shiver tugged at my shoulders. Harmony's laugh was always a little out of sync. It sounded stretched and distorted in spots, like a tape that had been left out in the sun.

Harmony looked like she had been left in the sun too. Maybe for her entire forty or fifty years. Her skin was a leathery tan, her hair a blond bush of frizz and her eyes a pale, bleached blue. She fingered the crosses and crystals hanging around her neck, her expression going blank when no one shared her laughter.

"Mom," began Wayne, setting the space gun carefully on the floor. "Why do you do these—"

"Oh, Waynie, my heart condition," Vesta cut in, the smile leaving her face. She clutched a hand to her chest and stared wide-eyed at Wayne.

Did she really think Wayne was going to fall for that old trick again? After all the times he had hauled her down to the doctor just to be told that her only heart condition was good to excellent? I smiled smugly. Then I noticed Wayne wasn't talking. I glanced up at his face. It was stricken. He had fallen for it. I felt the heat of anger flush my cheeks.

I grabbed Wayne's shoulder and shook it hard. After a couple of seconds he came out of it.

"Mom, I'm serious—" he began again.

"Hooboy, Wayne," interrupted a deep voice from behind Vesta. "Some trick or treat, huh? More like a *trigger* treat, if you ask me."

Vesta giggled at the pun and stepped away from the

doorway, revealing a heavily muscled, balding man who was at least as tall as Wayne, maybe even taller. And Wayne was well over six feet. The man's face looked like Wayne's too, with its large nose and heavy low brows. His eyes were navy blue, though, like Vesta's.

"Uncle Ace?" I guessed.

The man grinned, his homely face suddenly rendered comical. He stuck his hands into the air.

"I surrender," he growled. "You got me dead to rights, ma'am."

Then he stepped forward, bowed and grabbed my hand, pulling it up to meet his lips before I could resist. "Surrendering to you could only be a pleasure," he added and kissed my hand a second time.

I found it a strangely erotic gesture, especially coming from a man who looked like Wayne, only fifteen years or so older. I snatched my hand back, uncomfortable with the thoughts Ace's kiss had aroused.

"Uncle Ace, this is Kate Jasper," Wayne introduced belatedly.

"Yow! *The* Kate Jasper?" Ace said, stepping back in mock astonishment.

This time I smiled, thinking he'd probably keep on clowning until I did. "That's me," I replied.

"Well, come on in," he invited. He turned to the side and bowed again, sweeping his arm in a grand gesture toward Vesta's living room.

I took a quick glance up at Wayne's face. He was watching Ace with a shy, tentative smile that caught at my heart with its vulnerability. I grabbed his hand and pulled him past Harmony, who still stood in the doorway. I barely had time to glance at the roomful of tall strangers who filled Vesta's living room when Vesta herself reappeared. At least her space gun and mask were gone.

"So, now you've met Wayne's live-in girlfriend," she said to Ace, with a sneering emphasis on "live-in." "What do you think?"

I reminded myself to stay cool. Pretend to like Vesta, I thought. At least she hadn't called me "the adulteress," her usual term of affection for me. Or maybe it was disaffection.

Ace put his arm around Vesta's bony shoulders.

"She's a beauty," he said with a nod in my direction. Vesta's brows dropped into a frown. "But there's no one as beautiful as my Vessie," he added quickly. So, I thought, Ace was smart as well as funny.

Vesta laughed. "Ace, you'd say good morning to the devil if—"

"Aunt Vesta, you know what?" interrupted a tall, chubby young man walking toward us. His voice was high and insistent. "You don't say 'trick or treat' if you're the one opening the door."

I took a closer look and saw that he was more of a boy than a young man. It was his height that had fooled me. But the face on top of that tall body was soft and round with youth. The boy's blue eyes blinked anxiously through his thick wire-rimmed glasses.

"That's totally bogus," he went on. "You only say 'trick or treat' if you're the visitor—"

"This is my grandson, Eric Skeritt," Ace said, putting a hand on the boy's shoulder. The hand didn't seem to restrain the boy any.

"And anyhow, it isn't Halloween yet, you know," he went on. "And you know what else . . . ?"

"Eric is thirteen," Ace whispered over his grandson's lecture on Halloween. Then he rolled his eyes. A quick snort of laughter escaped me before I could cover my mouth.

I averted my eyes, glancing around the living room as Vesta snapped back at Eric. Her condo was efficiently arranged, with a large living room and kitchen downstairs and the bedroom area upstairs. The beige-and-white living room was filled with black leather chairs and sofas and glass-topped black-lacquered tables. But I was more interested in the members of the Skeritt clan, who stood around talking in small groups. I felt like I'd wandered into the land of the giants. Everyone in the room looked taller than me, including the other child present. But then, I am shorter than most, not to mention dark and A-line in figure. I turned back to Eric.

"So it's really totally bogus, you know—" he was saying.

"I heard a joke on the radio the other day," Vesta cut in. "Hire a high-school kid quick . . . before they forget they know everything." She let out a loud hoot of laughter.

Ace laughed with her. It was really pretty funny. Too bad the joke was at Eric's expense.

Eric drew himself up to stand on his tiptoes. "I am not in high school," he corrected her. "I'm in middle school."

It was nice to see Vesta with a friend in her own mental age group. Thirteen-year-old Eric was a good sparring partner for her.

"It's just like Christmas trees, you know," he plowed on. "They're totally bogus. They don't have anything to do with Christianity. . . ."

"Wanna meet some of the other inmates?" Ace whispered in my ear.

I nodded gratefully.

Ace put a meaty hand on my shoulder and guided me away from Vesta and Eric. I snuck a backward glance at Wayne, left behind with them, and saw with relief that his stricken expression had completely disappeared. He actually looked amused now as he listened to Eric lecture.

"My big brother, Trent Skeritt," Ace announced.

I swiveled my head back around in time to smile at the man Ace was introducing. Trent Skeritt returned my smile. At least I thought his was a smile. His teeth were showing. But somehow he didn't radiate the warmth that usually goes with the expression. Suddenly, my own smile felt stiff on my face.

"So glad to meet you, Mrs. Jasper," he said in a deep, sonorous voice. He stuck out his hand to shake mine.

His hand was cool, his grip firm but not too tight. I would have bet that Trent Skeritt did a lot of professional handshaking. He was a distinguished-looking man, as tall as the rest of the Skeritts but slimmer than Ace and Wayne, and less muscular. He had the heavy Skeritt brow too, over cool brown eyes, but the brow looked noble on him, aristocratic. Maybe it was his styled, silver hair. Or possibly the way he held his trim body erect.

"Please, call me Kate," I said, a beat too late to sound natural.

He nodded. "And please, call me Trent," he replied smoothly. He turned to the large white-haired woman, who stood behind him. "This is my wife, Ingrid," he said.

"So happy to meet Wayne's fiancée." Ingrid's greeting came out in a surprisingly resonant whisper.

She took my left hand in both of her moist ones and squeezed.

"Great to meet you too," I claimed inadequately, squeezing back as well as I could with one hand.

I smiled inanely and wondered who had told Ingrid that I was Wayne's "fiancée." Would Wayne have used the word? He of all people knew we had no wedding plans.

I squinted at Ingrid's face, noticing something familiar about her. She had a handsome face, blessed by good bones and friendly blue eyes. Barbara Bush, I realized—that was it. Ingrid looked like the former First Lady. And the superficial resemblance was strengthened by the similarity in the styling of Ingrid's white hair. And by the three strings of pearls she wore around her neck. Was she imitating the former President's wife on purpose?

"Lori," Trent called out. His voice wasn't loud, but there was a command implicit in its tone.

Ingrid dropped my hand gently and turned.

I followed her glance and saw a woman who might have been my age and a girl who looked about twelve or so sitting on a black leather couch across the room. The woman stood and waved. She was tall, probably close to six feet, with brown eyes and a long blond braid down her back. The girl stood too. Her movements resembled the woman's, but she had dark skin and features that proudly declared her African ancestry. The tall woman grinned at us and strode our way, her bracelets jangling as she approached. I could smell her perfume when she got within a yard of us. It was sweet and spicy. And strong. The girl followed along behind her.

"My daughter, Lori—" Trent began.

I missed the rest of his introduction as Lori enveloped me in a great big fragrant hug. Oh well, I thought, this was Marin after all, home of the hug as the correct gesture of greeting. Even for strangers.

"Are you Kate?" she demanded as she released me, the volume of her demand tempered by the welcoming grin on her face.

I opened my mouth to answer, but I wasn't fast enough.

"Wayne's told us all about you," she enthused, giving me less than an instant to wonder just what Wayne had told them. "Oh, I can see why he's in love with you. You have such a wonderful energy! And your aura." She closed her eyes for a minute. "Let me see," she commanded, putting her hands on my shoulders.

I took a closer look at Lori's face while she took a closer look at my aura. I could see a modified version of the Skeritt brow there. And the good bone structure from her mother. She was wearing a long, rainbow-striped woven top over an orange turtleneck and orange stirrup pants. Orange-and-turquoise beaded earrings quivered in her ears.

"Purple," she announced, opening her eyes. "Purple with hints of aqua and jade. Very higher-chakra. I'm impressed."

"Uh, thanks—" I began.

"Wayne says you own your own business. That takes a lot of juice, a lot of personal power. I really admire that. It's so . . . so . . ." She waved a hand in the air, jangling her bracelets and coming uncomfortably close to my face with her long red fingernails. "So vibrationally intense," she concluded. She looked down into my eyes expectantly.

"Do you own your own business?" I asked, feeling like a nosy insurance salesman. I really need to polish my social skills some day.

"I do massage," she answered, with another wave of her long fingernails.

"Oh," I said, wincing inwardly. "That's great." I could just imagine what a massage would feel like with those nails. Ouch.

"I'm really a healer on a more subtle level, of course. Mind, body, spirit. And the emotional body, of course. I've studied Chi-Lei Jung energy massage and holotrotpic breath work. And neuro-linguistic programming—"

"Grandpa says Mom should have a Ph.D. in New Age by now," commented the dark-skinned girl. Hers would have been a credible Tallulah Bankhead drawl except for the higher pitch of her voice. Her white teeth flashed in a quick grin.

Lori threw her head back and laughed, jangling her bracelets as she did.

"Oh, sweetie—" she began, reaching for her daughter.

"I'm Mandy Oliver," the girl interrupted. She jerked her head up at Lori. "Mom almost never remembers to tell people who I am." Her drawl sounded more affectionate than angry, though.

"Glad to meet you, Mandy," I said. And I was.

She was a pretty girl, already an inch or two taller than me. She had flawless taupe skin, a full mouth and her mother and grandmother's good bone structure. Her hair was pulled back into a shorter, more textured version of Lori's braid, revealing the slight heaviness of her brow. The heavy brow didn't spoil her face, though; it only served to give her liquid brown eyes a more intense look. In a few more years, I thought, she'll probably be truly beautiful. Not to mention taller.

"Mandy's an artist," Ingrid said softly before Lori could start up again. Her eyes were crinkled with a gentle smile as she put a hand on her granddaughter's shoulder.

Mandy reached up and stroked the older woman's hand. My own hands felt warmed by the unconscious sweetness of the gesture.

"My daughter, Lori, would rather go to New Age seminars for the rest of her life than actually work to get a good, solid education," Trent put in. He smiled as he said it, as if he was only teasing, but the sourness of his smile told me he was serious. The warmth in my hands faded.

"Oh, Dad," Lori protested, her bright smile wavering. "Please. You know real illumination doesn't come with a degree attached."

"Enough of family discussions," Trent told her quietly.

Lori opened her mouth for an instant, then closed it again, seeming to shrink a little from her magnificent height. I felt my own shoulders contract in sympathy.

Trent turned his polite gaze in my direction. "So, Kate," he said. "What kind of business do you have?"

"Gag gifts," I stated briefly, resisting the urge to tell him that it was none of his business what my business was.

I glanced over my shoulder, wishing Wayne or Ace were here with me. But they were standing by the door listening to Vesta and Eric. As I began to turn my head back, Vesta slapped Ace on the shoulder and he fell to the ground with a loud *whumph*.

My heart jumped. I turned completely around this time. Did Ace need help? What had Vesta done to him? Whatever it was, she thought it was funny. She was laughing out loud now. I took a step toward them, then felt a tug on my shirt sleeve.

"Don't worry," said Mandy. "They're just fooling around."

"Fooling around?" I repeated while my heart thudded madly.

Ace jumped up from the floor and put a choke-hold on Vesta. At least it looked like a choke-hold to me. But Vesta's hoots of laughter were too loud for a woman being strangled.

I turned back to Mandy.

"Uncle Ace pretends to be thrown on the ground," she explained, her brown eyes holding a look I couldn't quite identify. "He's really quite amusing. He used to be a wrestler, you know."

I nodded, just then remembering what Wayne had told me so many times.

"My little brother," Trent murmured, shaking his fine silver head. "He'll never grow up."

"Isn't Uncle Ace just splendid?" whispered Mandy. I studied her eyes. Her irises looked like molten Hershey's chocolate. Now I recognized the gaze she was aiming at Ace. She was in love.

"Too bad his grandson is so hideous," she added in her usual drawl.

Lori laughed. "Poor Eric," she said, hugging her daughter. "We can't all be as lovable as you, sweetie."

Trent's face relaxed into what looked like a real smile. Ingrid beamed. The four Skeritts stood there looking like one big happy, extended family.

Then Harmony came walking up to our little group.

"Hi," she said, her voice off as usual, a little too loud and a little too shrill. "Vesta said I should talk with you guys."

I looked into her blank, bleached eyes and tried to come up with a conversation starter. Lori beat me to it.

"I love your earrings," she said brightly. "Did you make them yourself?"

Harmony raised a hand to the cluster of tiny crystals and crosses that hung from her ear lobe. Life came into her eyes.

"Yeah, I made them," she answered softly. "They're really cool," she went on, her voice gaining speed and volume. "They keep the visitors away, right? The visitors are afraid of crosses. And crystals, right?"

"The visitors?" asked Lori, her brow looking almost like Wayne's as she furrowed it in confusion.

Harmony's face went blank again.

"Go on," prompted Vesta. I looked up, startled. I hadn't heard Vesta join our group. But she had, along with Ace, Wayne and Eric, who all stood a little ways behind her with somber expressions on their faces. Vesta was smiling widely, however, her teeth gleaming. The theme music from *Jaws* began playing in my head.

"Go ahead," Vesta purred. "Tell them about your visitors."

Harmony swallowed the bait. Light came into her burned-out eyes again. She even managed a tentative smile as she spoke.

"Visitors from outer space," she elucidated in an excited whisper. "They took me onto their spaceship three years ago. They only take certain ones of us, right? For testing—"

"You gotta be totally mental to believe that," Eric interrupted, his voice shrill with protest. And maybe fear. "I've read all about UFO's. They're totally bogus, you know."

Vesta laughed raucously. No one joined her. Harmony's face fell into blankness again. But her hands were alive, nervously touching and rubbing each and every one of the many crosses and crystals woven into the fringe on her leather jacket.

For a moment, no one seemed to have anything more to say, not even Eric. I had become used to Harmony's talk of

UFO's and midnight visits, but apparently this branch of the Skeritt clan hadn't been exposed before.

"They're very nice earrings," I told Harmony gently.

She didn't seem to be listening. She was lost in the world of her amulets.

"You shouldn't let Trent hear you talk about spaceships," Vesta advised Harmony. Her gleaming shark's smile had widened. She lowered her voice as she continued. "He had me put away for far less than that," she said, then turned the gleam of her teeth onto Trent.

"This is neither the time nor the place—" Trent began, his voice quiet and controlled. Maybe it was too quiet, too controlled.

"Shady Willows Mental Health Facility for over twenty fucking years!" Vesta shouted. The incongruous smile was gone from her face now. Anger squeezed her navy blue eyes into slits.

Trent shook his head coolly and calmly, folding his hands behind his back military style. He looked the picture of reason and concern except for the muscle that twitched along the right side of his jaw.

"Trent never meant to hurt you, dear," Ingrid whispered. Her eyes were wide and earnest. "He was terribly worried about you—"

"And no one came to help me in all those years," Vesta ground on, ignoring Ingrid entirely. "Not my darling brother Ace . . ." She paused to glare in Ace's direction. The color drained from his face on cue. "Or my sister Drusilla . . ." She pointed to a gray-haired woman across the room. Was that Drusilla?

Finally, Vesta turned to Wayne, her shark's smile appearing once more. "Or my own son, Waynie," she finished in a low, dangerous purr.

Wayne's body collapsed inward in slow motion. First his shoulders rolled forward. Then his chest deflated and his head bowed.

I was at his side in two steps, ready to catch him if his knees buckled. But they didn't. As I reached him, he took a deep breath and straightened his body.

"Mom," he said quietly. "You were sick."

Vesta's face darkened. Maybe Wayne wasn't supposed to have a speaking role in this scenario. "I certainly was after they put me on drugs!" she snapped.

"Now, Vessie," soothed Ace. "Wayne's always been good to you. Visited you once a week while you were in the hospital. Took care of you when you got out. You know how good he's been, don't you?"

"I don't know any such thing—" she began.

"Did I hear my name spoken in vain?" came a new voice, high-pitched and cheerful.

Vesta whirled on the speaker, the gray-haired woman from across the room. Drusilla, if it was Drusilla, was smiling as she moved to join us, apparently oblivious to the zone of tension she had entered on this side of the room. She motioned forward the two people who had accompanied her. One was a younger woman who wore a deep frown, the other a red-faced man who sported a bland smile.

"Now, Vesta," Drusilla caroled. "You've kept your new guest to yourself for long enough. You must introduce her to the three of us."

"God damn it, Drusilla—" Vesta began.

"Oh, just call me Dru," the gray-haired woman trilled. She was tall and slender, dressed in slacks and a gaily embroidered pink blouse. I caught a glimpse of the Skeritt brow under her curly bangs. And a glimpse of humor in the fine network of lines around her blue eyes. "And you must be Kate," she said, extending a hand.

Vesta crossed her arms with a loud snort, then set her face on glower for the duration.

"Good to meet you, Dru," I said enthusiastically, grabbing her hand and pumping. I'd shake the hand of anyone who could upstage Vesta.

"And this is my husband, Bill Norton," Dru went on.

I shook Bill's hand dutifully. He was probably about fifty or so, like his wife. He was good-looking in a WASP kind of way, with a classic profile and widely spaced blue eyes. But his skin was too ruddy for real good looks. And his expression too conversely colorless.

"And my daughter, Gail," Dru finished.

Gail didn't reach out to shake my hand, so I satisfied myself with a nod in her direction. She was as tall as the rest of the Skeritts. And on the plump side. Her face was plain, unremarkable except for the intensity of her brown eyes under aviator-style glasses. She stared at me, the frown deepening on her face. Had she heard Vesta's earlier remarks? And, unlike her mother, had she taken them seriously?

"Gail is a psychotherapist," Dru informed me with a giggle. "So you have to watch what you say around her."

I smiled. I figured it was a joke. Gail just stared. Maybe it wasn't a joke after all.

"I swear she takes notes," Dru whispered conspiratorially.

"So what do you do, Dru?" I asked.

"Oh, I'm comptroller of a mid-sized corporation," she said. Then she crinkled her eyes and added, "That's really just gobbledygook for a glorified bookkeeper, but it's sure fun to say." She let out a peal of laughter, so high and light it seemed to float up to the ceiling. "And my husband, Bill, is a realtor," she added. "Isn't that right, dear?" she prompted, turning to him.

He nodded without shifting his bland smile.

Maybe Bill and Gail didn't talk because Dru talked enough for the three of them, I speculated.

"And Wayne's told me all about your business," Dru bubbled on. "I really love the idea of joke gifts for accountants—"

"Bill Norton is Dru's second husband," Vesta interrupted, her shark's smile back in place. "She killed her first one."

- Three -

"Now, VESSIE," admonished Ace. "You know that's not true—"

"You have no right to say such a thing!" Dru suddenly shouted at Vesta. Her voice was high and tearful. And she wasn't smiling anymore. Without that smile, Dru's face and Vesta's showed a strong family resemblance. Dru jutted her head forward to glare at Vesta. Vesta jutted her own glare back. Skeritt brows dueled silently for an instant. Then Dru sighed and shook her head slowly.

"I loved my Raoul," she said softly, her voice trembling. "I would have never—"

"Well you damn well killed him with all your silly prattling!" Vesta snapped. "If that's love—"

"Now, Vessie," said Ace, putting up his hands like a referee. "There's no need—"

"Why do you always have to be so unpleasant?" Dru demanded of Vesta, her own glare back in place. "Why can't you—"

"What do you mean 'always'?" Vesta shot back. She smiled her shark's smile once more. "You haven't seen me for more than twenty fucking years. Remember? I was locked up—"

"And for good cause—" began Dru.

"Now, Dru," said Ace. "Don't you start—"

"The terrible things you say—"

"At least I never killed—"

"Now, Vessie—"

Their voices clashed and whirled like unshelled nuts in a blender.

I felt dizzy with motion sickness just watching them. Finally, I turned away. And came face to face with Dru's daughter, Gail. Her brown eyes were intent behind her glasses as she stared down at me.

"My father committed suicide," she told me in a clear, ringing voice.

"Your father?" I asked, glancing at Bill Norton in confusion. His face was still frozen in a vague smile as he watched his wife battle Vesta.

"Bill's not my father," Gail explained. Her voice had all the feeling of a robot. But her eyes . . . I looked closer and saw anger there. Then she stepped past me, toward Vesta.

"Aunt Vesta, why are you acting out like this?" she asked in the same clear, ringing tones in which she'd announced her father's suicide.

There was a lull in the battle as Vesta, Dru and Ace turned to face Gail. Vesta's face went slack for a moment; then she glared at the intruder.

"None of your damn business!" she answered succinctly.

"Why did you invite us here?" Gail asked, as if she hadn't heard the first response.

"Why shouldn't I?" answered Vesta. "My own loving family with all their precious secrets . . ." She let her insinuating words trail off and grinned.

"And?" prodded Gail.

"Never you mind, Little Miss Nosy," warned Vesta. She poked her long, bony finger into Gail's face. "All the generations have secrets," she added. "Even yours."

It was only then that I remembered Wayne. I spotted him where he had retreated, on a couch against the far wall. His brows were dropped low enough that the eyes were impossible to read, almost impossible to see. His face was blank. It might have been carved in stone. I sprinted over and sat down next to him, laying my warm hand on top of his cold one. Poor Wayne. No wonder he had been scared. This was awful.

Dru pulled her shoulders back and smiled brightly, as if she had heard my thought. She turned to her daughter. "It's all right, honey," she told Gail.

"But Mother—" Gail objected.

"Your Aunt Vesta's been through an awfully hard time," Dru explained. "We just have to try and understand." Then she turned to her husband. "Bill and I understand, don't we, dear?"

Bill nodded carefully and took a sip from a glass tumbler that had magically appeared in his hand some time after I had been introduced to him.

Vesta turned to Ace with a frown.

"As for you, little brother. Don't think you can get away with—"

Ace hit the floor with a loud *whumph*.

"Yow!" he cried in a falsetto. "You sure do pack a wallop, little lady!"

Vesta held her frown for an instant. The room was silent. Then she giggled.

Relief swept the room in an explosion of laughter and movement. I let out the breath I had been holding and watched as spines straightened and smiles blossomed. Gail's face, though, remained unchanged. She still stared at Vesta unblinkingly. Wayne squeezed my hand. I looked up and saw his eyes gazing back, alive again. The war was over. Or, at least, postponed.

"Buffet's in the kitchen," announced Vesta, her voice easy now, free of its earlier rage. "Let's eat."

There were no stragglers as she led us through the doorway into the kitchen.

It was a great spread. It had to be. Wayne had arranged for the catering himself. Sliced roast beef, miniature quiche Lorraines, Thai prawns and honey mustard chicken sat side by side with the vegetarian dolmas, herbed tofu-stuffed mushrooms and avocado sushi. Then there were the salads and the pastas. All artistically arranged on spotless white china laid upon crisp white linen that seemed to glow against the backdrop of vanilla-beige walls and teak cabinets.

As I spooned pasta primavera onto my plate, Mandy asked if I was a vegetarian.

"Mrmph," I agreed, my mouth full of avocado sushi. I swallowed. "And you?"

"Of course," she drawled. "I'm a complete vegan. Really, it's the only choice, when you think of the hideous conditions for all those poor little animals." I squirmed guiltily in my leather Reeboks. "Mom still eats chicken and fish," she continued, shaking her head.

Lori's skin pinkened. She sighed and with a great rattling of bracelets returned a chicken breast she had taken from the serving tray.

"I have a really splendid little kitty at home," Mandy told me. "His name is Catullus, after the Roman poet. I just adore animals. I wish I could have more, but Mom says one is enough." She sent her mother another look, one Skeritt eyebrow raised over a dark and lovely eye.

"Just think how lucky you are to have Catullus," Lori advised cheerfully. "I didn't even have a cat growing up. Dad was too worried about his precious garden for us to have animals."

Vesta reached for the piece of chicken that Lori had abandoned. "I remember the summer Trent came home after his first year of college," she told us, plopping the breast onto her plate. "He was more interested in the garden than me that summer." She winked largely at Trent. "Big Man on Campus. Big deal."

Trent smiled back coolly and speared a piece of roast beef. The muscle on the right side of his jaw was twitching again. I was glad he wasn't foolish enough to answer her. I wasn't ready for another round of arguments.

"Ace, on the other hand—" Vesta purred, turning to her younger brother. "Ace couldn't give a shit about the garden."

Ace blushed deeply, but like his brother Trent, he made no verbal retort. Was he embarrassed by her language? I wondered. Or was it something about the garden?

"I garden for a few bucks sometimes," whispered Harmony. She held an empty china plate tightly by its edges. I hoped it wouldn't crack. "That's how I met Vesta." Her voice took on speed and volume. "I was trimming this bush, right? Right out front here. And Vesta came out, right? Now she's my best friend. We're like sisters—"

"God picks your relatives," Vesta cut in. "Thank God you can pick your friends." She let out a hoot of laughter and headed out the doorway to the living room.

Harmony tilted her head and stared wide-eyed at Vesta's back until it disappeared. Then her hand began to twitch across the landscape of crystals and crosses on her jacket.

"Harmony, would you like some pasta?" I prompted gently.

She looked at me blankly for a moment, then held out her plate with the silent gravity of a child. I loaded it up with pasta and salad and dolmas. I had no idea what she usually ate. Or if she ate at all if no one told her to. She took her plate and followed Vesta's footsteps out of the kitchen into the living room.

"My father gave me Catullus," Mandy said into the silence. At twelve, she seemed to have the best conversational skills of the group. "He's an artist actually, really quite splendid."

"Lance Oliver," Lori added, flashing red fingernails as she waved her free hand in the air. "You may have heard of him." I shook my head, embarrassed that I hadn't. She went on before I could tell her I didn't follow the art world. "Oh, he's a truly spiritual man. His paintings are so healing. We're legally separated, but he hasn't abandoned us vibrationally—"

"Only financially," Trent cut in.

"That's not true, Dad—" Lori began.

I took a deep breath and carried my plate out into the living room. Most of the Skeritts were already there. Ingrid, Dru and Ace were packed together companionably on one black leather couch. Dru was laughing at something Ace was saying as she nibbled on her salad. Vesta leaned back in her easy chair, wolfing down roast beef and chicken, with Harmony at her feet like a large domestic dog. Harmony stared down blankly at her plate of food. Bill Norton sat by himself on another couch, sipping from his glass. His stepdaughter, Gail, was perched on a lone chair near the kitchen doorway. And Wayne and Eric sat eating side by side on the floor. I headed their way.

"You know what, Uncle Wayne?" Eric was saying. "They

have these totally weird contests in Alaska where they tie these great big weights to their ears . . ."

I veered at the last minute and sat down next to Bill Norton on the couch.

I asked him how he was doing. He nodded and smiled. I ate a stuffed mushroom. Bill took a sip of his drink. A couple of prawns and an untouched piece of roast beef seemed to be the only things on his plate. I asked him how the real estate market was doing these days. He shrugged and took another sip, still smiling. I ate my dolmas, pasta and salad, listening to the conversations tinkling and humming around me, then gave it another try. I asked him how long he and Dru had been married. Would Bill stomp his foot for the number of years like a trick horse?

No. He just shrugged again.

"I think I'll get some more of these great mushrooms," I said brightly and headed back to the kitchen, passing Lori and Mandy on their way out.

Trent was still in the kitchen, frowning down at his full plate. He was about as chatty as Bill. I asked him about his work as I scooped up mushrooms. He told me that he was to retire soon from his position as the dean of Fulton College. He didn't ask anything about me in return. He picked up a fork and inspected it closely instead. What was he looking for? Insects? Dirt?

"Nice talking with you," I murmured and left with my mushrooms.

Back in the living room, I was relieved to see that Mandy and Lori were now seated on the couch with Bill Norton. Lori's smile was looking strained as she talked at Bill. Silently, I wished her luck. Maybe she could read his aura or something.

"You know what else, Uncle Wayne?" Eric said to Wayne, still seated next to the boy on the floor.

"No, what?" Wayne answered. He even managed to sound interested.

"Tomatoes aren't really a vegetable, they're a fruit," Eric told him solemnly.

"That so?" Wayne commented encouragingly.

"And you know what else. . . ?"

Wayne was an exceptionally good-natured human being. There was no doubt about it. I wasn't, though. I didn't want to hear Eric's parade of amazing facts right now. I looked around and spotted a space consisting of a few inches to Ingrid's left on the couch that she shared with Dru and Ace. That was enough for me. I trotted over and squeezed in next to her.

"How nice to see you, Kate," Ingrid said in her resonant whisper. She held my hand for a moment and I found myself feeling inordinately warmed by the friendly gesture. "I was just telling Dru about our library programs," she went on, her voice full of excitement. "I volunteer at the library, you know—"

The chime of the doorbell cut her off.

"Kate!" Vesta shouted. She waved a fork imperiously. "Get the door."

My muscles tensed. I stared at the scowl on Vesta's thin face for an instant of rebellion. Pretend, I reminded myself. Pretend to like her.

I took a deep breath and smiled as I got up and opened the door.

I was glad I was smiling when I saw Clara Kushiyama standing there. Clara was the semi-retired psychiatric nurse that Wayne had hired to look in on Vesta twice a day. And as far as I was concerned, she was sanity incarnate. I looked down at her with special fondness at that moment. Her solid body was the first one I'd seen all night that was shorter than mine. And her wise and gentle Asian-American face could never be mistaken for a Skeritt's.

"Good to see you, my dear," she greeted me quietly. "How's our Mrs. Caruso doing tonight?"

"Is that you, Pearl?" Vesta shouted before I had a chance to answer.

"It's me," Clara sang back. She gave my hand a reassuring pat as she walked into the living room.

"You know why I call her Pearl?" Vesta asked the assembled Skeritts loudly. I resisted sticking my fingers in my ears. I already knew the punch line and I didn't want to hear it again. "Because she's sneaky, just like all the other Japs at *Pearl* Harbor!" Vesta finished up, shrieking with laughter.

No one joined in, but Vesta didn't seem to notice. Of course, the Skeritts had been here for a few days. They had probably heard the line before too. In any case, Vesta's rude remark had served to squelch all conversation. The room was silent as Clara tended to her charge.

I resumed my seat next to Ingrid on the couch and watched from behind as Clara spoke quietly to Vesta and checked her vital signs without disturbing Harmony, who still sat at her friend's feet. Clara's back was broader than I would have expected, maybe from all the years she'd spent lifting recalcitrant patients in various mental institutions. There were a few strands of gray in her black pageboy, but very little else that would have given away her sixty odd years of age.

"I'm having a party here," Vesta complained after a few minutes of Clara's ministrations. "You've done enough spying for one day, Tokyo Rose. Now go the hell away."

"Okey-dokey, Mrs. Caruso," Clara answered genially. "I'll see you tomorrow morning." Then she headed for the door.

Wayne jumped up from his place on the floor. "There's plenty of food," he growled awkwardly to Clara. "Like to stay and eat?"

"Waynie!" Vesta objected. "I said I want the spy outa here!"

"I've already eaten, but thank you, Wayne," Clara murmured cheerily. She gave his hand a sympathetic pat and left.

I'd be cheery too if I could leave, I thought enviously, as the door closed behind her.

"Mom!" Wayne whispered urgently as he stomped over to Vesta's chair. "Clara Kushiyama was born in America, same as you. She's never spied for Japan. She's never even lived there! And even if she had, you have no business insulting her. I've told you that. Kate's told you that. Why do you keep insulting her?"

"Keep your big fat ugly nose out of it," Vesta replied casually. "It's between me and Pearl." She waved her bony hand dismissively and looked down at Harmony.

"But—" began Wayne.

"I want my 'New Age' tea now," Vesta announced. "Harmony, be a good girl and go put the kettle on."

Harmony set her untouched plate on the floor and left to do Vesta's bidding.

Vesta dropped her own plate down beside Harmony's. "Somebody clear up this mess," she ordered and leaned back in her easy chair.

I started to get up, but Ingrid gently shoved me back onto the couch. "I'll be glad to clear," she whispered enthusiastically.

"I'll help you," I offered and attempted to get up again.

This time Dru shoved me back down. "You just relax," she trilled. "We'll take care of it."

I opened my mouth and shut it again as Dru took my plate. I knew it could be dangerous to argue with women of a certain age bent on exercising the best of good manners.

Harmony reappeared as Ingrid took a stack of plates into the kitchen. Harmony's face was tuned into an indistinct smile which wavered in and out of focus.

"I make Vesta tea every night," she announced shrilly. "I get the herbs at the health food store and mix them myself. They're all organic, right? Valerian, skullcap, chamomile, stuff like that—"

"And a little grass once in a while," Vesta broke in. She looked around the room as if daring someone to criticize her. I wasn't about to take her up on it. Now that Shady Willows was no longer over-medicating her, she was doing a good job on her own. "Harmony's my own home-grown organic expert on the New Age," Vesta added. "All I know is *old* age."

Harmony giggled dutifully. Dru chuckled a little on her way back from the kitchen.

"Herbalism is a real art form," Lori put in, bending forward encouragingly. "You have to be truly intuitive to create the right mixtures for the right people."

"No, you don't," shrilled Harmony, glaring now at Lori.

Lori's head jerked back. Her beaded earrings bobbed. "I just meant that you must be a very creative—"

"It's my job and you can't have it!" Harmony cried out. Her eyes were round with distress.

"Mom just meant—" Mandy began.

"Shh, sweetie," whispered Lori, standing up. "We'll just go help with the dishes. Okay?"

Ace pushed himself up off the couch as Lori and her daughter headed into the kitchen. "So, what say we have some real drinks?" he suggested heartily.

Harmony sat down again at Vesta's feet, her face resuming its usual blank expression as her hands resumed their trek between the amulets around her neck and the ones imbedded in the fringes of her jacket.

"I'll take a Scotch," said Trent, his deep voice reassuringly steady.

Other voices began calling out their orders. As Ace ran around writing them down on a little notepad, I slithered my way over to sit by Wayne on the floor.

"Can we go now?" I whispered in his ear.

"Just a little longer," he whispered back.

"Pretend?" I mouthed.

"Pretend," he mouthed back and kissed me sweetly.

"Kate!" shouted Vesta. I jerked back mid-kiss. "You like all this New Age, hippie stuff. Wanna try some of my tea?"

"No, thank you," I sang back cheerily. I had tasted her "New Age" tea once. It may have been both herbal and organic, but it tasted liked brewed sweat socks. Even Harmony didn't drink it.

"Anyone else?" Vesta asked the room at large.

No one responded in the affirmative. They had obviously tasted it, too.

"Bunch of fucking wimps," she said and grinned. I let out a deep breath. She was happy.

The teakettle shrieked. Harmony leapt up and ran to the kitchen with Ace in her wake.

Once Vesta had drunk her tea, cup after pungent cup from her special, lavender-enameled teapot, the evening went much more smoothly. Conversation resumed. Ace told jokes and proposed toasts. Plans to visit Mount Tam, Stinson Beach and Sausalito were discussed. The only recurrence of Vesta's earlier hostility was when she replied "feces" to Lori's earnest inquiry concerning her astrological sign.

An hour later, I was squinting through the lens of Dru's camera at the four Skeritt siblings. Ace had his eyes crossed and his tongue sticking out. Vesta was making rabbit ears in back of Trent's head. Dru tilted her face and winked flirtatiously.

I pushed the shutter button down. Click.

Ace put his arm around the two women. Trent leaned his head into the viewfinder. Click.

The two men stood behind their sisters. Vesta put her hand over her heart and frowned. Damn. I lifted my finger away from the button. Was it fake heart-attack time again?

"I don't feel so good," Vesta said. "Maybe we oughta call it a night." She was sweating, that was for sure. I'd noticed the drops of perspiration sliding off the end of her nose as I looked through the viewfinder. But she'd had a good workout that evening. At least her tongue had. And rage can be a very strenuous emotion. I looked over my shoulder at Wayne.

"Okay, everyone," he said quietly. "Time to go."

The Skeritts assembled to leave in an embarrassingly short amount of time.

Vesta had one more shark's smile for us all at the door. "I'll have more surprises tomorrow," she promised. "It's my birthday. Be here by nine. Now get outa here."

We got out of there. All but Harmony, who stood next to Vesta in the doorway as they waved us away into the cool night air.

Wayne was unlocking the Jaguar door when I heard a clear voice ring out somewhere across the darkened grass of La Risa Green.

"Why do you put up with it?" asked the voice. It was Gail. At least I thought it was. It was too dark to see her across the grass. And there was more feeling in her voice now than before.

"Vesta was very good to me as a child," came a high trill back. Dru. "She's had a difficult life, honey. More difficult than you may realize." A car door slammed.

"Oh, Mother," Gail protested. "You're too good—"

Another door slammed and all was silent. Then an engine started.

Wayne and I had our own, brief conversation as he drove south on Highway 101. He reminded me that Vesta's parents had thrown her out of her home when she became pregnant with Wayne. That her life had been miserable. That the beatings she had given him had sprung from that misery. That he just wanted her to be happy.

I gave him a long, hard look.

"I understand the things that happened to her weren't my fault," he countered. "Understand it intellectually—"

"But emotionally it's a different story," I finished for him wearily. "I know."

He turned his wounded face back to the road and didn't say another word for the rest of the drive home.

My cat, C.C., greeted us at our door with her usual yowl of disapproval. Wayne gave her a pat and shuffled down the hall to the bedroom. My answering machine blinked at me anxiously, filled with messages it needed to disgorge. There were a few business calls, a quick message from my friend Barbara, and another rambling one from my warehouse-woman, Judy. She wanted me to call her. Probably about her divorce, I guessed. When you run a small business with a handful of employees, you get to be dictator, therapist, teacher, referee and mother all rolled into one. Just for starters. Not to mention lawyer. Somehow Judy and her husband, Jerry, had gone from a trial separation to filing for divorce awfully fast. Now Judy kept asking me for legal advice.

I punched out the first two digits of her number.

"Kate?" murmured Wayne from behind me.

I turned.

"Sorry," he growled, looking down at his feet.

I put the telephone receiver back in the cradle and wrapped my arms around him.

"Hey," I mumbled into his chest. "We made it out alive. Let's celebrate."

And we did.

The phone rang at eight the next morning. I picked it up, expecting Barbara or Judy.

"I can't wake her up!" someone wailed.

– Four –

"WAIT A MINUTE!" I ordered the receiver. Adrenaline-fueled scenarios of disaster pumped through my mind. "Who is this?"

"It's not my fault, is it?" the voice replied in a whisper. "I didn't do anything bad, right?"

"Who is this?" I repeated, trying to infuse my voice with a calm I didn't feel. "Who can't you wake up?"

"Maybe the visitors got her," the voice went on, so faint I could barely hear it above the pounding of my own pulse. Visitors? The Skeritts were visiting. Or maybe . . .

"Harmony?" I guessed. "Is that you?"

"It's not my fault!" she wailed. Now I was almost sure it was Harmony on the other end of the line. And if it was Harmony . . . Damn. I took a deep breath as the imagined scenarios became more specific. And more frightening.

"Who can't you wake up, Harmony?" I asked in a slow, steady voice. "Is Vesta all right?"

"I don't know!" she shrieked. "I've been good, right? I just did what she told me—"

"Kate?" came Wayne's deep voice from behind me.

I put my hand over the mouthpiece and turned to him. He frowned a question at me.

"Harmony, I think," I whispered. "She's not making sense—"

He nodded and stuck out his hand for the phone. I hesitated for an instant. What if something really were wrong with Vesta? Could he handle it?

"It's okay," he told me.

I wasn't sure what he meant, but I decided to believe him anyway. I handed him the phone.

Ten minutes later we were dressed and in Wayne's Jaguar, doing eighty up Highway 101. He hadn't made any more sense out of Harmony's words than I had. But at least he was sure that it had been Harmony on the phone. And he was more than convinced that we needed to check in on Vesta. Immediately.

I watched his grim profile as he drove. I hoped Vesta was all right. I would even forgive her if this was another one of her jokes.

"Shouldn't we call 911?" I asked.

His eyebrows went up. "Yeah," he agreed. "Didn't think of it."

"Me neither," I admitted. "Not till now." I wriggled inside my seat belt uncomfortably. What if Vesta needed an ambulance?

"We'll call from the condo if we need to," he promised, and tromped the gas pedal even harder.

Unfortunately, it wasn't that easy. We had to get inside the condo first if we were going to use the phone. And while it was true that Harmony had opened the door when we'd arrived, it was also true that she'd left the chain lock securely in place. And there was no way either Wayne or I could squeeze through the two-inch crack between the door and the doorjamb.

"It's not my fault, right?" Harmony shrilled. Parts of her face kept appearing and disappearing through the crack in the doorway. A wide, bleached blue eye, the flash of crystals and crosses on an ear lobe, blond bushy hair. I even caught a glimpse of her hand around the neck of the wooden baseball bat she had carried the night before.

"Slide the lock open, Harmony," I ordered in the smoothest voice I could muster. Wayne and I had been issuing alternating versions of this order for what seemed like an eternity but was probably only a minute or two. I even wondered for an instant if I could stick my hand through the crack and unloose the chain. Not likely, I decided. That was exactly what the damn things were designed to protect against.

I put my face closer to the crack. The amulet-embedded fringes of Harmony's leather jacket danced before my eyes. The smell of sweat, leather, dope and patchouli drifted my way. But this time the sweat predominated. It was a heavy, sour sweat, the kind fear can produce. Or maybe she had just slept in her clothes all night. I drew my head back.

"Mom?" Wayne called out. "Mom, are you in there?"

"She won't talk to you, man," Harmony informed him. "She won't even talk to me."

"Is Vesta sick, Harmony?" I asked.

There was a short silence. I pressed my face up to the crack in the doorway once more. It looked like Harmony was nodding her head. "Vesta was really sick last night," she finally answered. "Throwing up all over the place around one in the morning—"

"Mom!" Wayne called out again, louder this time.

"It was awful, man. Just awful," Harmony went on, her words coming faster and louder. "I asked if she wanted a doctor, right? She said . . . she said . . ."

"What did she say?" asked Wayne. His deep voice seemed ready to explode with the effort of keeping it even.

"She said she'd had enough of doctors, right? And she said she'd had enough of me." Harmony's voice cracked, and I thought she wouldn't go on, but she did. "She told me to get out. So I went and slept in my car. I had to, right? That's what she told me to do. I didn't do anything wrong, did I?"

"No, you did just fine," I assured her. "Just fine." I took a deep breath and tried to remember the tricks I had learned while working in a mental hospital some two decades before. "How is Vesta doing now?" I asked in a steady, low voice.

But Harmony didn't seem to hear me. I caught a glimpse of her round blue eye staring through the crack in the doorway; then she started up again.

"Vesta kept talking about 'New Age' and 'organic' and 'herbal' and stuff. I think she mighta meant the tea, right?" Her voice grew shrill. "But I made the tea, right? Just like always. I get the herbs at the health food store—"

"How is Vesta doing *now*, Harmony?" I repeated in a louder tone of voice.

"I let myself back in at eight," she told me. "Vesta'd given me a key before, right? But she's real sick, man. She won't even talk to me." Her voice lowered to a whisper. "I think the visitors got to her," she breathed.

"If you let us in, we can protect you from them," I whispered back, hating myself for the necessary lie.

"I got my bat," she assured me. "No one can hurt me."

"But you're tired of holding that bat, aren't you, Harmony?" I said slowly. Softly. "Really tired. It would feel so good to let it drop—"

"I . . . I'm scared," she interrupted.

"Of course you are," I told her, keeping my voice steady though I wanted to cheer. It was the sanest thing she'd said yet. "You can't help but be scared, Harmony. Let us help you. Now, slide back the chain—"

The crack in the doorway closed for a moment and I thought I'd lost her. But then I heard the chain slide in the lock. And the door was open.

I wasted no time pushing my way through. Harmony stood aside, but she held her wooden baseball bat high and trembling in the air.

"Put down the bat," said Wayne, his voice soft and reasonable. He put his hand out. Harmony lowered the bat slowly, then handed it neck first to Wayne. He dropped it on the floor next to Vesta's water gun.

"Thank you, Harmony," he said solemnly.

"I'll be back in a second," I whispered and trotted across the living room, toward the stairs that led to the bedroom area.

If something were seriously wrong with Vesta—I couldn't even let myself think the word "dead"—I didn't want Wayne to see her and remember the sight for the rest of his life. I sprinted up the stairs and down the hall, pausing for an instant before I opened the door to Vesta's bedroom.

The smell hit me first. I gagged, then put my hand over my mouth and nose as I felt across flocked wallpaper for the light switch. I will not throw up, I told myself and took shallow sips of air through my fingers as my eyes adjusted to the bright light.

I saw the swirling gold and ivory shades of the flocked wallpaper first. And the four-poster bed. And then, Vesta. Her legs were tucked under her silken gold bedspread, but her upper body was twisted and sprawled out over the side of the bed as if she had reached for something and collapsed, her black hair pooling on the plush golden carpet alongside splashes of vomit. I closed my eyes and took another breath through my fingers. When I opened them again, I noticed her lavender-enameled teapot leaning on its side in the long, thick threads of gold wool inches from Vesta's outstretched hand.

The room began to shimmer. Only it wasn't the room, of course. It was me. I took a deep breath. That was a mistake. I clapped my hand over my mouth again. What if she was still alive? What if she needed help? I forced myself to step closer and saw the side of her face, gray and contorted through the veil of black hair. I held my breath as I stepped forward and reached down to check for her pulse. The skin on her arm was cool. The good news is she doesn't have a fever, I thought hysterically. I pressed my fingers to the inside of her wrist. The bad news was she didn't have a pulse either. Not one that I could find, anyway.

But what if she wasn't dead? An ambulance, I told myself. I need to call for an ambulance. Then I heard Wayne's heavy footsteps on the stairs.

I was at the doorway in three long steps and out in another, all dizziness forgotten. Wayne stood a few yards down the hall, his grim face looking as if he already knew what awaited him inside the bedroom. Maybe he did. Maybe Harmony had finally told him.

I put my hand up in warning as I walked to him. "Go back downstairs now," I said firmly. "Call an ambulance."

He didn't speak as he stepped past me. I backpedaled and placed myself in his path again.

"No," I told him. "Believe me, you don't want to."

He didn't choose to believe me. He picked me up ever so gently and set me back down by his side, then took the last step to the doorway.

He stopped there, staring in. He didn't gasp. He didn't make any sound at all. But as I watched from behind, I saw his body begin to sway like a tall tree ready to fall with the last cut of the ax.

I leapt to his side and put my arm around his waist, wondering if I could actually support his weight if he lost consciousness. He stiffened. At least he wasn't swaying anymore. I moved around in front of him. His brows were pulled low over blank eyes that stared over the top of my head into his mother's room. His face was plaster-white and unmoving, as if he were only a sculpted representation of himself.

I brought my hand up to stroke his shoulder.

"Wayne?" I prompted.

He didn't answer. My chest tightened. Where was he? He's in shock, I admonished myself. His mother is dead. Of course he's upset. But he wasn't just upset. He was gone. As far away as the lifetime mental patients I had nursed long ago.

I grasped Wayne's hand. It was ice-cold, and limp.

"Wayne, please," I tried. My throat was suddenly sore. "We need to call an ambulance." When I heard the tears in my own voice, I realized I was crying.

But Wayne didn't respond to my words or my tears.

I stepped behind him and pulled his arm hard in my direction. He allowed himself to be turned around, his feet shuffling slowly to accommodate the movement of his arm. But he never spoke, not then or later as I tugged him down the stairway. We were almost down when the doorbell rang.

"Don't answer that!" I shouted at Harmony.

But of course she did. And this time she didn't bother with the chain lock. I guided Wayne down the last of the stairs as three generations of Skeritts spurted into the living room in a buzz of conversation and laughter.

No one seemed to notice as I maneuvered Wayne into position in front of one of the couches and eased him down, like an old man, onto its black leather cushions. I kissed the top of his head, willing him to return to life soon. His curly hair was damp with sweat. *Please*, I begged silently, *let him be all right. Please—*

"It's not my fault, right?" Harmony's shrill voice cut through the babble of voices.

"What's not your fault?" asked Dru, smiling uncertainly at Harmony.

Suddenly, all the visiting Skeritts were silent and staring at Harmony. And at me. And finally, at Wayne.

"Hey, what's wrong with Uncle Wayne?" asked Eric. "He looks totally wasted."

"He's . . . he's had a shock," I answered, damning the telltale tremor in my voice. "But he'll be all right soon," I added. I looked into Wayne's eyes. They stared through me, unseeing.

"But—" Eric began.

"Ace?" I said, turning to the big man. "Can you take care . . ." I pointed at Wayne, unable to finish.

"Why, sure," he boomed, striding toward us, his face looking achingly like Wayne's as his eyebrows descended in concern. "But what's wrong—?"

"I have to make a phone call," I cut in. "I'll be back."

I waited impatiently as Ace sat down next to Wayne. Ingrid silently placed herself on Wayne's other side, and took his hand in hers. New tears burned in my eyes as I ran into the kitchen to find the telephone. It was sitting on the tiled counter by the refrigerator.

But Eric had followed me in. "Where's Aunt Vesta?" he asked before I could get to the counter.

"Vesta's indisposed," I told him. I suppose I shouldn't have been surprised that this wasn't enough to satisfy him.

"What do you mean, 'indisposed'?" he pressed.

"Please, Eric," I begged. "Not now. Go sit with the others."

I watched as he left the kitchen, hurt evident in the set of his shoulders. I'd make it up to him later, I told myself as I lunged for the phone. Later.

"What's wrong with Wayne?" asked a new voice at the kitchen doorway. Damn. It was Trent, looking trim and distinguished in a polo shirt and slacks.

"It's Vesta," I said. "She's very sick."

His brows shot up, brown eyes wide for a moment.

"Actually, I think she's probably dead," I went on. I had to tell someone or I'd never be able to get to the phone. "But I need to call an ambulance, just in case."

Trent nodded reassuringly, his face taking on the same Skeritt look of low-browed concern as Ace's had. "Heart?" he asked quietly.

I shrugged my shoulders impatiently. I wasn't ready to talk to anyone about causes. Not even myself.

"Shall I explain to the others?" he offered.

"Yes, please," I breathed gratefully.

He turned and went back into the living room. I heard the drone of his steady, resonant voice as I picked up the telephone receiver. Then a few gasps, a deep groan and a couple of high-pitched questions.

I punched out 9-1-1.

And heard a shriek of pure terror. Was that Wayne? I dropped the receiver back into its cradle and rushed into the living room, looking for Wayne past all the other members of the Skeritt family.

But it was Eric, not Wayne, who was shrieking. Eric stood at the foot of the stairs with his mouth wide and his chubby face distorted by fear. Ace jumped up and ran to the boy.

"She's dead!" Eric screamed. "I'm gonna hurl!" Then he sprinted toward the guest bathroom, with Ace galloping close behind him.

I turned my gaze back to Wayne. There was a little more color in his face, but his eyes were still dead. As Ingrid patted his hand gently, I turned away and took a step back toward the kitchen. The doorbell rang again.

Damn. Who the hell was left?

I yanked open the front door and saw Clara Kushiyama.

"Clara!" I shouted and wrapped my arms around her short, stocky body.

It took me less than a minute to whisper the details nonstop into her ear. Clara was halfway up the stairs when the phone rang.

Trent got to the phone first.

"Yes, there is an emergency," I heard him say calmly into the receiver. "Yes, a call was made." He put his hand over the phone for a moment. "Do we need an ambulance?" he asked me.

"Wait," I ordered and ran back into the living room.

Clara was descending the staircase, her gentle face solemn. And troubled.

"Do we need an ambulance?" I relayed the question.

She shook her head slowly. I heard a gasp from somewhere behind me, and a thin trickle of whispered conversation. I looked over my shoulder to see who was talking.

"But Kate," came Clara's voice, tugging my head back around with its insistence. "I'm afraid we need the police."

– Five –

"THE POLICE!" HARMONY shrieked. "No! You can't call the police. They'll blame me, right? I know they will."

Her hands were as agitated as her mouth. Moments before, her right hand had stroked a crystal at her throat while her left had fingered a clump of crosses hanging from her jacket fringe. But as she shrieked, both hands began racing from jacket fringe to necklace to earrings and back again, as if trying and failing to touch every amulet at the same time.

"The visitors will convince them," she bleated. They can do that, right? Then they'll blame me for everything—"

"There, there," Clara crooned softly, at Harmony's side in an instant. She reached up to stroke the taller woman's bush of blond hair. "You'll be just fine. Just keep breathing—"

"But why do we need the police?" demanded a new female voice from my left.

I swiveled my head and saw Lori, dressed like a parrot today in shades of bright green, scarlet and turquoise. But her face wasn't as cheerful as her clothing. She frowned and pointed a long, scarlet fingernail at Harmony. "What's wrong with—"

"I didn't do anything wrong!" Harmony wailed before I could answer Lori. It was just as well. I didn't have any answers.

"Of course you didn't do anything wrong," Clara told Harmony.

"Clara . . ." I began. I was going to ask her if she could handle Harmony. Then I remembered that handling psychiatric patients was what Clara did for a living.

Clara nodded briskly in answer to my implied question,

then put her arm around Harmony's waist. "You've had a hard time, haven't you, you poor little thing," she murmured. And suddenly Harmony, probably a full foot taller than Clara, did seem like a little thing as she slumped over the smaller woman's shoulder and began to cry.

"What in the world is going on here?" came a high-pitched voice from my right. I turned the other way and saw Dru. She tilted her head, her bright blue eyes looking more curious than concerned. This was probably more a function of her habitual smile than a real lack of concern, I told myself. "Has Vesta really passed away?" she prodded.

"Well, I—"

"An ambulance is coming," Trent cut in, back from the kitchen.

I swung my head around in his direction, only then remembering that I'd never relayed Clara's message not to send an ambulance.

"Oh, damn. I'm sorry," I mumbled inadequately and then remembered the second part of Clara's message. "Are the police coming too?" I whispered.

"I explained the situation quite carefully," he assured me in a calm and steady voice. His wife, Ingrid, walked up behind him and put a hand on his shoulder. He flinched and jerked his head around, then took a breath and turned slowly back to me.

"I'm certain they'll send whoever and whatever they think necessary," he finished quietly.

"Uh, thank you," I muttered, reserving comment on the unnecessary ambulance. Hopefully, necessary police would follow the unnecessary ambulance. Or were the police necessary? Had it been the tea—?

"Is there anything we can do for poor Vesta?" asked Ingrid in her sonorous whisper. Her eyes were red and blurred with tears, and her skin was blotchy.

I shook my head slowly, not having any other answer to offer.

"Oh dear," she moaned and pulled out a cotton handkerchief. "I'm so terribly, terribly sorry," she gurgled through it.

Trent sighed and closed his eyes for a moment, then put his arm around Ingrid as the sound of her weeping grew.

"Are you okay, Grandma?" asked Mandy, the drawl gone from her voice. She sounded like a twelve-year-old now, a frightened twelve-year-old.

Ingrid drew in a sodden breath and reached out to her grandchild.

I turned away and looked for Wayne. He was alone now on the black leather couch, still staring blankly ahead. I trotted over and plopped down next to him before anyone else could ask me any more questions. I had done my duty. The authorities had been informed. The rest of the Skeritts were on their own as far as I was concerned. Except for Wayne.

I watched his profile as I took his limp hand in mine and squeezed. He didn't even blink. My chest tightened all over again. Was he in a temporary state of shock? Or was his mind gone for good? Not for good, I told myself emphatically. That was just silly. I knew Wayne. He was rock-solid, sanity itself. Except, a shrill voice in my subconscious informed me, when it came to his mother.

"Wayne!" I whispered sharply.

He turned his head slowly in my direction, but his eyes looked through me. I felt a chill creep over me, tightening the skin on my arms and legs first, then prickling my back and scalp. The kind of chill that a nightmare brings when the dreamer suddenly sees demons blossom where a familiar form has been before. I wanted to scream myself awake.

"Please, sweetie," I whispered instead, squeezing his hand harder. If my own hands hadn't been so slippery with sweat, I might have crushed the bones of his fingers. At that point, I would have bitten him to get his attention.

"I—" The word came abruptly from somewhere deep in his throat. His eyes focused and grew moist at the same moment. "I can't," he rasped and jerked his head away to stare straight ahead once more.

"That's all right," I told him. I dropped his poor hand and kissed him on the neck. "That's all right." There was still someone in there. That was all I needed to know.

I took a big breath and turned my own moist eyes forward.

A few moments later, I noticed three pairs of eyes staring back.

Gail Norton was the most obvious. She studied Wayne and me through her aviator glasses as if we were laboratory rats. There was a hint of dissatisfaction evident in the flare of her nostrils and the asymmetry of her brows, as if we rats were not producing the results she had hypothesized. Suddenly, I wondered if she was actually a research psychologist, not a psychotherapist as her mother had told me. Somehow, I just couldn't imagine anyone pouring out their problems to Gail Norton.

Dru stood between her daughter and her husband, watching us a little less obviously out of the corner of one eye. She turned her head and whispered into Gail's ear. Gail's eyes didn't flicker. Dru turned back and reached out for Bill's left hand. His left was the only one available. He held a glass tumbler in his right hand. He gazed in our general direction with his usual bland smile.

I raised my hand and wiggled my fingers in a little wave just to let them know I saw them. Maybe their looks were meant to be friendly. Dru giggled and waved back. Bill toasted me with his tumbler. Gail continued to stare unblinkingly. Maybe she and Wayne could have a contest, I thought. I certainly wasn't interested. I looked away, over to the corner of the living room where Trent, Lori, Ingrid and Mandy had gathered.

At least they weren't staring at us. Ingrid's eyes were closed as she hugged her granddaughter to her. And all I could see of Mandy's head was her neatly braided hair. Trent and Lori's heads were thrust at each other, brows down. Were they arguing? A harsh whisper drifted my way.

". . . your mother is far too emotional—"

"Of course, she's emotional, Dad!" Lori whispered back fiercely. Her bracelets jangled as she thumped her hands onto her hips. "Anyone human would be emotional. . . ."

I tuned them out quickly and let my gaze travel to Clara and Harmony, who had taken seats on the other black leather couch. While Harmony sobbed Clara was murmuring something to her that I couldn't hear.

I closed my own eyes for a minute, suddenly very tired.

"It was totally gross, I mean really totally gross. . . ." a high-pitched voice was insisting.

Eric. That had to be Eric. But where was he? And where was Ace? I pulled my eyes open with an effort. They weren't in the living room.

"Why did she puke all over the place?" Eric asked. The kitchen. That's where his voice was coming from.

I heard the low rumble of Ace's answer but not his words.

"I never knew that people puked when they had heart attacks, Grampy," said Eric. "I thought they just like grabbed their chests and, you know, keeled over or something. But this was totally gross. . . ."

Eric was right as usual. The whole damn situation was "totally gross." No doubt about it. And his questions were on point too. Did people throw up when they had heart attacks? I didn't know the answer to that one. But I was pretty sure people sometimes threw up when they were poisoned. And Vesta had tried to tell Harmony about something, something New Age, herbal and organic. Could it have been anything but the tea? Then I thought of the teapot, lying inches from her hand. Ugh.

I felt a wave of nausea as I remembered the scene in Vesta's bedroom. And with the nausea came an unpleasant thought, one I hadn't wanted to consider before. If Vesta had been poisoned, the poisoner might well be someone in this room. But that was a big "If." She could have had a heart attack. Or . . . Or . . . Or what?

I looked at Wayne's unmoving profile. What was he thinking? Had he heard Clara say we needed the police? Was his mind jumping to the same conclusions as mine? Had he wondered yet if one of his family had killed his mother?

"And you know what else, Grampy?" came Eric's voice again, closer this time. I saw him trailing after Ace through the kitchen doorway. "The police may want to interview us all. They do that when a sudden death looks like totally bogus—"

The sound of an approaching siren stopped his flow of words. It stopped everyone's. The room was completely silent as we heard the siren grow louder. I took a deep breath and waited for the police.

But it wasn't the police who knocked at the door. It was a couple of paramedics, one stocky and female, the other lanky and male. Clara left Harmony on the couch and opened the door for them. After a terse conversation, she directed them upstairs as the rest of us watched.

The instant Clara disappeared up the stairs, Harmony stood up and started pacing. Pacing and rubbing her amulets.

"Harmony, would you like a massage?" asked Lori, her genial voice sounding strange in the silence. Her bracelets jangled merrily as she strode over to Harmony's side. "Massage can heal on an emotional, spiritual and—"

Harmony whirled to face her. "You!" she accused, pointing at Lori. "You're the one. You tried to take Vesta away from me, right?"

Lori's red nails flashed as she raised her hands and turned them palm out, as if to block a blow. "I never—" she began.

"It wasn't me that hurt her. It was you!" Harmony shouted. Her pale eyes were round in her face, no longer blank but alive with a feeling I couldn't identify. Malice? Realization? Hurt?

Mandy ran to her mother's side. "My mom didn't do any such thing, to you or to Aunt Vesta!" she shouted back, her high voice ringing out pure and clear.

"Thank you, Mandy my love," Lori said quietly. "You see, Harmony is just a little confused—"

"You guys are all against me!" Harmony wailed. She swept accusing eyes over everyone in the living room, her fingers beginning the great amulet hunt on her jacket fringes once more. "They sent you, right? They told you—"

And suddenly Clara was back, her arm around Harmony's waist. She murmured and soothed the younger woman into quiet as the two paramedics shuffled out the front door.

Then we heard the second siren.

When the doorbell rang, I jumped up to answer, hoping it was the police this time. After hearing Harmony's random accusations, I wanted first crack at the representatives of law and order. It might be crucial. If I could give them my own clear explanation of the events surrounding Vesta's death before they questioned anyone else, mine just might carry more weight. Now all I had to do was figure out what exactly my own explanation was. I opened the door. It was the police all right. The two uniformed men on the doorstep couldn't have been anything else but.

"La Risa Police Department, ma'am," announced the first one. He was a well-muscled man with a well-trimmed mustache and buzz-cut hair. He attempted a smile. It gave his face the look of a friendly Nazi.

"Hear you got a dead woman upstairs," said the second officer. He was tall with blow-dried brown hair. He didn't bother with a smile.

"I'll show you," I said briefly.

They introduced themselves on the way up the stairs. The one with the buzz cut was Officer Yoder. The blow-dried one was Officer Zappetini.

"Yuck!" said Zappetini when I pointed through the doorway in Vesta's direction. I was taking care not to look myself. I remembered Vesta's sprawling body all too well. Unfortunately, I could still smell the room without seeing it.

"Did you know the deceased, ma'am?" asked Officer Yoder.

"Uh-huh," I answered. "Her name's Vesta Caruso. She's my boyfriend's mother."

"Can we get outa here?" asked Officer Zappetini nasally. He was holding his nose.

Yoder gave him a cool look and went on. "Did you find the body, ma'am?" he asked.

I nodded, then changed my mind. "Actually, Harmony found her first," I amended.

"Who is Harmony, ma'am?"

"She was Vesta's—that is, Mrs. Caruso's—roommate," I told him. "Well, not exactly a roommate—I don't think she paid any money or anything, but she stayed in the guest room. Anyway, Harmony said Vesta was really sick last night. And Vesta was talking about the tea Harmony fixed her—at least I think that's what she must have been talking about—

Harmony said she mentioned 'organic,' and 'herbal' and 'New Age,' so it must have been the tea."

I paused for a breath. So much for my clear explanation of the events surrounding Vesta's death. Yoder stared at me, unsmiling. Zappetini was fanning the air in front of his face. My stomach felt funny all of a sudden. Maybe I should have let Harmony talk to them first.

I pointed into the room.

"See, there's the teapot," I whispered. "That's the one."

"That's the one what?" asked Yoder.

I looked into his cold eyes. Should I keep my mouth shut? Probably. But I couldn't. If someone had killed Vesta . . .

"I think her tea might have been poisoned," I said firmly. Yoder's eyes narrowed. "Well, it's a possibility, anyway," I added defensively.

Yoder looked at Zappetini. Zappetini looked at Yoder.

"Get Upton and Amador," Yoder said finally. He let out a low sigh as he turned back to me.

"Is there someplace where we can talk in private?" he asked.

"About time," Zappetini muttered as he descended the stairs. I wondered if he was going to get Upton and Amador. And who or what were Upton and Amador?

I opened my mouth to ask, then looked into Officer Yoder's eyes and changed my mind. "How about the guest room?" I suggested.

The guest room had changed since the last time I had seen it. It still had the same gold-and-ivory flocked wallpaper as Vesta's room and a double bed covered in a chocolate-brown spread. But now large pieces of newsprint were taped to the walls, even to the ceiling. And on each piece of newsprint there was a sketch in black ink of one or another of two objects. I recognized the bold black outlines of the crosses at once, but it was only when I realized that the sketches must be Harmony's work that I identified the other objects as crystals. She had rounded their edges, making them appear vaguely phallic rather than sharply prismatic.

"Whose work is this?" asked Officer Yoder.

I jumped. I had almost forgotten him as I stared at the drawings.

"Harmony's," I answered. "At least I think it is."

He sniffed. At first I thought it was a comment, but then I noticed the scent in the room. It was Harmony's scent of course. I couldn't smell any leather, but the odor of Harmony's sweat, patchouli oil and marijuana were evident. I guessed it was the latter component that Yoder was sniffing at.

I sighed and sat down on the edge of the neatly made bed. Yoder sat on the lone wooden chair and pulled a three-by-five spiral notebook from his breast pocket.

Twenty minutes later, he'd filled up every page in his notebook, front and back, and was writing in the margins. I had told him everything I knew about Vesta Caruso, explained her relationship to each and every person in the living room and recounted all that I could remember of the events of the last fifteen hours. I took a deep breath and congratulated myself. Everything was clear. At least I hoped so. I offered Officer Yoder a tentative smile.

"So," he said. "You harbored quite a dislike for your boyfriend's mother, didn't you?"

Maybe I had been a little too clear. I ditched the smile. "I didn't exactly dislike her," I began uncomfortably.

The doorbell rang again.

"Stay here," Yoder commanded and left the room.

I sat where I was and stared at Harmony's artwork for a while. I didn't have much choice. It was hard to find a spot on the walls or the ceiling that didn't have newsprint taped to it. Finally, I closed my eyes and began to worry in earnest. Did Officer Yoder actually think I had murdered Vesta? He couldn't, could he? Didn't he have to warn me if he did? Or maybe he just thought I was some kind of lunatic who imagined poison everywhere. Or—

I heard the door creak and opened my eyes in time to see Officer Yoder ushering in two newcomers. One was a tall, cadaverously thin man with a fringe of red hair around the edges of his otherwise bald head. He rotated his head on his shoulders as if his neck was bothering him. The second was an equally tall, black woman with a round, freckled face. She flashed me a toothy grin. Both were wearing navy blue suits.

"Ms. Jasper, this is Detective Sergeant Upton," Yoder said with a nod to the thin man. "And Detective Amador—"

"We need more chairs," the detective sergeant interrupted. He drummed his fingers on the side of his thigh. "Amador, tell him to get more chairs."

"Officer Yoder, get the man more chairs," Detective Amador ordered.

As Yoder left the room, Upton turned his gaze in my direction. Well, almost in my direction. Actually, he was looking somewhere over my left shoulder.

"Tell her she's going to have to start from the beginning and tell us everything over again," he said out of the corner of his mouth.

"Ms. Jasper, you're going to have to start at the beginning—" Amador began.

"Got it," I told her.

Upton aimed a fierce glare over my left shoulder. Then he began popping his knuckles.

Was I supposed to pretend I didn't hear his orders to Detective Amador? I turned to her and tilted my head in a question. She grinned and winked back.

I was relieved when Officer Yoder brought in three kitchen chairs. He offered a note of sanity to the scene in the guest room as he set the chairs down, two of them with their backs to the bed and the other one facing the first two. Upton told Amador to tell me to take the lone chair facing the bed. She did and I did. Then they sat down simultaneously and the questioning began.

They ran through everything I had told Officer Yoder and more, with Detective Amador relaying Detective Sergeant Upton's questions to me as he tapped his feet, rotated his head, popped his knuckles and drummed his fingers. After a while, I got used to the arrangement. It gave me a chance to think out my answers, for which I was grateful. But it took twice as long to get through the exercise, for which I was not grateful. By the time they began asking me about Wayne, I was tapping my fingers and rotating my own head.

"Ask her how the boyfriend felt about his mother," Upton said.

I waited for Amador's relay before telling them that they would have to ask Wayne himself.

"Ask her if the boyfriend knew where the tea was kept."

Again, I said I didn't know. They would have to ask Wayne.

After the fifteenth or twentieth time that I told them they would have to ask Wayne, I started wondering if Wayne was going to be able to answer them. Damn. Why hadn't I just left it alone? Maybe they would have believed that Vesta had merely suffered a heart attack. Maybe she had.

Then they got onto me. Ask her how she felt about her boyfriend's mother. Ask her if they ever argued about the mother. Ask her if she would have liked to see the mother back in a mental institution. Ask her . . . Ask her . . . Ask her . . .

"Tell her she can leave," Upton said finally.

It was an act of real willpower to remain seated until Detective Amador relayed the order. But I did. And I let Officer Yoder escort me downstairs, nodding obediently as he told me to keep quiet when I joined the others.

We reached the bottom of the stairs and I saw that everyone was sitting down now. Well, everyone except Officer Zappetini. Zappetini stood with his back to the front door and his arms crossed over his chest as if daring someone to try and leave.

Wayne, Ace and Eric were on one black leather couch, all staring straight ahead. And for once, Eric was quiet. But then, so was everyone. Dru, Bill, Ingrid and Trent were crowded onto the other couch. Each of them held their elbows pointing inwards and their hands clasped together as if to avoid touching any more than was necessary. Lori and Mandy sat cross-legged on the floor a few yards away from Gail, who had stretched her legs out and was staring at the ceiling. And Harmony was sitting in Vesta's big black easy chair with Clara perched beside her on the armrest. Harmony's face looked oddly content as she leaned back in the big chair, maybe even triumphant. I subdued an incipient shiver and walked over to Wayne's couch.

Ace moved over without speaking and I squeezed in between him and Wayne. I touched Wayne's arm lightly, wishing I could talk to him, alone and at length.

"Harmony Fitch," Officer Yoder called out. "Please come with me."

The look of contentment on Harmony's face was instantly transformed into panic.

"No!" she cried. "I didn't do nothin' wrong. I just made her the tea like always, right?"

"We just want to talk to you," Yoder told her gently. He bent over Harmony and held his arm out for her to take. Suddenly, he looked like a human being instead of a Nazi.

"It'll be fine," whispered Clara.

Harmony took his arm and allowed herself to be guided up the stairs, all the while protesting in a shrill voice.

"Vesta was my friend. She told me stuff, right? I wouldn't do nothin' to hurt her. She didn't even like these guys. They'll tell you lies. They always tell lies. Vesta said—" And then her voice was gone as a door closed.

I took one last look at Wayne's stiff profile, then leaned back against the couch and closed my eyes.

A picture of Vesta bloomed in my mind's eye, not as she had been when I found her body but as she had been when she was alive, her intense, bony face alert and smiling. And I realized I would miss her. The thought was so astounding, it popped my eyes open. I would miss Vesta.

For all the abuse the woman had heaped on Wayne, even on me, I realized that I had learned to . . . not to like her exactly . . . but maybe to enjoy her company occasionally. Vesta hadn't followed the rules. If the emperor wore no clothes, she was the first to point it out. And every now and again, her nasty comments were the very ones I would have liked to make myself if I hadn't been so damned polite.

I turned to Wayne, wanting to share the realization, and then remembered Officer Zappetini. I sighed loudly. They couldn't arrest me for that. Then I closed my eyes once more and sank back against the cushions of the couch, urging my mind to contemplate future gag gifts instead of suspicions of murder. It didn't work.

Harmony's shrill voice sounded on the stairs some minutes later. Officer Yoder escorted her back to her chair, then turned toward our couch.

"Wayne Caruso," he called out. "Please come with me."

Panic grabbed my heart and twisted. I couldn't breathe. Was Wayne ready to be interviewed? He turned to me for a second, and I saw intelligence in his eyes. Then he rose to his feet, bending over at the last moment to give me a kiss on the forehead before he followed Yoder up the stairs.

By the time Wayne returned, I had imagined everything from his arrest to his execution. Not to mention my own. And that was in between telling myself everything would be all right and berating myself for having raised the issue of poison in the first place. But Wayne's color looked good as he returned to sit beside me. And his steps were sure. He wasn't shuffling anymore.

He clasped my hand gently as he sat down, and even looked into my eyes for one blissful instant. Then he turned his gaze straight ahead again. I wanted to scream.

"Clara Kushiyama," Yoder was calling. "Please—"

"Officer Yoder," I interrupted. "May we leave now? We've both been interviewed and—"

Wayne clasped my hand again, this time not so gently.

"It's okay, Officer," he growled. "We'll stay."

I stared at him with my mouth open. He kissed my upper lip. I shut my mouth. And kept it shut for three more, endless hours.

The police interviewed Clara and each of the Skeritts and their spouses, one by one. Trent, Ingrid, Dru, Ace and Bill went first. Then the second generation, Lori and Gail. Then Mandy went up with Lori at her side. And finally they called Eric. Eric leapt up off the couch. Ace got up more slowly to accompany him.

"You know what?" Eric said to Officer Yoder.

"No, what?" Yoder replied. He smiled at Eric. I smiled too. Yoder had made a big mistake.

"You gotta read me my rights," Eric told him. "Or else the whole thing is totally bogus—"

"Only if we suspect you of a crime—" Yoder corrected him.

"No, no," Eric insisted. He was on his tiptoes now, squirming with righteousness. "You gotta read me my rights. It's called the Miranda ruling. It's totally cool. See, there was this guy named Miranda and—"

"Don't worry about it," Yoder advised, no longer smiling.

"You know what else?" Eric said.

Yoder shook his head impatiently.

"You're supposed to have this little card. And then you pull it out of your pocket, you know, or else it's totally bogus—"

"Only if we suspect you—" Yoder tried again.

"No," insisted Eric. "You gotta tell me all this cool stuff. Like I have a right to an attorney—"

"Okay!" Yoder shouted. "You have the right to remain silent . . ."

– Six –

Officer Yoder's reading of the Miranda rights was definitely
the highlight of the morning. It would have been nice to clap
warmly for his performance and then rise from our seats to
leave, but Wayne wasn't up for it. He wasn't up for leaving
fifteen minutes later either, after the final interview had been
conducted and the visiting Skeritts had departed. Or even
after Clara had finally quit the scene. Maybe this refusal to
decamp was some kind of necessary penance for him, part of
his unique grieving process. But for me, it was just aimless
torment.

We sat, glued to the black leather couch and watched,
along with Harmony, who leaned back in Vesta's easy chair to
stare at something only she could see in the space above her,
as a continuing cast of characters from the police department
buzzed in and out of Vesta's condo. Even the coroner's office
had sent an investigator, one Jenny Quintara, a plump
brown-skinned woman who seemed almost suspiciously
serene in the face of death.

It wasn't until after Vesta's body had been zipped up tightly
in a plastic bag and carried out the front door on a stretcher
that Wayne finally stood. And when he stood, his movements
were like an invalid's, slow and tentative. I jumped up beside
him and together we climbed the stairs to the bedroom area
one last time. Officer Yoder and Detective Amador were in
the hallway outside the guest room, whispering intently.

"Tell me what you find out," Wayne barked, his voice
rough with disuse.

Yoder's head jerked up, startled.

"Please," Wayne added in a softer tone.

Amador was unruffled by the request. "We'll keep you informed," she said with a flash of a smile. Then she turned back to Yoder.

Wayne grunted.

My eyes traveled to the door of Vesta's bedroom. It was shut now, with a red coroner's seal glued across the doorjamb. I felt a surge of nausea.

"Well, goodbye then," I said quickly and took Wayne by the elbow. It seemed to take forever to get back down the stairs and across the expanse of the living room carpet.

As I pulled the front door open, I heard Harmony's shrill voice call out from behind us.

"Thank you ever so much for comin'," she said, her voice lilting in a mild Southern accent I had never heard on her lips before.

I looked over my shoulder. Harmony was smiling widely, her teeth gleaming. Who did that grin remind me of? Vesta, that's who, I realized with a shiver. Harmony had Vesta's shark smile down pat. Damn, that was spooky. I grabbed Wayne's hand and pulled him through the doorway, out into the sunlight.

"God, Wayne," I whispered as he shut the door behind us. "Do you think she's really crazy?"

He shrugged without saying anything and walked toward the car. I suppressed a groan, struggling between sympathy and impatience. After spending the entire morning in silence, I was ready to talk, trauma or no trauma.

"Come on, sweetie," I prodded, trailing after him. "We gotta—"

"Hi there!" a voice boomed from behind us.

I jumped straight up into the air and turned as I came back down. It seemed to me that I flew high enough for an Olympic pole-vaulting medal, but I might have just imagined it. I didn't have a pole anyway.

"Name's Paul Paulson," announced the man with the booming voice, a chubby blond whose tan face was stretched into an all-American smile. "I'm Vesta's next door neighbor. I've been wondering what all the fuss was about." He tilted his head and stared at us enticingly out of boyish blue eyes.

Wayne turned and subjected Paul Paulson to a 100-watt Skeritt glare.

"Mrs. Caruso's passed away," I said quickly. "We have to get going now."

"Oh, hey. That's too bad," Paulson said. He wrinkled his forehead in a frown for a moment, then smiled again. "Hey, you're her son, aren't you? Are you going to sell the condo?"

Wayne had the right idea. I added my glare to his. But it didn't stop Paulson.

"Well, I always say, when the universe hands you lemons, make lemonade," he went on. "So when you sell that condo, you might want to think about investing in land develop-ment." He pulled a business card out of his pocket and pressed it into my hand. "You know, predeveloped land is a dynamic growth opportunity for creating wealth—"

"We really have to get going," I said and took Wayne's hand in mine. In tandem, we turned and strode toward the Jaguar.

"It's been really nice talking with you folks," Paulson called out amiably from behind us.

When we got to the car, I asked Wayne if he was up to driving. He grunted and got in the driver's seat. I took this combination of sound and action as an affirmative.

Paulson waved heartily as the Jaguar pulled away from the curb. I didn't wave back. Nor did Wayne.

I wanted to be sensitive to Wayne's feelings. So I held out for three whole minutes, until we were on Highway 101 heading south, before asking him if he wanted to talk.

He grunted again and pulled into the fast lane. I took this grunt as a negative since he didn't say anything immediately afterwards.

I settled back in my seat and tried to think of something pleasant as we whizzed down the road. Uninvited, Vesta's lifeless body swam into my mind's eye, twisted and sprawl-ing, her black hair pooling on the golden rug. For a moment, I could even smell the vomit. My stomach fluttered, then clenched. What a horrible way to die. Nobody should have to die like that. My eyes burned with the effort to hold back tears.

"Harmony," Wayne said abruptly.

"What?" I yelped, caught off guard. The impending tide of tears receded.

"Harmony made the tea," he muttered impatiently. He pulled into the next lane to pass a Volkswagen that was creeping down the highway at the speed limit.

"And you think Harmony killed your mother?" I prompted.

He shrugged. "Harmony or someone else. Someone poisoned Mom." His voice shimmied on the final word.

I pretended I didn't notice the shimmy. "Are you sure she was murdered?" I asked carefully. I wasn't sure. And I would have bet the police weren't sure either.

He nodded emphatically. "Mom always said she had a heart problem, but she didn't. You know that." He turned his head for an instant and shot me a fierce glance. "No other major health problems either. Nothing that could kill her. I had the doctor check her time and time again. She was poisoned. Had to be."

I opened my mouth to say that Vesta had certainly made plenty of people angry, then closed it again. Now that Wayne was talking, I didn't know how to respond. This was his mother we were talking about.

Wayne didn't seem to notice my silence. "Remember last night?" he went on. "Mom said she didn't feel well. It was an hour or so after she drank the tea."

I had forgotten, but now I remembered. Vesta had put her hand over her heart. She had been sweating, sweating profusely. And we had just walked out and left her there. Damn. My chest contracted, suddenly making it hard to breathe. I snuck a look at Wayne. If I felt this guilty, then how did he feel?

A rasping sound came from his throat, as if to answer my question. His face crumpled. He took a wheezing breath and tightened his grip on the steering wheel. The veins on his hands stuck out blue and ropy.

"Are you all right?" I asked. Ask a stupid question.

He nodded affirmatively as he wheezed. Get a stupid answer.

"It's okay to cry," I said gently, wondering an instant later

if crying while driving was actually such a great idea.
Especially at seventy miles an hour.

The question was moot. He didn't cry for the rest of the trip
home. Or say another word. But at least he had stopped
wheezing by the time he pulled into our driveway.

He set the parking brake, took off his seat belt and pulled
the key out of the ignition. Then he just sat there immobile,
staring straight ahead.

"Wayne?" I prodded.

"I'm the only one who ever took care of her," he growled.
"I have to take care of her now. Have to find out what
happened. Someone killed her. Can't let that go by. Bad
enough what happened at Shady Willows." He paused. He
was breathing hard again. "More than twenty years over-
medicated—"

"That wasn't your fault," I argued impatiently.

"I should have done something!" he shouted. His words
reverberated in the enclosed space of the Jaguar. I stared at
him open-mouthed. Wayne never shouted.

"I . . ." he began again. He stopped, overcome. His
sentence turned into a long, painful wheeze.

"Oh, Wayne," I whispered, my own tears beginning to fall
now.

I turned awkwardly in my seat and put my arm around his
shoulders. I heard a sob and pulled him toward me.

"It's all right," I told him.

And then he began to cry, wheezing at first as he fought the
tears back, but finally letting go. He put his arms around my
neck and leaned into me as he gulped and sobbed and keened.

I don't know how long we sat there, crying in the front seat
of the Jaguar. But finally he spoke again, his deep voice still
rough with emotion.

"I have to know for sure," he said, pulling away to lean
back in his seat. "I have to know who did it and why."

"Harmony," I proposed instantly. "She made the tea. She
knew that Vesta was sick and didn't call a doctor." But even
as I said it, I didn't really believe Harmony was the murderer.
Why would she have told us about the tea if she was guilty?

"Clara," Wayne countered softly.

"Clara!" I yelped. "Not Clara—"

"She's a nurse, Kate," he argued. "Has access to drugs. Knows how much would be lethal."

"But why would she kill Vesta?" I challenged. "And why would she want to call the police if she did?"

He shrugged his shoulders and was quiet for a moment. "Don't know why," he admitted finally, his tone bitter. "Guess I just don't want it to be one of my family."

"Do you want to talk about your family?" I asked carefully. "Motives, opportunity, all that stuff?"

"Have to, I guess," he answered succinctly. His eyebrows lowered. "Could be any of them. Especially the older generation." He stared out the window for a few more moments, then added one word: "Secrets."

"Like what?" I asked eagerly.

He shrugged again. "Who knows?" he growled. His eyebrows dropped even lower. "Mom was locked up over twenty years ago. If she was killed over an old secret, it would've had to have been Dru, Ace or Trent."

"Why?" I asked.

"Because no one else was old enough," he explained. "Lori was in junior high then. I was just starting college. And Gail was in grammar school."

"Well, Vesta—your mother—sure jumped all over Dru about her first husband," I said thoughtfully. "And she gave Trent and Ace a pretty hard time for letting her get locked up."

"And me," Wayne mumbled. I stole a look at his face. He was pale again and staring. I was losing him.

"Remember what your mother said about all the generations having secrets?" I added quickly, trying to divert his impending withdrawal. "That means it could be anyone. Lori or Gail for instance. Harmony's mad at Lori for some reason. Maybe she knows something about Lori that we don't. And Gail is weird enough to do anything, as far as I'm concerned."

Wayne grunted.

"Then there're the spouses," I went on, glad for the grunt. "I can't imagine Ingrid killing anyone. Not with all her crying. Or Bill for that matter. I can't imagine Bill planning much of anything but getting his next drink. Still, maybe to defend someone they loved . . ." I let my sentence drift off tantalizingly.

Wayne didn't even grunt. He just sat and stared out the window silently.

"Even Eric or Mandy could have done it," I said desperately. "Look how Mandy defended her mother. And Eric—we think he's funny, but everyone laughing at him can't make him feel very good about himself. And Vesta made terrible fun of him."

Wayne didn't grunt. He didn't blink. I wasn't even sure if he was breathing. I might as well have been talking to myself.

"Let's go inside," I suggested with a sigh.

Wayne shuffled in after me without a word. I told myself that he was doing as well as could be expected. One good cry wasn't going to be enough to erase the memory of his mother's violent death. Or her violent life for that matter. I wondered what he was thinking. I wondered if he needed a therapist. I didn't seem to be doing him a lot of good myself.

"Do you want to lie down, sweetie?" I asked him softly.

He jerked his head to the side and back, then sat down on the living room couch, a homemade denim-and-wood model that was probably even less comfortable than Vesta's black leather one. He fixed his eyes ahead. At first I thought he was just staring into space again, but then I followed his gaze to the box. The great big box sitting in front of the couch, tied up in an oversized pink bow. The box that contained the mink coat Wayne had bought his mother for her birthday. Damn. Today would have been her birthday.

"Wayne?" I prompted.

He didn't answer. I patted his hand and kissed his forehead.

"I'm here if you need me, sweetie," I whispered and tiptoed across the entry hall to my office, where the answering machine was blinking.

The machine was far more talkative than Wayne. First, there was a message telling me I'd won an all-expense-paid trip to Las Vegas. And following that, there was an ominous message from my new accountant asking me to return her call on Monday. Then I heard a couple of hang-ups, and finally, another message from my warehousewoman, Judy. She needed to talk about her divorce. I realized guiltily that I had never answered her call from the night before.

I looked across the entry hall to the living room, where Wayne still sat unmoving.

"I'm going to phone Judy now," I called out.

He made no objection. I sighed and punched in Judy Mulligan's number.

"Jeez, Kate," Judy said once she knew it was me. "You wouldn't believe what Jerry's done!"

"No. What?" I asked on cue.

"Well, we were going to do a friendly divorce. You know. Using one of those do-it-yourself divorce books. We don't have any kids or any major property. . . ."

"Uh-huh," I said and flopped down into my comfy Naugahyde chair. I could see Wayne from here. And I was pretty sure this was going to be a long telephone call.

". . . everything was going just fine. We each made lists of what property we wanted. Just the little stuff, you know. But when we got to the dogs, Daisy and Poppy . . ."

I wondered if Wayne would be scarred for life. I didn't feel too hot myself, I realized suddenly. I was lightheaded. It was past lunch time and I couldn't remember the last meal I'd eaten. Then I did remember. It had been last night's buffet. Ugh.

". . . two of the cutest little dachshunds you've ever seen," Judy went on. "You've met them, haven't you?"

"Who?" I asked.

"My dogs, Kate!"

"Yeah, yeah. Right," I assured her. "Nice dogs." Actually I had seen the pictures that Judy carried in her wallet at least a dozen times before I actually met the dachshunds. Poppy and Daisy. Judy ate, breathed and sneezed those dogs.

"Jeez, I raised them from puppies, you know," she said indignantly. "Jerry never fed them or anything. And now the son of a bitch wants them!"

"Oh, dear," I answered. My cat, C.C., strolled into the

living room and stretched. I wondered if she'd heard the news about Judy's dogs.

"I talked to an attorney about getting custody and she said there is no custody for pets," Judy rattled on. "She said that technically the dogs are community property! Property! My little Poppy and Daisy." C.C. jumped onto Wayne's lap and yowled. Wayne didn't move. C.C. sniffed his face curiously. Did she wonder what was wrong with Wayne? Or was she just hungry?

"Maybe you guys could agree to let the dogs decide," I said absently. Wayne continued to stare straight ahead. At the box or through it, I couldn't tell which. C.C. yowled into his face.

"How?" Judy asked, hope in her tone now. The tone woke me up. Why did I always try to solve other people's problems? I had to learn to keep my mouth shut.

"Never mind," I said quickly. "It was a stupid idea."

"No, it wasn't," she said eagerly. "We could set it up so that Jerry and I come into the room at the same time and then see who Poppy and Daisy come to first."

"But—" I began.

"Jeez, it's brilliant, Kate," Judy said. "Thanks.

And then I was listening to the dial tone. I hung up the phone and sat watching as C.C. jumped off Wayne's lap and tiptoed gracefully around his feet, sniffing.

Was Wayne going crazy? How long would he sit on the couch and stare like that? For another hour? Another day? Or would it be a lifetime?

My body began to shake. I pushed myself out of my comfy chair. I had to do something. Throw up, cry, scream. Something, anything. I strode into the living room, still shaking, and stood directly in front of Wayne, blocking his view of the box.

"Wayne, I'm scared," I said.

– Seven –

WAYNE DIDN'T REACT to my words. He just continued to stare past me, or maybe through me, at the gift box.

"Wayne, I said I'm scared!" I shouted finally. I rationalized that my shouting would be therapy for him. Shock therapy. Or would it just make things worse to divert him from his own pace, his own process?

"What?" he asked faintly. He pulled his head up slowly until his eyes looked into mine, seeing me now.

"You're scaring the hell out of me," I told him. "I don't want you to go crazy."

"Sorry," he whispered as his gaze drifted back down to the box.

"Wayne!" I shouted again, not caring for the moment whether or not it was therapeutic for him, only that it was for me. "Talk to me!"

He shook his head violently as if to awaken himself, then brought his eyes back up to focus on my face.

"I'm not going crazy, Kate," he announced brusquely. "At least not until I've found Mom's killer."

He glared then, a full-browed Skeritt glare. His back stiffened. His shoulders straightened. Gone was the vacancy of withdrawal. He looked determined now. And angry. I restrained myself from throwing my arms around him in celebration, not wanting to jinx the transformation.

"I'll have to talk to everyone," he said quietly, rising from the couch as he spoke. "Hear what they say. Watch their reactions. Find out who had access to poison."

"Are we sure it was poison?" I asked cautiously.

"Ninety percent sure," he replied, still glaring but alive

now. Alive, intelligent, and leaping to conclusions. "Wish I knew what kind of poison we were looking for. Whoever the killer is must have found it here in Marin. Or else brought it with them from home."

I nodded thoughtfully. I hadn't thought about the access issue. Where did one find poison? Pictures of ant stakes, hemlock leaves, dripping syringes, castor beans, prescription bottles and bleach bottles flipped through my mind in rapid succession.

"Have to talk to Harmony and Clara for sure," Wayne went on. "But first," he added grimly, "my family. I'll call the hotel."

He strode across the entry hall to the phone and dialed. Before his finger punched the final number he turned to me.

"This'll keep me sane," he whispered in explanation.

I nodded my understanding.

"Okay?" he asked quietly.

"More than okay," I assured him. My voice was trembling, but I didn't care. "Much more," I finished happily.

He turned back to the phone and punched the last number just as C.C. began to meow from the kitchen.

I took a deep breath and went to feed her. I realized how hungry I was while scooping out Baked Tuna and Sardines Fancy Feast. It smelled good to me, really good. I was wistfully imagining how a little bite would taste when Wayne hung up the phone.

"Lori says they're all on their way downstairs for a late lunch," he told me. He took his keys from his pocket and started toward the front door. "The Old Burl Cafe."

"Good," I said. "Let's join them. I'm hungry enough to eat hotel food."

He stopped in his tracks. "No, Kate," he growled as he turned back to me. "Don't want you getting hurt. I'm doing this alone."

"Oh no, you're not," I snapped. Then I put my hands on my hips and glared. It wasn't a Skeritt glare, but it was still powerful. Wayne squirmed in place. "This isn't some kind of John Wayne western," I went on. "I'm going with you."

"But—"

"Do you think it would be any better for me to sit here waiting for you and worrying?" I demanded. I didn't give him a chance to answer. "Of course not. And anyway, if we go together, we'll both be safe."

"But—" he tried again.

"I'll get my purse," I told him.

"You're impossible," he muttered under his breath.

I gave him a big smile. "Aren't you glad?" I asked.

The corners of his mouth twitched upwards for an instant, but only for an instant before he seemed to remember why he wasn't smiling that day. His eyes looked stricken, and then he was glaring again.

I grabbed my purse and we headed out the front door.

The Old Burl Cafe stuck out from the bottom story of the Redwood Grove Inn like an open drawer. There wasn't a living redwood in sight outside the cafe. And the wood grain inside the restaurant looked more like pine than redwood. But there was plenty of greenery. Potted ferns hung everywhere. A smiling hostess walked up to greet us.

"Lunch," she inquired. "For two?"

"Kate, Wayne. Over here!" Lori called out before I could answer.

Three tables had been pushed together to accommodate the Skeritt family. The tables were covered with red-checked cloths whose cheeriness contrasted dramatically with most of the faces floating above them.

Bill was wearing his usual, vague smile. And Dru greeted us brightly as we sat down between her and Ace, but her face didn't retain that brightness once she had spoken. Even Lori's effort at her usual positive-thinking grin looked strained. The rest of the crew looked like survivors of a train wreck. Or maybe that makes them sound too happy.

I shot a friendly smile across the table at Ingrid. She whispered back a "hello," the tail end of which was lost in a sniffle. Her eyes were swollen nearly shut. Mandy sat on Ingrid's left, watching her grandmother with obvious concern in her chocolate-brown eyes. Trent sat on Ingrid's right, ignoring everyone as he frowned down at the red-checked tablecloth. I turned to greet Ace and Eric on Wayne's other side, but gave up the effort. Both of them were lost in thought, not happy thoughts either, judging by their expressions. Gail didn't look any more unhappy than usual, though, as she studied us through her glasses.

The table was as quiet as a Zen retreat. And about as much fun. No one spoke a word until the waitress came. And even she seemed anxious, standing a good yard away to take our orders, and handing us our plates fifteen minutes later with the wariness of a novice zoo keeper feeding the bears. I had just bitten into my California BLT on whole wheat, hold the bacon—the California element presumably being the avocado—when Wayne broke the silence.

"I believe my mother was murdered," he announced quietly.

Damn. I wished he had warned me. By the time I looked up from my sandwich, all the faces at the table seemed to be wearing the same expressions of open-mouthed surprise. Except for Gail, who stared as usual. Then the mouths began to move.

"Murdered?"

"It couldn't be!"

"I thought it was her heart."

"Someone killed Vesta?"

Gail was the first to react with coherence. She bent forward and scrutinized Wayne, a trace of a smile on her plain face.

"Very interesting," she observed. "I wondered if you would allow yourself to consider the possibility. The rest of us are pretending everything is fine."

"Oh, you're just teasing," said Dru. It wasn't clear whether she was speaking to Wayne or to Gail. She giggled nervously. "Vesta had a heart condition. We all know that. Don't we, dear?" she appealed to her husband.

Bill nodded graciously

"There, you see," she concluded brightly. "She had a heart attack."

"Oh, Mother," Gail protested. "Why must you always deny any—"

"My mother didn't have a heart condition," Wayne interrupted. He spoke slowly, his deep, quiet voice taking on the sound of absolute truth.

"Not any heart condition that you knew about, perhaps," Trent suggested a few beats later.

Wayne scowled in his direction.

Trent ignored the scowl and continued in a resonant voice that rivaled Wayne's for authority.

"You must realize that your mother was mentally unbalanced," he said. "Have you asked yourself yet if she might have committed suicide?"

"My mother didn't commit suicide," Wayne growled.

Trent sighed and shook his head slowly. He turned to Gail for support.

"Isn't it true that suicidal people often become manic immediately before they . . ." He paused tastefully. "Before they do away with themselves?"

Gail shrugged her shoulders. "It's possible, but I—"

"Someone killed Vessie?" Ace asked wonderingly before Gail could finish her sentence. From the sound of his voice it appeared that Wayne's words had only now seeped through to his consciousness. He looked around the table, staring at each of us in turn. I wondered what he was looking for.

Ace's eyes came to Ingrid. She let out a long sob and buried her face in her handkerchief. He continued to stare as the big woman stood and dropped her napkin onto her untouched salad. She pushed her chair back. It crashed to the floor.

"Excuse me," she whispered. Then she turned and ran awkwardly in the direction of the rest rooms.

Mandy jumped up and loped after her.

"Mama?" said Lori, her bracelets jangling as she rose and straightened her mother's chair. She turned and glared at her father for a moment before following her mother and daughter out of the room.

And then miraculously, Bill spoke.

"I'll have another beer," he said to the waitress, who had appeared sometime during the commotion.

I looked into his face. His bland smile widened. I looked away with a shiver. Was he laughing at all of us?

"You know what?" Eric said into the ensuing silence. "I *thought* Aunt Vesta might have been murdered. I mean, this is totally awesome. We could figure it out and then—"

"Are you sure?" Ace broke in. At first I thought he was speaking to Eric, but then I saw that his eyes were on Wayne.

Wayne nodded his head slowly. Ace's eyes creased into a glare.

"You know what else?" Eric said. "We could like—"

"This is all getting too silly," Dru interrupted, her high voice shrill now. She laughed unconvincingly. "No one has been murdered—"

"But they have, Aunt Dru," Eric insisted. His eyes glittered with excitement behind his glasses. "Don't worry. It's totally cool. We can do tests and take fingerprints and—"

"Be quiet, Eric," Ace commanded in a stern voice.

Eric turned to his grandfather, apparently shocked by his tone of voice. I could see why. Ace was acting nothing like the amiable clown I had met last night.

"But—" Eric tried again.

"Quiet," Ace repeated.

By the time Ingrid, Lori and Mandy returned from the rest room, the table was completely silent. Some of us were still eating. Some of us had never started. Wayne and Ace ignored their untouched sandwiches. And Dru, who had just moved a french fry from one side of her plate to the other, was now moving it back. But all of us were watching each other, staring directly or glancing furtively, but watching all the same. When Ingrid sat down, our eyes traveled to her blotchy, ravaged face. Mandy took her seat by her grandmother's side and picked up a fork. Lori sat next to her daughter and frowned.

"Wayne," said Lori quietly. "I had an intuition." Some of the usual animation returned to her voice as she continued. "Actually, I was doing a healing meditation, and my higher self spoke to me—or maybe it was channeled—but anyway, the voice said 'harmony,' and I realized what it meant." She waved one hand in the air excitedly, flashing scarlet nails. "At first I thought it was advice—you know, like I needed more harmony in my life—but then I realized it might mean Harmony, Vesta's friend. That she was the murderer."

You could see relief ripple around the table. Heads lifted. Eyes lit up.

"I'll bet you're right," Dru trilled with a bright smile. "That girl is out of her head. If anyone killed Vesta, she'd have been the one to do it."

Trent nodded sagely.

"What do you think, honey?" Dru asked, turning to Gail.

"It's always easier to blame an outsider, isn't it?" Gail replied.

She sure knew how to kill a conversation. The people at the table went back to eating and watching in silence.

But some spirits are irrepressible. A few minutes later, Eric spoke again.

"You know what?" he said, craning his head toward his grandfather hopefully. "I think we oughta go to Mount Tamalpais after lunch. It'd be totally cool."

Ace looked at Wayne.

"Fine with me," Wayne muttered.

So we went to Mount Tamalpais. All of us.

Most of the Skeritts decided to ride in Uncle Ace's van. It could seat seven comfortably, or eight a little less comfortably. Nine was pushing it. So I invited Eric to ride with Wayne and me in the Jaguar. I had plans for him. He accepted without objection.

Ten minutes later, Wayne was guiding our car up Highway 1 toward the mountaintop. I was feeling carsick. Or maybe my California BLT hadn't set too well on top of fear and suspicion. But Eric chattered easily from the back seat, even reading to us from a Marin guidebook as we went.

". . . all kinds of totally famous people have visited," he was saying. "Sir Arthur Conan Doyle—you know, he's the Sherlock Holmes dude—visited Mount Tamalpais in 1923, it says here. And—"

I took a deep breath to combat my nausea, and then interrupted him.

"I'll bet you know where everyone in your family lives and what kind of cars they're driving," I said, with as much audible enthusiasm as I could muster. I took another breath. "Information like that might be important to the murder investigation," I went on.

"Really?" he squeaked, his high voice even higher with excitement.

"Really," I assured him.

"Wow," he breathed. "You know what? I know *all* about everyone. . . ."

By the time we turned onto Panoramic, Eric had told me that he and his grandfather both lived in the Los Angeles area. They'd traveled to the reunion in Ace's big beige Volkswagen van. Trent and Ingrid lived north of them, in Paso Robles. They'd driven up in their blue Volvo station wagon, picking up Lori and Mandy in Santa Cruz on the way. Dru, Bill and Gail had flown down together from Oregon and were sharing a white Toyota rental car.

I wasn't sure if any of this was actually important, but the question of access to poison had brought the further question of transportation to mind. And even if it wasn't important, it was worth it to see Eric happily reeling off everything he had observed and more.

"They're all like totally weird," he said as we passed a lookout point and saw the San Francisco skyline below us, partially shrouded in fog. "Even Grampy is acting weird. He's totally grouchy. And he usually isn't. He used to be a professional wrestler, you know." He paused to look out the window. "My dad's a stuntman . . ." he continued.

My mind tuned out as I focused on not throwing up.

". . . and you know what else?" he was saying for the fortieth time as we turned into the parking area. "When they do a scene where a guy jumps through a window, it's really spun sugar. Isn't that totally cool?"

I agreed that it was totally cool as Wayne parked the Jaguar in the lot just below the mountain summit. Then I stepped queasily out the door and breathed in the wind-chilled air, waiting for my stomach to realize we weren't moving anymore. I took a few steps to the edge of the lot to look out at the panoramic view of San Francisco and the coastline below it. Not many parking lots have such a view. Or such a wind.

A gust filled my jacket, flapping back its sides. I grabbed the cloth and zipped it up before I could be borne away like the flying nun. I turned and saw Wayne, digging his hands into his pockets as he leaned into the gale.

"Oh boy, is this totally cool or what!" Eric shouted over the wind.

I nodded and put my hand up to shield my eyes. The wind had whipped up a dust cloud that looked sneaky enough to slip grit into my eyes. It gathered momentum, whirling leaves and discarded food wrappers into its center.

Ace's van pulled into a space next to the Jaguar as the dust cloud moved on and a new symphony of gusts took its place. The van door slid open and Skeritts poured out. Mandy looked as sick as I had felt a moment ago. But Lori was grinning as she jumped from the van.

"Can't you just feel the healing power?" she asked of no one in particular. She spread her arms and twirled in the wind, her long blond braid streaming out behind her. "Mandy, my love," she called. "Let's fly with the spirits of the air."

Mandy rolled her eyes but followed her mother as she trotted toward a manzanita- and oak-covered slope with her arms outstretched.

"My, isn't this lovely?" Dru called out a moment later. She rubbed her arms, inadequately protected in a silky lavender blouse, and looked out toward the city. Bill stood beside her, treating the view to the same bland stare he gave everything else.

Ingrid emerged next. And Trent.

". . . come for a walk," Trent was saying. "It'll do you good. Ace tells me there's a short trail that leads around the mountain."

Ingrid shook her head. "I'll stay here," she told him, her swollen eyes forlorn. She shuffled to one of the redwood benches that looked out from the parking lot and sat down, her back to the panoramic view. "I can watch everyone's things!" she shouted.

Dru was quick to take Ingrid up on her offer. She handed

Ingrid her purse, then grabbed Bill's hand and headed off in the direction of the visitors' center. I could hear the tinkle of her voice on the air as she went, but I couldn't make out her words.

Trent took one look back at Ingrid and stomped off in a different direction, his hands clasped stiffly behind his back. As I watched, I felt a nip of pity for the man. He was a petty tyrant in my opinion, but he seemed to be a lonely one.

"Better than TV, hmm?" a voice commented in my ear.

I jerked my head around and saw Gail's watchful eyes all too close to mine. I could have licked her glasses at this distance. She had a near smile on her face. I made an effort to return it, shivering in the cold wind.

The van door slid shut with a loud clunk. Ace locked it and made his way over to Wayne. I was glad to see Ace put his arm around his nephew's shoulder. He said something to Wayne that I couldn't hear. Wayne turned to look at me.

"Kate?" he began. "Okay if . . ."

The rest of his words were swallowed by a new dust cloud whirling by. But I nodded and waved. The two men lumbered away together like a pair of bears.

Then it was just the four of us: Gail, Eric, Ingrid and me.

I turned back to Ingrid. Her eyes were puffy and bleak as she stared out at the parking lot.

I motioned Eric over. He trotted to my side eagerly.

"Do you think you can cheer your Aunt Ingrid up?" I asked him.

"Sure!" he shouted.

"Go for it," I told him and patted his back.

"Aunt Ingrid, you know what?" he said. "Mount Tam . . ."

"See you guys later," I called out with a quick farewell glance in Gail's direction.

I dropped my purse by Dru's, at Ingrid's feet, and hoofed it down to the beginning of the loop trail. I was alone, with only the wind for company. Finally.

– Eight –

THE LOOP TRAIL is my kind of trail: gorgeous, paved and short. Located within a Frisbee's toss of the mountain's summit, the trail circles Mount Tamalpais in less than a mile. And the views are spectacular all the way around. I trudged off into the wind, stopping at each break in the manzanita to let my gaze wander greedily over the ridged Marin hills, across the Bay Bridge to Oakland and back, and into San Francisco. I could see the elongated Transamerica pyramid among the more conservative rectangles of the downtown San Francisco skyline. I could even pick out one orange tower of the Golden Gate Bridge, the green of Golden Gate Park and the white of the houses on the avenues below, which stretched all the way to the fog-covered Pacific Ocean.

It was heaven. Not only the views, but the escape from the tendrils of emotion that seemed to reach out from each and every member of the Skeritt family. The whole damn family was crazy, I decided uncharitably. A gust of wind slapped the side of my face, as if in reprimand. Except for Wayne, of course, I amended silently. I could feel my chest loosening for the first time that day as I strolled and studied the greens and browns of the Tiburon Peninsula. Even the wind seemed to whistle a happier tune as it blew past me. Heaven was short-lived, though. I heard voices coming my way, and tensed.

"Goddamn wind got me again," someone sputtered. Then, "Ow! Stop for a minute. I gotta take my contacts out."

"We're almost to the end," another voice cajoled.

The owners of the voices came into view, walking toward me from around the curve of the mountain. A suntanned young man in khaki shorts held one hand cupped below his eye as he pulled at his eyelid with the index finger of his other hand. An even tanner young woman looked on. I smiled and took a long, cleansing breath of cool air, relieved that I wasn't looking at anyone connected with the Skeritt family.

"Oh, hello," the young woman greeted me belatedly. "Beautiful day, isn't it?"

"Gorgeous," I agreed and passed around them carefully, crowding up against the guardrail as the young man probed his eye with his finger. Ugh.

The view changed color as I trudged on. There was more blue at first, the blue of the San Francisco Bay. And then more shades of green and beige, with a sprinkling of white and terra-cotta rooftops sparkling in the sun. It was calmer on this side of the mountain, the fierce wind just a memory.

Then the rooftops disappeared and all I could see was the green of the hills and the blue of Bon Tempe Lake. There was no guardrail here, nothing but me and the land. And a lone hawk floating on the updraft. Alone like this, I could almost imagine Marin as it must have been before people. I leaned my head back and let the sun warm my face for a few moments.

Then, from somewhere behind me, I heard a rock skittering off the side of the mountain. And something else. Was that the scuffling of footsteps?

I turned to look. But the trail behind me curved around the mountain into invisibility about thirty feet away. And abruptly, the scuffling sound was gone too. All I could hear was the thrumming of invisible insects overlaid with the pounding of my own pulse.

My body tensed all over again. Relax, I told myself. But then the memory of all the things that I was walking around the mountain to avoid dumped down on me like a landslide. Vesta was dead. Wayne withdrawn. And the Skeritts, one of them possibly a murderer. My mouth went dry. I was perched on the edge of a mountain. And there were no guardrails. I wasn't happy to be alone with the land anymore.

I took a deep breath and thought about tai chi. Not about the meditation or exercise benefits, but about the martial arts applications. I heard another footstep. It was unmistakable, now that I was listening for it. I centered myself and let my weight sink down until I was rooted on the path, then took an instant to wish that the guy with the dirty contact lens was back.

Another footstep sounded, and the edge of a figure became visible around the curve of the mountain. It was Gail Norton.

"Hi there," I called to her, my voice embarrassingly high. I lowered it. "Enjoying the trail?" I asked.

She didn't answer as she strode toward me, frowning. She just stared, her brown eyes cool under her aviator glasses. I hadn't actually realized before how cool brown eyes could be.

"Nice view—" I tried again.

"I have to talk to you about Vesta's murder," she cut in brusquely.

I forced my face into a smile and hoped she wasn't confessing.

"I need to talk to an outsider," Gail pressed on. Her frown cut even deeper into her face as she spoke. "Everyone else seems to be in complete denial. And they're not just denying the possibility of the murder, but their own feelings toward Vesta as well. And her feelings toward them."

She stared at me expectantly.

"You mean feelings of anger?" I hazarded.

"Yes, anger," she agreed. Her face lit up in a pleased smile. It made her plain face seem lovely for a moment, but only for a moment. She resumed her frown as she went on. "Anger and hatred. Obviously, that's why Vesta staged this reunion. She was a very disturbed woman, but she was certainly in touch with her feelings. That explains *her* behavior. But how about the rest of the family? I keep asking myself why they agreed to come."

"Well, why did *you* come?" I asked her, hoping that her answer wouldn't involve a quick shove over the mountainside.

A blush flooded her face as she clenched and unclenched her fists. Uh-oh. I let my arms float up a few inches, ready to defend myself if necessary.

"My significant other left me," she muttered finally.

"Oh," I said. "I'm sorry." I let my arms float back down and wondered who or what her significant other had been. A cat? A professor maybe, as dry as herself? Or how about someone of the opposite temperament, a punk rock musician or a street artist—

"But back to this reunion," she said before my imagination could take full flight. "A dysfunctional family like my mother's can produce an alcoholic if the conditions are right. In fact, it has." As she paused, I tried to remember. Wasn't there another aunt out there who was an alcoholic? Or did she mean someone else? "Or it can produce a caretaker person-ality, an obsessive-compulsive, a full-blown psychotic. Just to name a few types. And it can produce them for generations to come." She bent closer to me, peering into my eyes. "But right now, I'm wondering if it produced a murderer."

I peered back into her eyes, wondering if I was looking at that murderer. I took a deep breath.

"Do you suspect anyone in particular—?" I began.

"You know what?" came a voice from behind her.

I looked up, startled by the new voice. But Gail was more than startled. Her eyes flared wide open with fear for an instant. Then she whirled around to face the speaker. It was, of course, Eric.

"Don't sneak up on me like that!" she yelped. So much for the dispassionate therapist.

"I didn't sneak up on you!" he argued. "That's totally bogus. I just wanted to tell you guys something—"

"Well, what is it?" she demanded.

Eric glared at her. "I don't want to tell you anymore," he said with as much dignity as a boy of thirteen squirming on his tiptoes can muster. "Never mind."

"Eric, please be reasonable," she said, regaining her therapist's cool. "If you have something to say . . ."

I turned to look out at the green hills again, to stare at the blue of the lake. But the magic was gone. I couldn't imagine myself alone here anymore. I began walking again.

I was glad to see the rear end of the snack bar when it came into view, signifying the end of the loop trail. As I headed back to the parking lot, I could hear Eric and Gail arguing behind me. Actually, I only heard pieces of their words on the wind, which had returned in nearly full force now.

Ingrid was still sitting on the redwood bench, her back to the view. Her eyes were half closed, drowsy now. She didn't look as miserable as before. Dru and Bill were sitting alongside her, faced in the opposite direction. Dru was uncharacteristically quiet. But not for long.

"Oh, Kate. There you are," she trilled, swiveling her head around when I picked up my purse. "This is such a peaceful place to just sit and look out. It must be twenty years since I've been here." She stood up and turned her whole body toward me. "Oh, look. Here comes Lori. Yoo-hoo!" she called out.

Lori and Mandy came trotting up all bright-eyed, with leaves in their hair, looking like multi-generational wood nymphs. As the wind blew their way, Lori opened her arms as if to embrace it. Her bracelets jingled ecstatically.

"Yes, oh wind!" she sang out. "Yes."

Mandy giggled. But then, abruptly, her face grew grave.

I followed her gaze. Wayne and Ace shambled across the parking lot, the somber expressions on their low-browed faces almost identical. Death was back. Lori let her arms drop slowly.

It was a long and quiet wait for Trent to show up. When he did, we all loaded up in our respective vehicles for the winding drive back to the hotel. Eric rode with us again, treating us to an extended reading of his Marin guidebook.

All I wanted was to go home when we dropped Eric off with the others at the Redwood Grove Inn. But Dru insisted on a guided tour of their lodgings. Besides the Old Burl Cafe, the inn boasted a bar (dark wood grain decor with lots of ferns), a lobby (oyster-beige walls with a giant redwood carving of a frolicking dolphin), a pool (complete with pool chairs and granite statuary), and identical rooms (sand-beige with evergreen-green drapes and bedspreads).

"Nice, very attractive," I was saying for the third or fourth time. "But it's getting late. We really have to go."

"Why don't you have dinner with us?" Dru suggested, her blue eyes sparkling. With mischief or pleasure, I couldn't really tell. "The others are probably going to eat in that dreary old restaurant downstairs, but Bill and Gail and I thought we'd be adventurous. Get some Thai food maybe."

I looked up at Wayne and saw to my amazement that he was nodding. "Sounds good," he growled without smiling.

My whole body clenched. I wanted to scream. I wanted away from these people! This wasn't investigating. This was torture.

I was feeling a little better an hour later when our Por-Pia Tod spring rolls finally came. At least they were vegetarian. Dru had thought ordering vegetarian would be "really fun," and neither Bill, Gail nor Wayne raised any objection.

". . . so I worked myself up from a lowly bookkeeper to the comptroller of a corporation," Dru was saying, thus completing the story of her adult life.

"Very appropriate, Mother," Gail commented. "For a controlling person like yourself."

It was only when Dru laughed that I realized Gail had made a joke.

Bill saluted his stepdaughter with his fourth glass of wine. They didn't serve hard liquor here.

I dipped my spring roll into the sweet and sour sauce and bit in. It was hot and crispy, bursting with shredded veggies, tofu and bean sprouts. I stole a look at Wayne, hoping he would eat too and was relieved to see him pop a whole spring roll into his mouth and chew. It was the first food he'd had since the buffet the night before. Maybe Dru's stream of social babble was what he needed to hear now.

"I just wanted to tell you how really, really terrible I feel about poor, poor Vesta," Dru cooed, her cheery, freckled face taking on as solemn an expression as it would allow.

Wayne paled, but continued to chew.

"Jesus, Mother," Gail said, shaking her head. "Your sense of timing—"

"Now, honey," Dru admonished. "You have better manners than that. Doesn't she, Bill?" Bill blinked in answer. "You certainly didn't learn to swear like that from me."

"But—"

"Vesta was a very, very good big sister to me," Dru continued. She smiled, a faraway look worthy of Katherine Hepburn lifting her gaze. Was this an act? "There was a girl in my fourth-grade class, Ruthie Thompson, who used to make my life miserable with her teasing and taunting. Well, I told Vesta about it and Vesta collared the girl, collared her good." Dru's laughter tinkled merrily. "Ruthie never made fun of me or my parents again."

"Why would Ruthie—" I began, wanting to ask about the Skeritt family elders. What was it that made them something to make fun of? Or made them dysfunctional parents from Gail's point of view? But Dru was on a roll.

"For my fifth birthday," she rattled on, "Vesta dressed up just like a clown in the circus, and put on a show for me and my little friends. She was thirteen, I think. She made her costume out of a bunch of rags that Ma was going to throw away. And Ace did gymnastics." Dru clapped her hands together like the five-year-old she must have been then. "Handstands, somersaults, flips. Even Trent helped. He held the hoop for Ace to jump through."

When Dru's eyes refocused, they landed on Wayne. "I just wanted to make sure to give you some good memories of your mother," she said softly.

Wayne nodded. I reached under the table for his hand. His face didn't change as he gave my hand a quick squeeze and then reached out for another spring roll. My stomach relaxed a little.

"Vesta was always such a good sport," Dru told him, her voice upbeat again. "She wouldn't want you to brood over her death."

"Mother," Gail objected, coolly this time. "Just because you're ready to deny your own feelings doesn't mean you can project your attitudes onto Wayne. . . ."

Gail and Dru argued through the servings of Tofu Tod (deep-fried bean cakes with chili sauce), Pad Pak (sautéed vegetables), Praram Pak (vegetables in peanut sauce), and Pad Ped (vegetables in curry sauce). Neither of them appeared to be particularly angry, though. In fact, their fighting words seemed almost affectionate. Bill drank and watched, nodding occasionally at Dru's appeals for agreement. Wayne ate, slowly and without apparent pleasure, but taking sustenance all the same. And finally, the long meal came to an end.

I let out a long breath, imagining freedom soon, and reached into my purse for a credit card. A piece of paper was shoved in on top of my wallet. I pulled it out. It was a sheet of hotel stationery. Across the top it read "Redwood Grove Inn" in script. And across the bottom in block letters, "LET SLEEPING DOGS LIE. WAYNE WILL BE HAPPIER THIS WAY."

I stopped breathing as I shoved the stationery back into my purse. My heart marched into my ears, boots pounding, as my mind ran in circles. Was this a threat? And then, through the pounding, I heard my name being called.

"Kate?"

I looked up and saw Wayne frowning at me.

"Are you all right?" Dru asked. Then I noticed that it wasn't just Wayne. Everyone was looking at me.

"I'm fine," I lied. It was hard to get the words out. My throat felt too tight. I remembered to breathe again. "Just had a thought for a new gag," I added.

"Oh, I would just love to work for your gag gift company," Dru trilled. "You know, I actually sold a few ideas to Hallmark in my time."

"Oh, did you?" I said politely, on automatic now. Had Dru put the message in my purse when she picked up her own handbag back at the mountain? Or maybe Ingrid as she "watched" them? Or Eric? Or just about anyone else, for that matter. I had no idea who had gone near my purse while I walked around the loop trail.

"I had a teeny little idea for a line to go on one of your bookkeeping cups," Dru told me, bending forward eagerly.

"Oh, what was that?" I asked obediently. I prepared a smile in advance.

"Bookkeepers are a credit to their ledgers," she whispered. "You can have it for free."

"Gee, thanks," I whispered back.

*   *   *

C.C. greeted me with a friendly yowl when we got home. Or maybe it was just a hungry one. I picked her up and peered into her face. C.C. is a small black cat with white markings. A white spot that looks like a mini beret is balanced over her right ear, and another spot that could pass for a goatee covers the bottommost point of her chin. She squinted her eyes at me, looking far wiser than she probably is.

Should I tell Wayne about the note? I wondered at her. Should I take it to the police?

Wayne had been silent all the way home, lost in his own thoughts. If he had said anything at all to me, I probably would have shown him the note. But he didn't.

C.C. meowed into my face, reminding me that she was a cat, not an advisor. I set her on the floor and looked for Wayne. He had settled down on the couch again to stare at the box that held his mother's birthday coat. Oh, well.

I snuck across the entryway into the far corner of my office. Wayne couldn't see me there from the living room couch. Then I pulled the hotel stationery back out of my purse. "LET SLEEPING DOGS LIE. WAYNE WILL BE HAPPIER THIS WAY." On the second reading it sounded more like friendly advice and less like a death threat. But what did it mean? Who were the sleeping—

"Kate?" came Wayne's voice from across the way.

I shoved the note back in my purse guiltily. Tomorrow I'd deal with it, I told myself. Show it to Wayne or not. Show it to the police or not. But deal with it somehow, no matter what.

"What is it, sweetie?" I asked, trotting back to the entryway.

"Got some calls," he told me, pointing to my answering machine. At least he was talking. I played my messages.

The first one was from my warehousewoman, Judy. I groaned and went on to the next one.

"They're gonna get me too!" someone's voice wailed.

– Nine –

THE VOICE ON the answering machine dropped to a whisper. "Where are you guys?" it asked. It said something more, but I couldn't quite understand the words. I stopped the tape.

Wayne walked up behind me. "Who is it?" he growled.

"Wait a second," I told him. I rewound the tape partway. Then I turned up the sound and played it again. Now I could hear the whispered words clearly.

". . . are you guys?" it asked. And then, "I'm scared, I'm so scared. It's not fair!" Abruptly, the voice had turned loud and shrill, vibrating the tinny speaker into distortion. Hastily, I turned the sound back down. "It was the visitors, right? They got Vesta, right? And now they're gonna get me. . . ."

It was Harmony. It had to be.

"Come on over, okay?" the message finished up after a few more minutes of babble. Then we heard a dial tone.

I turned to Wayne.

"Call or go over?" I asked brusquely.

He sighed and closed his eyes for a moment. He didn't need any more stress, I realized. Or distress, for that matter.

"I'll call," I told him softly and tapped out Vesta's number.

"Harmony Fitch residence," the voice on the other end of the wire answered cheerfully.

"Harmony, this is Kate," I said. Then as an afterthought, "That is you, Harmony. Isn't it?"

A long, high-pitched giggle answered my question. I guessed that Harmony wasn't scared anymore. I also guessed that her upbeat mood was at least partly due to chemicals. Well, at least Wayne and I didn't need to visit and cheer her up.

"Are you all right now?" I asked her, just to be sure.

"Wouldn't you like to know?" she asked back, her words in singsong like a child's.

At first, I thought she was just being cute. But then I wondered if there was a hidden meaning to her question. With Harmony, there often was.

"Do you need to tell me something?" I asked cautiously, not wanting to be drawn into one of the Alice-in-Wonderland conversations that Harmony and I had gotten into in the past.

"Vesta willed me everything, right?" she said and giggled again. "Her condo is mine now."

I opened my mouth to tell her that will or no will, the condo was still Wayne's, just like it had been when Vesta was still alive. He made the payments. He owned it. But I couldn't bring myself to say it.

"She willed me her secrets too," Harmony added. This time she didn't just giggle. She laughed, a low, spooky laugh that Vincent Price would have been proud of. I could almost see her hugging herself, her pale blue eyes glowing phosphorescently in the dark along with her crystals and crosses.

Stop that, I told myself, rubbing the goose bumps that had risen on my arms.

"What secrets are you talking—" I began.

"I'm having a party," she interrupted. "Tomorrow morning at ten. All the Skeritts will be here, right? I want you guys to come too."

"Have you actually asked the Skeritts?" I prodded, not sure if this party had any more claim to reality than her alleged ownership of the condo.

"Oh, they'll come," she assured me. "Ace and Ingrid promised me, right?"

Ace and Ingrid probably felt sorry for the poor woman, I thought. So did I, for that matter.

"We'd love to come," I told her.

"It'll be real cool, right?" she said.

"Right," I agreed as she hung up. I just hoped I wasn't lying.

"Well?" said Wayne once I put down the receiver.

"We're going to a party," I told him.

His eyebrows rose.

"At the condo. Harmony—"

Then the doorbell rang. It looked like it was going to be one of those Saturday nights. Not one of those fun Saturday nights, one of those strange ones.

Ace was at the door, a lopsided grin on his homely face. Once more, I was struck by his physical resemblance to Wayne. He had Wayne's low brows and large nose, even his height and build. The build wasn't so surprising, though. Ace probably worked out. I knew Wayne did. The only major differences between them were eye color, fifteen years or so and a receding hairline. And Ace's silly smile. I couldn't imagine Wayne smiling like that.

"Hey," said Ace as he walked through the doorway. "I hoped you two would be here." Then, "Wow! Great living room!"

I always forget what my own living room looks like until I see it through a visitor's eyes. Now I saw it through Ace's eyes: the swinging chairs suspended by ropes from the high, wood-beamed ceiling; the pinball machines; the one and only couch, homemade in wood and denim; the piles of mismatched pillows; the overflowing bookshelves and overgrown plants that always looked so out of place against the standard, tasteful backdrop of white walls and beige carpet. And a more recent addition: the huge box with the pink bow which now sat in front of the couch.

I could tell the instant that Ace saw the box and realized whose present it had been meant to be. The smile disappeared from his face, leaving it dark and frowning. Now he really looked like Wayne.

"So," I demanded, a bit more impatiently than I intended. "What's up?"

Ace looked down at his feet and muttered something I couldn't make out. I turned to Wayne for a translation. But Wayne's eyes were staring again, staring at the box. I promised myself I'd get rid of the damn thing the minute he went to sleep that night. If he ever did go to sleep. Then I wondered if you could return a mink coat and get your money back.

I don't know how long we would have stood there, immobilized, if C.C. hadn't come upon the scene. But she did, trotting up with a great show of purpose to sniff Ace's legs.

"Hey, little kitty cat," he called out and bent down to pet her.

She yowled in greeting and flopped down on her back to be fondled.

Ace returned her yowl and then threw himself down onto his own back, sticking his arms and legs up into the air.

C.C. was astounded. A very human, wide-eyed look of incredulity passed over her face. And then she pounced. Ace wrapped his arms around her and pretended to wrestle her to the ground. C.C. was in ecstasy, growling and yowling and clawing his arms. I was glad someone was having a good time here.

"Why don't you have a seat, Uncle Ace?" I suggested after C.C. jumped out of his arms and pounced on him for the third time.

Ace jumped to his feet with his silly smile back in place. He brushed the cat hair off his pants legs. His shirt sleeves were shredded.

"Didn't mean to bother you," he said. "Just thought I'd come over and maybe talk a little." He looked at Wayne uncomfortably.

Wayne looked back, a hint of curiosity in his face. What the hell did Ace want? Whatever it was, it probably had more to do with Wayne than me, I decided.

"Well, I'll let you two talk, then," I told them. "I need to call Judy back."

I walked over to the phone and called my warehouse-woman. I knew her number by heart now. I turned to look at Ace and Wayne as the phone rang. Ace had taken a seat on the closest swinging chair, his back to me, and was pushing off with his feet. Wayne had returned to the couch. Neither of them was speaking.

"Hello," came Judy's voice.

"Hi," I said back. "This is Kate—"

"Kate, you wouldn't believe what that son of a bitch

pulled!" she shouted without further introduction. "We did like you said. You know, decided to see which of us the dogs came to. But Jerry cheated! He smeared hamburger on his hands first, so of course they came to him."

I clicked my tongue sympathetically, and glanced over my shoulder again at Wayne's motionless profile and the back of Ace's head.

"I said it was fraud and invalidated our agreement," Judy told me. "But now he's saying I can take one dog and he can take the other. He wants to split them up!" The outrage stretched her voice into the higher registers. "Little dogs that were together from birth . . ."

I heard a low murmur coming from the living room as Judy ranted on. Was that Ace speaking? I turned to see, but I couldn't tell by the back of his head.

". . . don't know why he even wants the dog in the first place," Judy was saying. "He didn't care before—"

"Maybe you could get another dog," I suggested.

"Another dog?" said Judy, her voice confused. She paused, then went on eagerly, "Oh, you mean a ringer!"

"'A ringer'?" I repeated, warning bells going off in my brain. "What do you mean, 'a ringer'?"

"That's a great idea, Kate," Judy said, ignoring my question. "I'll go to the pound and get an imposter dog that looks like Poppy. Or maybe Daisy. Jerry doesn't really care about them. He won't be able to tell the difference. Then I'll leave the ringer at Jerry's and he'll think it's the real thing—"

"I'm not sure this is such a good idea," I tried.

"I'll do it, Kate," she bulldozed on. "I'll go to the pound tomorrow as soon as they open!"

"But—"

"Thanks, Kate," she said. "You're a great boss."

"But don't you think—" I began, then closed my mouth.

I was listening to the dial tone. Judy was going to get another dachshund. I was a great boss, all right. I'd done it again.

I turned to look into the living room again, wondering if I should call her back. Then I noticed that Ace was gone. And Wayne was still sitting on the couch staring at the birthday present. I took a big breath and marched into the living room.

"Do you mind if I move this?" I asked Wayne, tapping the corner of the box with my toe.

He shrugged his shoulders. I took that as a go-ahead and wrestled the box down the hallway and into the back room. It wasn't easy. It was a big box, too big for me to get my arms around. But a few minutes of kicking, sliding and shoving did the trick. And the kicking part felt pretty damn good after a day of shock and frustration. Then I went back to the living room to sit next to Wayne. He was still staring, only now he was staring at the spot where the box had been. Damn.

"So, what'd you guys talk about?" I asked in a voice that was cheerier than I felt. Much cheerier.

He shrugged again.

"Well, what'd you talk about earlier at Mount Tam?" I tried.

"Didn't talk," Wayne muttered, his face vacant.

I held in the burn that was warming my face. I knew he was still hurting. But I wanted him to talk to me. Ace wasn't just his favorite uncle anymore. He was a murder suspect.

"Did Ace mention Harmony's party at the condo tomorrow?" I asked.

He shook his head.

I took a deep breath. The doorbell rang again.

This time it was Clara Kushiyama, Vesta's nurse. Vesta's former nurse, I corrected myself silently. At least she was more direct about her purpose than Ace had been.

"I came by to see how Wayne was doing," she told me in a whisper as she breezed through the doorway, her kind, moon-shaped face filled with obvious concern. I felt something loosen in my shoulders as I looked into her eyes. Maybe it was responsibility.

"He's not doing too well," I whispered back, with a nod in his direction.

Clara patted my hand sympathetically. A moment later, she was sitting next to Wayne on the couch. She didn't look at his face but instead joined him in gazing straight ahead, speaking as if to the air.

"I know how painful grief can be," she said, her voice as

gentle as a lullaby. "When you're in it, it seems like the pain will never pass. But it does, slowly, lessening with each tear of remorse, with each cry of rage."

Wayne continued to stare ahead, but I could see moisture in his eyes now.

"My husband died five years ago," Clara continued. "I thought I would never be able to live afterwards, but I did." She reached over and patted Wayne's hand. A tear trickled slowly down his face. "I just wanted you to know that you will get past the worst of the pain," she finished. "It won't go on forever. You can let go now."

He nodded his head violently in silent acknowledgment.

"Do you want to talk?" she asked him.

He shook his head even more violently and put his hand over his face.

"Need to be alone," he said, squeezing out each word painfully. My own throat felt sore just hearing him.

"Kate, my dear," Clara prompted. "Why don't you show me your kitchen."

"Huh?" I said. And then belatedly, "Oh, yeah, the kitchen. How would you like some tea?"

A little while later, Clara was sitting at the kitchen table and I was putting the kettle on the stove. I heard a long sob from the living room. My feet carried me toward the doorway, the kettle still in my hand. I didn't know I was carrying it. All my senses were tuned in on Wayne. I heard a low whimper. My heart contracted.

"He'll be fine, Kate," Clara said quickly. "Let him be alone for a little while."

But my legs were still urging me forward. Slowly, I forced them to turn and take me back to the kitchen stove. Think of something else, I told myself as I set the kettle on the burner. But the only other thing I could think of was Vesta.

"Do you think Vesta was poisoned?" I blurted out finally.

"I'm not really sure," Clara answered slowly. She frowned for a few moments. "But I'm afraid she might have been," she added.

I nodded my head. I could still hear Wayne crying.

"Harmony's gone over the edge," I said loud enough to drown out the sound.

"Harmony was very dependent on Vesta," Clara observed. "And in her own way, Vesta was dependent on Harmony. They fed on each other's problems."

"They smoked a lot of dope together," I added. "I always thought that was kind of strange. Vesta voluntarily medicating herself like that after all the years of involuntary over-medication."

"Not really so strange," Clara said quietly. "Vesta was used to a lot more medicine. And she had too many feelings she couldn't deal with on her own. The drugs helped."

The teakettle began to sing.

"I'll miss her," Clara sighed, as I turned it off. "Vesta was a fighter. She was getting better all the time. She'd have been okay." She shook her head slowly. "I don't know about Harmony, though," she added.

"Could we pay you to look in on Harmony like you did with Vesta?" I suggested, feeling suddenly lighter with the idea. "I'm worried about her."

"So am I," Clara told me. "I've looked in on her once already today. But you don't have to pay me."

"But we should," I insisted, wondering how much Wayne had actually paid her to look after Vesta. Did I have enough money to back up my proposal? "Harmony thinks she's going to be able to stay at the condo—"

A long, keening sob broke into my consciousness. All my muscles tensed.

"He'll be all right, Kate," said Clara, on her feet in an instant. She reached up and put an arm around my shoulders. "You can't control his process of grieving. All you can do is be there for him. Don't expect to be able to do any more."

And then I was crying too.

"There, there," Clara said. "Sit down and have a long cry. It'll do you good."

A few minutes later she was gone. We never did have any tea. And my sinuses ached from crying. But she was right. I did feel better, lighter at least. Maybe that was why Ingrid cried so much. Crying, I thought, the new addiction.

"Kate?" came a voice from the kitchen doorway. I turned and saw Wayne, his eyes red under his overhanging brows. "You okay?" he asked.

I nodded.

"You?" I asked back.

He nodded.

I gestured toward a chair across the table. He sat down. And began talking.

"Been trying to remember," he said. "Can't remember a lot. We lived over a bar for a long time. Mom worked there." He was talking faster than usual, speeding through his words. "My uncles both gave her money periodically, but she spent it. Clothes, fancy dinners. I don't know what."

He shook his head and went on. "And then it'd be gone and we'd live on peanuts and pretzels from the bar. And pancakes for dinner. I thought the pancakes were really fun the first few times. Didn't know we were eating them 'cause we were poor. And then there was a man. Some guy from the bar. Mom was laughing and flirting, happy finally. She said he was going to marry her. But he didn't. Turned out he was already married."

He sighed and looked down at the table. I kept my mouth shut. I could tell he had more to say.

"Mom was really angry after that," he growled. "I tried to make her happy, but it got harder and harder. She was so angry. Even Uncle Ace couldn't cheer her up." He swallowed. "When I left for college, she flipped out. It was my fault. I didn't even find out in time to help her. She was already in the hospital under medication when I got there."

He looked up from the table. "And Kate," he whispered. "I wanted her dead so many times. I loved her, and I wanted her happy. And I wanted her dead."

- Ten -

"BUT YOU DIDN'T kill her," I said.

Wayne didn't answer me. He was looking down at the table again. I felt my pulse pop into gear and accelerate.

"But you didn't kill her," I stated again, loudly this time. "Right?"

Wayne looked up at me, eyebrows raised.

"You didn't, did you?" I asked, an involuntary tremor creeping into my voice.

"Of course not," he answered brusquely. His eyebrows dropped back into frowning position.

"Wayne, listen to me," I said, once my pulse had slowed again. "Killing someone and wanting them dead are two different things."

His eyebrows sank even lower. "Very different things," he growled in assent. "Very different."

And that was the end of that conversation.

I headed into my office to do some paperwork while Wayne resumed brooding. I had a feeling I'd better do what I could now. If we were going to be poking our noses into Vesta's death, I was bound to lose some work time in the next couple of weeks, and I couldn't afford it. In my business, October counted as the Christmas season. The late Christmas season.

I picked up an inventory summary for coffee mugs. These were my biggest items. Mugs with shark handles for the lawyers, caduceus cups for the doctors, little silver safes for the bankers, bull and bear cups for the stockbrokers; the list went on and on. They were all made and hopefully sitting safe and unbroken in my warehouse. But would I need more? I had to order them now from the manufacturers if I did.

My stomach began to hurt like it did every year about this time. The inventory had to be just right. Too low and I wouldn't be able to fill my customers' orders. Too high and I would be stuck with excess inventory that would eat up my slender profit margin, the margin I lived on. I reached for my files from the year before. The instant my fingertips touched manila, the doorbell rang again.

The memories of the whole terrible day flooded over me as I got up to answer the bell. I forgot all about profit margins as the hurt in my stomach turned to nausea. It was almost ten o'clock on Saturday night. Who was at the door now?

"Howdy-hi," said Felix as I opened up. Damn. I should have guessed he'd turn up sooner or later.

Felix Byrne was my friend Barbara's sweetie, and more recently, her roommate. He was also a reporter, a pit bull of a reporter. Looking at his slight body and soulful eyes, it was all too easy to forget the inquisitional fervor that burned beneath his unimposing exterior. Not to mention the insensitivity.

"Found another friggin' body and just forgot to tell me, huh Kate?" he accused angrily. Angrily and loudly. I put my finger to my lips, trying to shush him. It was useless. "I don't friggin' believe this," he ranted on. "How come you never tell me these things—"

"Stop it, Felix," I interrupted, putting a hand on his chest to shove him out the door. "Wayne's here. It was his mother—"

"I know," he replied with a smile that seemed as big as his whole face. He ducked my hand and tried to push past me into the house.

I stepped in front of him quickly, blocking his path. Experience had taught me that early intervention was the best policy when confronting Felix.

"Don't you want to know what the pork patrol has to say about it?" he whispered enticingly.

Actually, I did want to know. I took a quick look over my shoulder, hoping that Wayne hadn't heard the commotion. But it was too late. He was already there, looming behind me.

"Well," growled Wayne. "What did they say?"

Felix looked up over my head, and his smile faded. But he still tried to negotiate. "Hey, Wayne," he said. "I'll tell you if you tell me—"

"No deals," Wayne boomed. "What did the police tell you?"

"The cops think it's probably suicide," Felix said hastily. "Or maybe murder."

"Suicide?" I repeated, wondering. I hadn't really considered the idea when Trent had mentioned it earlier. But Vesta wasn't a happy woman, that was for sure. And she hadn't allowed Harmony to get help—

"My mother did not commit suicide," Wayne said quietly. Too quietly. I looked over my shoulder again. His face was grim, his eyes invisible under frowning brows, his mouth a thin, angry line.

He was probably right about Vesta, though, I thought as I turned back. She wasn't the suicidal type. On the other hand, if she had committed suicide, I was sure she'd do it in a way that would cause the most trouble. My breath caught in my chest. Had she been unhappy enough to kill herself?

"Police figure out the cause of death yet?" Wayne asked.

"Listen, big guy," said Felix, an ingratiating smile forming on his face. "Before I give you the rundown on our men in blue, maybe you can tell me—"

"Answer my question," Wayne ordered.

Felix answered Wayne's question. He wasn't completely insensitive, at least not with someone bigger than he was.

"Cardiac arrest secondary to ingestion of poison," he rattled off. "The porkers don't know what kind of poison yet. They're like friggin' doctors, you know. They ask a lot of questions, but when you try to get anything out of *them*, they just say they're waiting for the lab results." He sighed and shook his head slowly and sadly.

"What else?" Wayne prodded, apparently unimpressed by Felix's display of feeling.

"Holy Moly, give me a chance," objected Felix. He looked up at Wayne, sighed again and went on. "Coroners did the gross autopsy already," he told us. "They sent the blood, urine and tissue samples to a lab. Lab's gonna test the tea dregs too."

My mind got stuck on the tissue samples. Oh God, that was awful to think about. Nausea rose into my throat. Poor Vesta.

"Anyway," Felix went on. "The poop is that one Hermoine Fitch—calls herself Harmony—did the deed if anyone did. They're saying she's a real looney-tunes. And she made the tea—"

"But she's the one who told us Vesta was sick," I found myself arguing. "And she told us herself that she didn't get a doctor. And that she thought it was the tea." Felix was smiling again. Damn. I wondered if he had a tape recorder going. "Why would she tell us all that if she did it?" I finished weakly.

"'Cause she's nuts," he answered succinctly. "So, I hear the looney-tunes was living with Vesta. Is that true?"

"That's enough," said Wayne. "End of interview."

"Come on, Wayne," Felix cajoled. "You and all your friggin' relatives were there partying when she drank the tea in question, weren't you?"

"Good night, Felix," Wayne said.

"Hey, big guy!" Felix protested. "Give me a friggin' second, will ya? So, when's the funeral?"

"Time to go, Felix," I told him. "Say hello to Barbara for me."

He frowned. "Ever since we moved in together, Barbara's been grouchier than a camel on steroids—"

"Gee, that's too bad," I said and pushed him gently out the doorway. He didn't try to duck this time. I shut the door and locked it quickly, then turned to look at Wayne.

But Wayne had gone. I caught one glimpse of his stiff shoulders, and then he disappeared down the hallway.

I found him in the bedroom, taking off his clothes. My pulse beat a little faster as he unzipped his pants, then slowed again as he crawled into bed in his underwear, pulled up the covers and stared vacantly at the ceiling. I told myself that this was the time for compassion not lust, all the while hoping the two might not prove mutually exclusive.

"Wayne?" I said softly.

He looked in my direction.

"Can I do anything—?"

"No, Kate," he said. "Just want to sleep. Not your responsibility. Okay?"

"Okay," I agreed, willing the emotion out of my voice. My responsibility or not, all my muscles were crying out to touch him, to hold him, to do something to make him feel better. I took a deep breath and told my muscles to knock it off. Then I went back to work.

A few hours later, I tiptoed back into the bedroom. Wayne's eyes were closed, but the stiffness of his body told me that he wasn't really sleeping. Still, he didn't open his eyes when I whispered his name. I lay down beside him, convinced I would never be able to sleep again.

And then it was Sunday morning.

I placed a quick call to the La Risa police while Wayne was showering. A man's bored voice told me to bring the note I'd found in my purse down to the station. I began to tell him that it was connected with the Caruso case, then decided not to in mid-sentence. Wayne and I had a date with Harmony at the condo. I wouldn't have time to visit the police anyway. I thanked the man on the phone and hung up.

The phone rang before I even had a chance to lift my hand from the receiver. At least it was easy to pick it back up that way.

"Hey, kiddo," said the voice at the other end. "Are you okay?" It was my friend Barbara Chu. My friend and self-proclaimed psychic.

"I'm fine," I said quickly. We were due at Harmony's in half an hour. I didn't have time to talk to her.

"Well, I'm getting this weird death vibe—" she began.

"Come on, Barbara," I cut in. "You've been talking to Felix. Admit it."

There was a brief silence. "Felix and I are not speaking," she informed me coolly.

"What?"

"I should never have moved in with him," she told me, the coolness fading as outrage filled her voice. "Kate, he is so weird! How come I never noticed before?" I nodded in passionate agreement. Luckily, she couldn't see me. Or maybe she could. You never know with psychics.

"He's eating all this greasy food," she went on, her voice vibrating with disgust. "I just know he's going to end up with gout again. I mean, even his computer screen is greasy! Jeez-Louise, he's gross. Why didn't I notice how gross he was before I moved in with him? And cheap. You wouldn't believe it—"

She stopped mid-sentence. For a moment, I thought we'd been disconnected. Then she started back up.

"Is it murder again?" she asked quietly.

"Probably," I said. I lowered my voice. "It's Wayne's mother—"

"The Wicked Witch of the West?" she breathed.

I nodded.

"Poor Wayne," she sighed. "Listen, I'll try to get over there to do a healing on him when I get a chance." She paused. "Oh, there he is," she told me. "He's not in great shape, is he?"

I looked over my shoulder. Sure enough, Wayne was standing there as silent as he had been all morning. His face was as rigid as stone and nearly as gray.

"How do you do that?" I demanded of Barbara.

Her chuckle floated over the phone line.

"Ready, Kate?" Wayne asked absently. I looked down at my drop-seat pajamas. Damn. He hadn't even noticed.

"See you later, kiddo," Barbara said breezily.

Wayne and I weren't the first ones to arrive at the condo, I realized, spotting Uncle Ace's van parked nearby as we pulled up to the curb in front of La Risa Green.

"Do you think they're all here?" I asked Wayne as we got out of the Jaguar.

He shrugged.

There was one advantage to Wayne's nearly complete silence, I thought, gritting my teeth. He hadn't reproached me for taking twenty minutes too long to get ready for Harmony's party. At least not verbally. It was harder to interpret the meaning behind his grunts, glares and shrugs.

"So, are you ready to party?" I asked as we walked up the well-groomed path to the condo's front door.

He shrugged again.

I rang the doorbell.

Harmony opened the door a crack and peered out. The odor that wafted our way was her usual sour, smoky potpourri, but somehow she looked different. It was the dress, I realized, as I gazed through the crack in the doorway. I had never seen Harmony in a dress before. But she was wearing one today, a black silk number that I recognized as one of Vesta's. It looked strange under Harmony's crystal-and-cross-encrusted leather jacket.

"Hey, it's Kate and Wayne, right?" she shrilled. She opened the door wider. "Come on in, man," she invited with a shaky bow.

I caught a flash of white as she bowed, the white of her muscular calves and bare feet. Harmony wasn't wearing her boots today either.

"Everyone's here, right?" she whispered as we stepped over the threshold. At least she didn't greet us with her wooden baseball bat this time. It was sitting harmlessly on the floor next to the door, along with Vesta's water gun.

Harmony grinned at us tremulously, her bleached blue eyes drifting in and out of focus.

I focused my own eyes on the people in the living room. Harmony wasn't lying. All of the Skeritts were present. And none of them were smiling. The muscles in my shoulders tightened. This wasn't going to be a fun party.

"Look at the wall," Harmony ordered loudly, pointing behind me.

I turned to look. The east wall of the living room was layered in sheets of newsprint, each sheet bearing one scrawled, black outline of a cross or crystal.

"Pretty cool," she whispered in my ear. "Right?"

- Eleven -

I PEEKED INTO Harmony's pale blue eyes and saw the quivering of hope there, the kind of hope that quivers in a dog's eyes when it brings you something wet and smelly from the beach. I forced an appreciative expression onto my face.

"Very nice," I told her. "You must have put a lot of work into the drawings."

"I had to do them really fast," she whispered. Her hand drifted up to a crystal-and-cross cluster hanging around her neck. "To protect the room, right?"

Maybe her rush to produce the drawings explained the wobbliness of the black outlines. I would have never recognized the crystals if I hadn't known ahead of time what some vaguely phallic shapes were meant to represent. Even some of the crosses were hard to identify. They looked more like four-legged amoebas, with their rounded edges and less than exact right angles.

"But I have plenty of protection now that I'm Vesta," Harmony added. She straightened her shoulders and smiled. The smile looked familiar.

"Now that you're Vesta?" I repeated, taking a closer look at her. Her leathery brown face looked tighter than usual, even gaunt under her blond frizz of hair. And her hands were trembling. In fact, it looked as if her whole body was trembling.

"Vesta gave me her life," she explained simply.

My stomach churned unhappily. Was this a confession?

"It was in her will," Harmony continued. "Isn't that cool?"

"When you say 'will,' do you mean—" I began.

"Kate and Wayne," came a hearty voice. "Good to see you."

It was Uncle Ace, grinning as if this were a real social occasion. He put a meaty hand on Wayne's shoulder.

"How're you doing, kid?" he asked.

Wayne shrugged slowly. His eyes stared out ahead of him, unseeing. The grin faded from Ace's face.

"Listen, Wayne—" he began, his voice a low growl.

"You know what, Aunt Kate?" came Eric's voice, advancing on me from Ace's side.

"What?" I asked, turning to the boy. At least he was cheerful.

"I got this totally awesome book at this really cool bookstore last night," he said, his voice high with excitement. "It's all about poisons." His voice dropped to an insistent whisper. "See, I've got it like totally figured out. Aunt Vesta musta been poisoned. That's why she puked . . ."

I looked around the living room quickly, wondering who else could hear the boy's words. Wayne, Ace and Harmony had turned toward him, clearly listening. But the rest of the Skeritts were apparently oblivious, occupied with their individual family groups. Trent and Ingrid stood with Lori and Mandy at the far end of the living room in front of one of the black leather sofas. Lori was waving her hands and talking loudly about healing through chakra work. A few feet away, Dru was saying something to Bill and Gail that I couldn't quite make out.

". . . gonna figure it out and then I'm gonna tell the police," Eric was saying. "All the poisons have like totally different symptoms—"

"Eric!" Ace interrupted sharply. "Not now."

"But Grampy—" Eric objected.

"Come talk to me in the kitchen," Ace ordered.

The boy followed him to the kitchen, sputtering, "But, it's totally awesome."

"You guys want some food?" asked Harmony softly, recalling me to her presence. And to Wayne's.

Wayne shook his head no. Harmony's face turned to mine. Her pale blue eyes were wide in her tan face.

"You'll have some food, right?" she said to me. Her voice wasn't soft anymore. It was loud and shrill.

"Well, I—" I began. I wasn't sure I wanted to eat whatever food Harmony had cooked.

"Come on," she said and grabbed my arm. Her grip was a strong one. As she led me to the center of the room, I wondered if she got that grip from gardening.

"See, I fixed it all up," she told me, her shrill voice taking on speed. I looked down and saw the plates of food laid out on the black-lacquered coffee table. "It's the best, the very best," she went on. "I can afford the best now, right? I can do what I want. I'm protected now. . . ."

Her words pinged off my ears as I scanned the food. There was a plate of what looked like roast beef, the edges of the slices curled and grayish, sitting on a bed of limp, browning lettuce. And some miniature quiches, mashed up next to a handful of drying mushrooms and dolmas. A sour smell drifted up from a plate of heaped chicken, and with it, the realization of what was spread out on the table. It was the remains of Friday night's buffet dinner. I wondered if any of it had been refrigerated.

"So whaddaya want?" Harmony demanded. "You can have anything you want, man. Anything! Just like Alice's Restaurant." She giggled. "Isn't this far out—?"

"I'm not really very hungry," I interrupted.

Harmony's eyes widened until I could see the whites all the way around her pale irises. Her hand went to a crystal on her jacket, then moved onto a clump of crosses. Damn. Probably no one else had taken her up on her offer of food, either. Who knew if it was spoiled? Or poisoned, for that matter.

"It looks very nice," I lied. "But I just had breakfast." That wasn't true either.

Harmony looked down at the food as her hand raced across the familiar territory of her jacket.

"That's okay," she whispered.

I looked down again. There was a plate of rye crackers on the table. And a few clusters of red and green grapes.

"Well, maybe a cracker," I said. Crackers had to be all right, didn't they?

Harmony brought her eyes back up. "They're really good crackers," she whispered eagerly. "The best, right?"

I picked one up and sniffed it. Crackers didn't generally spoil. They just got stale. And it would be pretty hard to poison a cracker, wouldn't it? I certainly hoped so as I took a bite.

It tasted like a slightly stale rye cracker.

"Great," I told Harmony. "Delicious."

Harmony clapped her hands together and giggled happily.

I decided to live dangerously. I picked up a cluster of pale green grapes and popped one in my mouth. It tasted good to me.

"Kate, how lovely to see you," Dru trilled as I stuffed a few more grapes into my mouth.

I turned to her and mumbled a greeting through the grapes. Dru's bright blue eyes were sparkling this morning. And her voice was full of good cheer. It certainly hadn't taken her very long to get over her sister's death. Behind her, her husband, Bill, wore his usual expression of bland congeniality. Her daughter, Gail, didn't look very happy, though, as she stared at us.

"You sure you don't wanna have something to eat?" Harmony asked Dru. She looked into the older woman's eyes as if issuing a challenge. Dru averted her gaze.

"Oh, dear," she murmured, putting a delicate hand to her flat stomach. "I'm afraid I just couldn't eat another bite."

Harmony glared at Dru for a moment longer, then suddenly smiled again, a wide smile that exposed large, yellowing teeth.

"You think you're better than me, right?" she hissed. "You and your poor, dead husband."

The color drained from Dru's face, leaving it white under its sprinkling of freckles.

Harmony widened her smile, her shark's smile. Vesta, I realized. She was smiling exactly like Vesta had on Friday night. Goose bumps formed on my arms.

"Did you kill him so you could marry that drunk?" she demanded, pointing in Bill's direction.

Bill's eyes narrowed in his red face for a moment; then the

congenial mask settled back down again. But Dru was not so invincible. Her mouth gaped open, then closed convulsively.

"Why are you doing this?" she asked Harmony softly, her voice thick with impending tears. Or maybe anger. "We've never done anything to—"

"Perhaps we should leave now," came a calm, resonant voice from Dru's side. Her brother Trent had come to the rescue. He stood ramrod-straight with his hands clasped behind his back as he glared at Harmony reprovingly.

Harmony turned her smile in his direction.

"Isn't this amazing?" a voice whispered in my ear. I jumped, startled. It was Lori. I don't know how I missed her approach. Just the smell of her perfume should have warned me. "It's like Vesta has taken over Harmony's body," she continued in my ear. "Maybe she's a walk-in. They say that a stronger soul can take over a weaker one—"

"And you, Mr. Big-Man-On-Campus," Harmony said to Trent, drowning out Lori's words. "You think you're such hot shit, right? Well, Vesta was on to you—"

"That is quite enough," Trent interrupted. His voice was low but commanding, his gaze intense under lowered brows as he stared at her.

Harmony's shark's smile disappeared as she stopped talking. But her eyes were still alive and flickering with something that looked like rage as she glared back at Trent. Was Harmony the one who poisoned Vesta, after all? Perversely, I had believed her innocent because she was crazy. But I hadn't seen this side of her craziness before.

Mandy walked up to Lori as Harmony and Trent continued to stare into each other's eyes.

"Mom," she whispered insistently. "This is really, really hideous. Can't we leave now?"

"Just a little while longer, sweetie," Lori whispered back, her eyes still on Harmony. "Maybe you could draw for a while," she added. "You brought your sketch pad, didn't you?"

Mandy sighed loudly. When her mother didn't respond, the girl marched away. But I noticed that she did pick up a pad of paper as she sat down on one of the couches.

"Everything that was Vesta's is mine now," Harmony announced abruptly, still looking into Trent's eyes. Then she turned to Dru again. "Everything," she repeated. "Including all the family secrets."

"I think this has gone far—" began Trent. But this time his words weren't enough to cow Harmony.

"You'd better shut up," she advised loudly, pointing her finger into his face. Trent straightened his shoulders and smoldered, but he didn't say anything more. Apparently satisfied, Harmony twisted her neck to look over my head. I turned to follow her gaze and saw Wayne standing near the door with Ace. I wasn't sure which man she was looking at.

"Just remember what I've said," she finished in a low voice. "I know everything that Vesta did."

The condo was silent for a while. If Harmony was trying to imitate Vesta, she had done a damn good job. She'd certainly impressed me. But apparently she hadn't impressed everyone.

"You seem to be feeling very threatened, Harmony," Gail observed quietly. Her intense eyes were watchful under her aviator glasses. "Could you tell me why?"

Harmony turned to her, eyes wide again. She didn't look like Vesta anymore. "Shut up!" she shrieked at Gail. "You'll ruin everything. Just shut up!"

And then she turned and ran, across the living room and up the stairs.

No one said anything until we heard a door slam upstairs. Then everyone seemed to come back to life.

Trent stepped over to Gail's side and the two of them began to whisper. I caught the words "acute paranoia" from Trent and "completely out of touch with reality" from Gail and then Lori started up again.

"Wow!" she said in a tone that seemed to mix awe and something like admiration. "What a trip!"

I nodded absently. What had Harmony meant by all of that?

"What sign do you think Harmony is?" Lori asked me.

I shrugged, a long slow shrug borrowed from Wayne's repertoire. I looked over my shoulder at him again. Ace was bent forward, telling him something. Something serious from the expression on both men's faces.

"She's a Scorpio, I'll bet," Lori answered herself happily. "Mama, what do you think?" she asked.

I brought my head back around. Ingrid had joined us.

"Poor, poor woman," Ingrid whispered mournfully. Her eyes were still red, but at least she wasn't sniffling. "I've tried to be friendly to her, but I guess I just don't understand—"

"You know what, Aunt Ingrid?" Eric broke in.

Ingrid turned a kindly smile his way. It looked good on her face, better than the tears had.

Eric flowered under her gaze. "I'm learning all about poisons," he told her eagerly. Eagerly and loudly. Ingrid's smile crumpled. "You know, some dweebs think poisons are hard to get, but they're all around us. Totally easy to scarf. Cleaning stuff and pesticides, even plants. They're some totally awesome poisons right in the garden: foxgloves, deadly nightshade, oleander, Oriental poppies." He bounced on his toes. "And medicine. It's real easy to overdose on the stuff that the doctor gives you—"

The doorbell rang, cutting him off.

We all turned to the door as a group. Why didn't anyone go to answer it? Wayne and Ace were just staring, as if the door were alive and would answer itself. I started toward it myself as the second peal rang out. But Harmony had come back down the stairs by then. She swept across the living room with her head held high, white legs flashing under Vesta's black dress.

"Clara," she said as she opened the door. "Come in and have something to eat, okay?" The words were right, but the voice wasn't. It was too high in both pitch and volume.

"Okey dokey," Clara answered good-naturedly. "I'd like a little bite."

Harmony led her to the coffee table with its latter-day spread. Clara picked up a rye cracker. I wondered if she had used the same reasoning as I had in making the choice. The crunch when she bit into the cracker was clearly audible in the otherwise silent room.

"Well, this is very nice, Harmony," Clara told her. She

patted her hand gently and added, "But I mustn't keep you from your other guests."

Harmony nodded, then drifted toward Ace and Wayne. It was a good choice.

"How're you holding up, Harmony?" Ace asked in a voice that sounded genuinely concerned.

"Vesta always liked you," Harmony whispered, loudly enough to be heard by everyone.

The whole room seemed to let out a breath that had been held too long, and conversations sprang up again.

"So it's totally cool, Aunt Ingrid," Eric said. "Grampy says I can't use any specifics, but there's like a zillion ways you can poison someone. . . ."

"Kate," Clara greeted me as she walked my way. "Can we talk?"

"Sure," I answered enthusiastically, only too glad to get away from Eric, to get away from all the Skeritts.

I followed Clara upstairs. The red coroner's seal was still on Vesta's bedroom door. It gave me a queasy feeling to walk past it. And I felt even more queasy when we went into Harmony's room to talk. The drawings of crystals and crosses had multiplied since I had last been in her bedroom. The walls, and even the furniture, were completely covered in newsprint now.

Clara lifted a pile of paper from the wooden chair and set it gently on the floor. I followed her lead and carefully moved some of the paper on the bed aside so I could sit on its edge.

"Harmony is in worse shape than I thought," Clara murmured, getting right to the point. She looked down at the floor, her moon-shaped face wrinkling with worry. "The poor little thing may need hospitalization. Do you know if she has any relatives? Any friends?"

"I don't know," I said, hoping that Wayne and I weren't the closest thing.

"She shouldn't be alone," Clara told me.

"Well, at least she isn't talking so much about being abducted by UFO's," I said. Clara brought her eyes up to look into mine.

"You know, my dear," she said softly, "Harmony's claim of

abduction isn't all that unhealthy. It may be a way of making sense of whatever personal trouble she's been through. Or perhaps she actually was abducted. It doesn't really matter. It's real to her. And it's a fairly harmless fancy." She looked down at the floor again. "But this obsession with Mrs. Caruso and her relatives scares me. Harmony showed me her stomach this morning. She's carved a V into it. To let in Vesta's spirit, she told me."

"Uh-oh," I breathed.

"I cleaned the wound and bandaged it," Clara assured me. "It wasn't very deep, but still." She sighed. "The poor thing isn't eating either. I think it may have been Mrs. Caruso who encouraged her to eat. One day won't hurt her, but I have a feeling . . ."

Clara shook her head as her words trailed off. Then she stood abruptly and replaced the paper that had been on the chair.

"I just thought you ought to know," she said briskly. She leaned down and patted my shoulder. "We'll talk more later."

As Clara and I walked back down the stairs together, I wondered what you had to do these days to get someone admitted to a mental institution. Harmony certainly seemed to be a danger to herself. But was she a danger to others?

As if in answer, the Skeritts were all heading out the doorway when we got to the living room. I heard Dru's voice tinkling a last goodbye, and then the door slammed. Harmony sat in Vesta's easy chair, her knees pulled up to her chest, her eyes vacant.

"Why don't you and Wayne get going, dear?" Clara whispered in our ears. "I'll take care of Harmony."

I followed her advice and led Wayne out the door, only glancing back once. Clara was stroking Harmony's frizzy blond hair.

"There, there," she crooned. "You'll be all right, my little one—"

I shut the door softly behind us. Unexpected tears sprang up in my eyes. I shook them away.

"What happened while I was upstairs?" I asked Wayne as we walked to the car.

He shrugged his shoulders. I looked into his eyes. He was staring again. Maybe he and Harmony could start a club.

We were getting into the Jaguar when Lori came running toward us, waving her arms in the air.

"Wait up, you guys!" she shouted. "Wait up!"

– Twelve –

LORI CONTINUED TO wave her hands as she ran toward us, her red fingernails glinting in the sun.

"Hey, you guys!" she shouted, and then she was less than a yard away from the Jaguar. I could even hear her bracelets jangling.

I bumped my head as I jumped out of the car. But I barely noticed. My heart was beating too loudly.

"What's wrong?" I demanded, suddenly afraid. "Has someone else been hurt? Has somebody died?"

"Died?" Lori repeated, dropping her arms. Her forehead was wrinkled in confusion for a moment before comprehension smoothed the wrinkles away.

Then she giggled. "Of course nobody died," she said. "Dad and I just wanted to know if you'd like to go to lunch."

Lunch? As the sound of my beating heart subsided, my head began to hurt where I had bumped it. What was with these people? Wasn't Harmony's party enough visiting for the day?

I felt Wayne's presence behind me and turned to see him scowling over my head at Lori.

"Uncle Ace is taking Eric and Mandy to see the Bay Model in Sausalito," Lori babbled on. "He says it's a scale model of San Francisco Bay and the Sacramento-San Joaquin delta. A whole acre! And Aunt Dru wants to go into San Francisco with Bill and Gail to shop, so we thought we'd—"

"Lunch would be fine," Wayne growled abruptly.

I swallowed a groan and turned back to Lori. She was frowning now too, as if she had just noticed Wayne's black mood.

"I know you must be feeling really terrible about your mom," she said, her voice subdued for a moment, but only a moment. It got loud again as she went on. "But you shouldn't worry too much. I mean, I looked at her aura and it was this terrific orange, full of strength and adventure. Whatever incarnation she's in now, I'll bet she's enjoying it more than we can even imagine."

Wayne sighed. I snuck a quick peek over my shoulder. His eyes were shut, his hands clenched into fists by his sides. I had a feeling he was trying to keep from crying. Or maybe he was just trying to keep from throttling Lori.

"So where do you want to go to lunch?" she asked brightly.

"Mushrooms," Wayne barked.

"Pardon?" said Lori, her eyes widening. Somehow, Wayne had made the word into an expletive.

"It's a restaurant," I explained hastily and gave her directions. Then I got into the Jaguar with Wayne and slammed the door.

Lori and her parents followed us to Mushrooms in their Volvo station wagon.

"Wow!" said Lori as soon as we walked in. "I love it."

Mushrooms was located between two art galleries, in a windowless cavern that had been a welding shop a decade earlier. It didn't look like a welding shop anymore, though. Backlit fish tanks had been set into the pale blue walls of the restaurant, casting an eerie, undulating glow over the room. The only other lights were the soft, rosy shell-shaped fixtures on the tables. Overall, the effect was that of being underwater. Taped background music, of whales singing, enhanced the illusion.

I had never quite understood what the decor had to do with mushrooms. But the food was good, much of it vegetarian, nearly all of it featuring the fungus in its many forms.

"This is so incredibly serene," Lori went on as our eyes adjusted to the dim light. "All that wavy water. Water's very healing, you know. And the whales are so meditative—"

"Five for lunch?" asked our host.

Wayne and I nodded simultaneously. Once we were seated, Lori continued.

"Dolphins and whales are leading the way to peace," she told us. "There's no mistaking their vibrations. . . ."

I looked over the Mushrooms menu, glad that Lori was so chatty. It made up for Wayne's silence. And for her parents' silence, I thought. Trent was studying his menu in the soft light as if it were a legal document. Ingrid hadn't even opened hers yet. She just stared at its cover.

"Oh, they've got teriyaki mushroom kebabs, Mama," said Lori. "You'll like those."

"That sounds fine, dear," Ingrid whispered absently. Then she seemed to remember that this was supposed to be a social occasion. "Wayne," she said in a stronger voice. "Don't you own a restaurant yourself?"

"Yes," Wayne answered her. So much for conversation.

I turned to him, glaring at his scowling profile. He was the one who wanted to have lunch with these people. I assumed that was because he hoped to learn something about Vesta's death by talking with them. But he wasn't talking, goddammit.

He turned my way, as if he had heard the thought. His brows were low, but I could still see the pain in his eyes. Suddenly, I was ashamed. His mother was dead. How could I have forgotten the emotional reality of that fact?

"Wayne owns more than one restaurant," I filled in for him, trying to put some enthusiasm into my voice. "And a couple of art galleries too."

Trent nodded approvingly, setting down his menu. "Didn't you take a law degree?" he asked Wayne.

"Yes," Wayne answered.

"Wayne has a degree, but he's never practiced law," I expanded. I didn't try to explain why. The Bay Area was filled with people with law degrees. If they all practiced, they'd probably end up with only each other for clients. "What about you, Trent?" I asked instead.

"I have an M.A. in education," he answered with a smile that looked genuine. His face looked softer now, relaxed. "I was a placement counselor at Fulton College for many years and then the Dean of Students."

"And now he's the head dean," Lori finished for him. She

gave her father an affectionate wink. "Pretty impressive, huh?"

"Pretty impressive," I agreed.

"Dad's got a lot of personal juice," Lori went on. "So does the whole family. Aunt Dru's a high-powered comptroller now. And Uncle Ace owns a string of gyms."

"I never thought Ace would go anywhere with his wrestling," Trent admitted. He shook his head ruefully. "But he made a good income while he could, and then he invested it wisely. He's a wealthy man now."

"Mandy has a crush on him," Lori said.

"On Ace?" asked Trent, his tone unbelieving.

Lori nodded.

Trent let out a rough bark of laughter.

"Oh, you mustn't laugh, dear," said Ingrid. "Mandy seems quite taken with Ace. And that poor boy, Eric, has a crush on Mandy."

"And Mandy thinks he's just hideous, of course," Lori added, drawling the word "hideous," as her daughter would have.

We all laughed at that, all but Wayne. And even his scowl had lessened just a little.

The conversation that had lurched so awkwardly before seemed to flow more smoothly after that. Once the waiter had taken our orders, Trent talked a little about Fulton College. He seemed very proud of his school, but insisted he was looking forward to his retirement. Lori was more volubly enthusiastic as she explained some of the more obscure principles of goddess energy to us. Even Ingrid put in her two cents worth about her work with illiterate adults.

I was actually enjoying the company by the time our mushrooms arrived.

"Well, these are really quite good," Trent said in surprise as he tasted his mushrooms Stroganoff.

Lori and her mother praised their mushrooms too (curried and teriyaki) as I took a bite of my own (Szechuan style over udon noodles). Yum. Hot and sweet and sour, all at once. Then Lori started in on a class in Taoist healing that she had attended recently. I let her words flow over me like warm water as I ate, sneaking glances at Wayne every so often. I felt something loosen in my shoulders as he began to fork lemon mushrooms, chicken and rice into his mouth.

Later, as we said goodbye in the parking lot, Ingrid took me aside, tugging gently at my elbow.

"Don't worry about your Wayne," she whispered. "He'll be better in time."

I let out a sigh without meaning to. Was I that obvious? Then I said, "Thank you," and turned to go.

But Ingrid was still holding my elbow. Did she have something else to say? I turned back. She gazed down at me with reddened eyes.

"What is it?" I asked.

"I . . ." She faltered.

My chest tightened with dread. What was she going to tell me? I liked this woman. She wasn't going to confess, was she?

But all she finally said was, "I wanted to thank you for coming to lunch with us," and, "I wanted to apologize. I know I've been bad company. I get weepy sometimes. And Trent hasn't been at his best. He's not really so cold and tyrannical most of the time. It's just the years he's spent smoothing over other people's problems at Fulton. He really does deserve his retirement." She reached for my hand and squeezed. "I'm just glad we were able to relax together, dear."

And with that she turned to join Trent and Lori waiting in the Volvo. I let myself breathe again, glad Ingrid hadn't said anything about Vesta's death. Or had she?

There were two messages waiting for us when we got home. The first was a call on the answering machine for Wayne, from the coroner's office. The second was a potted plant tipped over in the living room. That was a message for me from C.C. She had taken to this form of communication lately when she felt unappreciated.

"C.C.!" I shouted threateningly.

But of course, she was nowhere to be seen. I got a whisk

broom from the kitchen and began sweeping the loose dirt back into the pot as Wayne called the coroner's office.

I listened as he muttered "voice mail" and punched out more numbers, then told his name to someone on the other end of the line. After a few more brusque answers he actually strung together a full sentence.

"Was it murder?" he demanded.

I straightened the pot and patted down the loosened soil, listening even harder, but there was only assorted rumbles of assent from Wayne's end of the conversation now. Finally, he said goodbye and hung up.

I walked around in front of him and put my hand on his shoulder gently.

"Well?" I asked as quietly as I could, reminding myself that it would be inappropriate to grab his shoulders and shake the information out of him if he didn't answer me. But surprisingly, he did answer.

"Coroners are finished with her body," he said. His face was stiff as he looked down at me, his eyes hooded and cold. "I'm supposed to call the funeral home to make arrangements tomorrow."

"Oh, sweetie," I whispered, not knowing what else to say.

"Man I talked to is an investigator for the coroner's office," he went on. There was no hint of feeling in his voice. "Man wouldn't say much. The lab hasn't done all the tests yet. Told me preliminary tests seemed to indicate cardiac glycosides. Some kind of poison found in plants." Wayne paused and took a breath. "Man said he'd send me a copy of the investigative report, but only more lab tests would show what happened for sure."

I reached out for his hand. It was wrapped into a fist.

"Someone killed her, Kate," he said. Feeling flooded into his eyes. "Probably someone in my family. I have to find out who."

I put my arms around his neck and drew his head down to my shoulder. When I felt the heaving of his body, I knew he was crying. We stood that way for what seemed like hours.

Finally, Wayne pulled his head back. "Have to make funeral arrangements," he said in a whisper. "Have to decide.

Do we have a religious ceremony? Flowers? A funeral procession? A buffet?" His voice cracked. "How am I going to decide?" he asked, his voice a child's in that moment.

"It'll be all right," I said, keeping my arms around him. "I'll decide. We'll keep it simple. No buffet—"

"It was her birthday, Kate. How could they have killed her on her birthday?" He stood up straight, breaking away from my arms. "No procession to the graveyard. I'll go to visit her grave alone . . . once I know who killed her."

I nodded, shivering in spite of myself. The kind and gentle man that I had loved for the past three years was an avenging angel now. Would his tender side ever return? Of course it would, I told myself.

"I have to keep them here till I know," his voice ground on. "We'll wait a few days for the funeral. They'll stay for that. Whoever killed her will wait for the funeral, at least." He slammed his fist into his palm. I winced. He hit his hand again.

"Wayne," I said. "Please don't do that."

He looked down at me as if seeing me for the first time. "Don't do what?" he asked.

"Don't hit . . ."

But he wasn't looking at me anymore. The moment was lost. He was looking out over my head now.

"Wayne?" I said. He didn't hear me.

"I have to watch them, listen to them," he whispered. "All of them. All of them together."

And then he was using the phone again.

– Thirteen –

"WHO ARE YOU calling?" I asked.

But Wayne didn't answer.

I was pretty sure I could figure it out, though, by listening to his side of the conversation. He seemed to be arranging dinner for the whole Skeritt family, with someone on the other end of the line, probably Ace from the sound of it. Ugh. I didn't know if my stomach could handle another family meal. I felt a little better when I heard Wayne propose his own San Francisco restaurant–art gallery, La Fête à L'oiel, as the site for the meal. At least the food would be well prepared there. Tasty, tasteful, and more important, poison-free.

"What time's dinner?" I asked when Wayne hung up the phone.

"Six o'clock," he replied absently. Then his brows had descended completely, blotting out any feeling in his eyes. "Need to think for a while," he announced quietly and shuffled off to the living room couch, where he resumed sitting and staring into space.

I watched him for a few minutes, wishing for once that I owned a TV set, one that I could put in front of him so that he would at least *look* comfortable staring that way.

I shook off the thought and took a peek at my watch. It was just one o'clock on Sunday afternoon. Time to get to work, I decided, and sat down at my desk to face the towering stacks of paper that Jest Gifts had spawned. I didn't even sigh, afraid the sudden gust might topple those towers.

Wayne was still in position on the couch when I got up more than four hours later. I looked into his blank face, hoping, but doubting, that all his time spent thinking had helped him.

"Come on, sweetie," I said softly, reaching out my hand to help him up. "It's time to get dressed."

"Oh my, but don't you two look nice!" Dru greeted us as we walked into the foyer-cum-gallery of La Fête à L'oiel.

I damn well hoped I looked nice. I was wearing the most expensive piece of clothing I owned, a velvet jumpsuit by Liz Claiborne. And Wayne was in a suit and tie. La Fête à L'oiel was as upscale as a BMW. On second thought, make that a Mercedes, or maybe even a Rolls. Designer dresses and suits, high heels, Rolexes and real jewels predominated. It was not a place I would be inclined to visit without Wayne.

"Well, you sure look great," I responded a beat later, pumping some warmth into my voice. Not that I was lying. Dru's tall thin body looked elegant in a lavender silk dress. She fit right into this room with its pricey artwork and well-heeled patrons. Ingrid did too, in her linen suit and pearls. Even Lori had dressed up her colorful handwoven top with a few more bracelets and an extra dab of perfume, if my nose was any guide.

Gail, on the other hand, wore an uncompromising man's dress shirt over twill pants. And Eric and Mandy were in jeans.

The men were all in suits. Even Ace.

"So tell me about the place, kid," he said to Wayne, rolling his massive shoulders, as if uncomfortable in the confines of his suit jacket.

Wayne mumbled something so low that I didn't even catch it standing next to him.

Ace's smile dimmed for a moment, then relit. "Inherited it, didn't you?" he tried again.

Wayne nodded, his chin sinking toward his chest as he did. Damn. Why hadn't I made the connection before? Wayne had inherited the Fête along with his other restaurants and galleries from his former boss, Scott Younger, a man whom Wayne had cared for and been unable to protect against murder. And now Vesta was dead too. Wayne thought it was all his fault, every last little bit. I knew that as well as I knew that shark ornaments would never go out of style for attorneys.

"Wayne managed this place before he inherited it," I said, my voice sounding too high and loud for the room. "And all the other restaurants and galleries too. He's done a really great job——"

"You seem defensive about this place," Gail cut in quietly. I looked into her serious brown eyes, not sure if she was talking to me or to Wayne. "Does it have unpleasant associations for you?"

All I could hear was the low murmur of the other patrons in the room in the instant after Gail spoke. That and my blood pulsing in my ears. I willed myself not to turn my eyes to Wayne at my side, not to grab his hand. That would *really* look defensive.

"Oh, Gail, honey," Dru protested hastily. "Don't you be so stuffy now. This isn't your office. This is a lovely, lovely place. And I bet you haven't even so much as glanced at the paintings on the wall."

"I wasn't being stuffy, Mother," Gail replied, turning her gaze away. "I was just——"

"I love this collage," Lori interjected. I turned to her gratefully. She was pointing at a conglomeration of plaster fragments, red paint, string and graffiti on bare canvas. "It's a real fusion of energy, almost like lucid dreaming. . . ."

"I think the photos are very nice," Ingrid whispered behind us.

"You know what, this one's totally excellent . . ."

"Well, I think it's hideous . . ."

And then everyone seemed to be talking at once, their voices blurring into a noisy hum as the Skeritts spread out to look at the paintings, photographs, collages and sculptures displayed around the room.

Only then did I turn my eyes to Wayne. He stood perfectly still with his eyes closed and his head bowed, looking like a sculpture himself, though far more representational than anything else in the room. A Rodin figure of tragedy perhaps, clothed in a business suit. I grabbed his hand.

"It is *not* your fault," I whispered emphatically into his ear. "None of it. You are a kind and responsible person, dammit. Stop blaming yourself!"

His eyes popped open. He looked at me for a moment, then said, "I'll set up dinner," and pulled his hand away.

I watched him walk toward the dining room. As he reached the entrance, he looked over his shoulder for an instant.

"Thank you," he mouthed and then he disappeared through the doorway.

"Aunt Kate," Eric called from behind me. "You gotta see this one. . . ."

I spent the next twenty minutes viewing headless torsos, toeless feet, string art, improbable photographs and more improbable paintings, all the while wondering if I should get Wayne into therapy. Or myself. I knew there were support programs for the loved ones of the deceased. I just hoped there were programs for the lovers of the loved ones of the deceased too. There had to be, I decided. This was California, after all.

Luckily, the food at La Fête à L'oiel was far more attractive than the artwork. At least in my opinion. Wayne had set up a special table for the whole family in the back of the dining room, shielded by discreet shoji screens. Crisp white linen draped the table, which gleamed with silver, china and glassware.

Once we were all seated, a man and a woman in matching tuxedos showed up to attend to our food desires, offering the carnivores all variety of fish, poultry and meat, sautéed, baked, layered, pounded, smoked and/or stuffed with touches of Dijon, thyme, tarragon, green peppercorns or raspberry. And then there were the sauces. Dru *oohed* and Trent *aahed*, and the carnivores ordered.

Then the tuxedos turned to the vegetarians. Ratatouille, white bean salad, asparagus in pastry with dairyless béchamel sauce, baked beans à la Charente, artichokes vinaigrette, pasta and vegetables with sauce velouté. I lost count of the choices. Mandy and Lori and I agreed to split a little of everything. And then, surprisingly, Eric changed his order to join us.

"Vegetarian food is totally healthy, you know," he said, with a quick sidelong glance at Mandy.

"Of course it is," she said dismissively. Then she seemed to soften. "If you're really interested, I've got a copy of *Diet for a New America* by John Robbins at the hotel. It's a splendid little book."

"That sounds totally awesome," Eric breathed.

By the time he made it through the savory pepper-and-chestnut soup, Eric was a dedicated vegetarian. By the time he had eaten his salad, Mandy had talked him into renouncing dairy products as well. I wondered how long it would take the boy to realize that ice cream was a dairy product.

Wayne waited until the entrees were served to bring up Vesta's funeral. Dru had just speared a piece of grilled duck in green peppercorn sauce. Trent was slicing into his rack of lamb Dijon on thyme jus. And I was just breathing in the tantalizing scent of sauce velouté.

"Been thinking about the services for Mom," Wayne said quietly, lifting his tortured eyes to scan the table slowly. Ace gulped down the food he had just put in his mouth. I heard the sound of silverware being laid back down hastily. "Maybe you can help me," Wayne went on. "You're all staying for the funeral on Wednesday, aren't you?"

"Of course we are," Ingrid and Dru assured him, their distinctive voices raised together in uneven unison.

"Wouldn't miss it, kid," Ace promised a half a beat later.

Trent nodded solemnly. Even Bill averted his bland gaze for a moment, touched by some unknown emotion.

I put down my own fork in amazement. I'd never known Wayne to be manipulative before. It wasn't his style. But somehow he had just talked the suspects into staying three more days. Maybe all that thinking this afternoon *had* helped him.

Then I noticed the way Gail was staring at him. I would have bet she was the only other person at the table who knew what he had just done.

"I've got an idea," Lori said eagerly. "Maybe we could do something with the Tibetan Book of the Dead."

Trent groaned and shook his head.

"Oh, dear," Ingrid whispered. "I don't think that would really be a comfort—"

"Maybe some music, though," Dru chimed in. "Vesta always did love music so. Chopin—wasn't it Chopin she loved?" she asked, turning to Ace.

"Chopin," he agreed, his blue eyes sparkling. Were those tears? "And opera. Caruso especially. Remember how she loved . . ." His voice trailed off. He looked down at his coq au vin abruptly.

"You know what?" said Eric. "Caruso was Aunt Vesta's name, Grampy. Isn't that totally weird? I mean, here's this guy she liked so much and that's her last name."

Ace was blushing now. Trent cleared his throat noisily. I wondered if Lori or Gail realized that Vesta had never been married, that she had chosen the name Caruso for herself when she became pregnant with Wayne. I couldn't tell by either of their attentive faces.

"Well, I think Caruso's a perfectly splendid name," Mandy said, filling the silence. She looked over at Uncle Ace with a hint of adoration in her chocolate eyes.

"Oh, me, too," Eric agreed eagerly.

"Have you thought about a minister yet?" Ingrid asked.

Wayne shrugged his shoulders. Now that he had them talking, he had slipped back into his cocoon of silence.

"Vessie was never very religious," Ace put in softly. "Don't think she ever went to church, did she?" He turned to Wayne.

Wayne shook his head.

"But still," Ingrid insisted. "She must have been a Christian. You were all raised in the Christian faith, weren't you?"

Ace tilted his head and grinned. "I guess you could call Baptists Christian," he drawled.

Dru giggled, then added, "Ma and Pa sure thought so, anyway."

Trent rolled his eyes. I wondered what Ma and Pa Skeritt had been like. I thought about asking, but Ingrid was still pursuing the religion issue.

"How about a nondenominational minister, then?" she suggested.

Wayne nodded. I did too, glad someone knew how to handle this.

"And flowers," she went on, taking full charge. "Too bad we aren't close enough to bring some from home."

"Those florists charge you an arm and a leg," Dru agreed. "I picked my own when Raoul died." Her face drooped into sadness for a moment.

A man in a tuxedo came around the screen and looked at our still full plates.

"Is everything all right here?" he asked.

"Everything's fine, George," Wayne assured him, then waved him away.

"Here we are, letting all this good food go to waste," Dru said, her tone high and aggressively cheerful. Her face wasn't drooping anymore, but it looked a bit strained at the jaw line. "Now, what would Ma and Pa have said to that?"

"Eat up or else," Trent shot back. A hint of a smile tugged at one corner of his mouth.

Dru giggled into her napkin.

"And be sure to clean your plate," Ace followed up in a falsetto.

Then everyone seemed to be laughing, Lori and Dru the loudest. Ingrid beamed at the table at large.

The Skeritts really felt like family now, I thought as I cut into the delicate asparagus-filled pastry. They hadn't seemed to get along so well on Friday night, though. But then again, Vesta had been alive on Friday night.

I bit into my asparagus, pushing away thoughts of murder. It was delicious, rich with the béchamel sauce. The pasta with sauce velouté was even better. And the baked beans! Only the French could have thought to bake them in cognac, garlic, herbs and red wine.

I began to realize that I shouldn't have worn my Liz Claiborne jumpsuit after all, as I took my last bite of fresh fruit compote. I could feel the velvet straining over my full belly. Oh, well. Maybe I'd be able to lose the added pounds if I skipped lunch for the next two weeks.

"Boy oh boy, was that good!" boomed Ace, patting his own belly happily.

"Truly magnificent," Trent intoned ponderously.

"And we're not finished yet," Dru announced, draining her coffee cup. She grinned and reached into her oversized handbag. "Guess what I've got," she challenged.

Ace was the first one to try. "Alka Seltzer," he hazarded. Dru shook her head, laughing.

"Even better," she whispered. "Guess again."

"Candy?" Eric tried.

She shook her head.

Cocaine? Pornography? The poison that had been used to kill Vesta? I kept my own guesses quiet.

"For heaven's sake, Dru," Trent protested impatiently. "Just get on with it."

Dru pressed her lips together in a pout for an instant. Trent rolled his eyes. Finally, she got on with it.

"Ta da!" she trilled and pulled a black volume tied with black ribbons out of her big bag. "I've got the family picture album."

Trent groaned.

"You didn't," Ace protested, but he was already on his feet and circling around behind her to look.

Gail and Bill pulled their chairs in closer to Dru as the rest of us filed around and squeezed in behind her. I shoved my head forward under Wayne's armpit, the only way I was going to be able to see around this family of giants.

Dru pushed her place setting aside and laid the album in front of her. Then she opened it with a theatrical flourish.

A bride and a groom stared out at us from an old black and white photo. Neither one looked very happy. I saw now where the Skeritt brow had come from. The groom's eyes were invisible under the heavy thatch of his brows. Even the bride's brow was unusually low. Maybe that's what had attracted them in the first place.

"Wow, totally cool," Eric breathed. "Who are these guys?"

"Your great-grandparents," Dru answered. "On their wedding day."

"How come they look so totally unhappy?" he asked.

"Not unhappy," Dru corrected him as she turned the page. "They were just, well . . . just serious."

"Oh, come on," Gail snorted.

The next picture was of a small child seated in a formal pose with hands folded, staring at the camera gravely. He, or she, didn't look very happy either.

"So, who's this one?" Eric asked eagerly.

"Your great-uncle Trent," Dru told him.

"Oh, Dad!" Lori squealed, pushing in closer. "You look so cute! I never knew you were a cute baby."

Ingrid smiled softly at her husband.

"Turn the page," Trent ordered gruffly.

There was another small child on the next page, looking remarkably similar except that this one was smiling.

"Mom?" asked Wayne softly.

"Yes, honey," Dru whispered. "That's your mama."

I looked closer. The child's smile was sweet and dreamy. Hopeful. I had never seen an expression like that on Vesta's adult face. My heart contracted suddenly. How had Vesta come to lose that sweetness?

Dru turned the page again and Ace grinned up at us. Another turn and Camille looked out with a dazed expression on her little face. Another and Nola was in her place, looking quizzical. And then, the baby of the family, Dru, beamed at us.

"A real looker, even then," Ace teased her.

Dru giggled and flipped to the next page, a group shot of all the children. Trent was the tallest, looking thin, teenaged and aloof in the background. Vesta was maybe a foot shorter than Trent, and Ace another foot shorter than she was. Little Camille and Nola were holding hands. And Dru was sitting on the ground with her doll.

"So those are my great-aunts, Nola and Camille, right?" Eric said, pointing at the girls holding hands. He didn't wait for a confirmation. "So how come they didn't come to the reunion?" he demanded.

"Camille is a drama teacher at a college on the east coast," Dru answered. "She couldn't get the time off."

"Oh," Eric said. "How about Aunt Nola?"

"She has, well . . . a little health problem," Dru answered slowly.

"What kind of health problem?" Eric pressed.

"Never mind——" Trent began.

"She's an alcoholic," Gail cut in brusquely. "She's in treatment."

Dru turned the pages more quickly after that. As the family shots went by, I heard Mandy whisper, "hideous clothes," and Eric whisper back something that sounded like, "a total dweeb parade." Then there were the inevitable graduation photos, and finally, a picture of another bride and groom.

"Me and Raoul," Dru whispered, then sighed tragically.

Gail flipped the page impatiently, then heaved her own not so tragic sigh at a baby picture of herself. The pages moved faster after that. We saw Gail grow up from a sullen toddler to a sullen adult, and then the album was closed.

As everyone returned to their seats, I excused myself to go to the rest room.

I was in one of the stalls, struggling through that long refastening process peculiar to jumpsuits when I heard the bathroom door swing open.

I hooked the side piece and the front piece and began buttoning the front. Funny, I thought. Whoever came in hadn't gone to a stall. I snapped the neck. I couldn't hear them washing up either. In fact, I couldn't hear any movement at all as I pulled the belt around my waist and buckled it.

I stood there in the cubicle, perfectly still for a moment . . . and couldn't hear a damn thing. I could feel my heart thumping in my chest, though. Maybe I just *thought* I heard someone come in, I told myself.

I took a deep breath and pressed my eye up to the crack of the stall door. I saw a woman standing a few feet away with her back to me, a heavyset woman in a pair of twill pants and a man's dress shirt. Gail Norton.

– Fourteen –

"I KNOW YOU'RE in there," Gail said softly. The hair went up on the back of my neck. I pressed my eye closer to the crack in the stall and watched her turn slowly around, her plain face expressionless except for the intensity of her gaze behind her glasses.

I kept silent in spite of her words. Or maybe, because of them.

"Are you afraid of me?" she asked, her voice neutral.

Damn right, I thought. You're a mighty strange woman.

"Do you think I'm the murderer?" she prodded.

The instant she named my fear, I began to feel foolish. Even if she was the murderer, what was she going to do? Poison me by force in the ladies' room?

"Just a moment," I called out. I flushed the toilet a second time, hoping she would interpret my earlier silence as mere lavatory modesty.

I took one last peek out the crack, then grabbed my purse, centered myself as best I could, and opened the stall door.

"What's up?" I asked in what I hoped was a cheerful tone.

The tone was wasted on Gail. She stared at me morosely as I washed my hands.

"It's this family," she said finally.

"This family," I repeated without inflection. I didn't need a degree to play the therapist game.

She sighed. "They're all so screwed up," she told me.

I nodded solemnly as I reached for a paper towel.

"Aunt Nola's an alcoholic," Gail said, her voice a drone. "Do you know, I was in my twenties before I'd even heard about her." She sighed again. "Nobody ever talked about

Aunt Vesta while she was institutionalized. They're all in complete denial."

"Complete denial," I repeated.

"None of them will cop to the truth," she went on. There was still no feeling in her voice. "None of them. Ace clowns around. I asked him once why he throws himself on the ground like that. Do you know what he said?"

I shook my head.

"He said, 'Didn't you see the other guy?'"

"Interesting," I commented, turning my face as I threw away the paper towel so she wouldn't see my smile.

"Uncle Trent is a control freak. And he intellectualizes everything he can't control, including the fact that he has a bliss-ninny for a daughter and a surfer dude for a son."

"A surfer dude?" I repeated, really curious this time.

"Yeah, Larry's in his thirties now," Gail told me. "Never went to school. Never had a regular job. He was in Australia, the last time I heard. His life's goal is to surf on every coast in the world."

"Hmm," I said, wondering if Larry was motivated by an unconscious desire to thwart his father. Playing therapist was beginning to do something to my mind.

"And Mom just denies and represses. And smiles. Little Miss Sunshine." Gail heaved a final sigh and slipped back into silence.

"What was your childhood like?" I asked softly.

"My father committed suicide when I was three," she answered. Then she grinned. It was not a happy grin. "How was your childhood?" she asked in turn.

I pushed the bathroom door open, deciding I didn't want a career in psychotherapy after all.

"After you," I said politely.

Wayne was quiet on the way home through the city. He had insisted on driving again. I didn't argue with him. I had come to realize that he needed to act now, even if the action was as trivial as driving. Or as significant as investigating his mother's murder, for that matter. I was too full to drive, anyway. I wasn't even sure I could have stretched my arms over my stomach to the wheel.

We were on the Golden Gate Bridge when he finally spoke. "Who do you think it is?" he asked.

"What?" I said, startled. I had been lost in the view of the lights across the water. The outline of the Bay Bridge looked like a jeweled circus tent at this distance.

"Who did it, Kate?" Wayne murmured. "Who's the murderer?"

"I . . . I don't know," I answered unhappily.

"Okay," he said. I could hear a volume of disappointment in the one word.

"But we can talk about it," I followed up quickly. "We can share ideas."

"Okay," he said again. The word sounded better this time.

"You first," I prompted.

He was silent for a few minutes. I thought I had lost him again. But I hadn't.

"There's the family," he said finally. "Can't rule out anyone so far. Ace, Trent and Dru. Their spouses, their kids, their grandkids."

"But we can limit it to the family members that were actually present, can't we?" I suggested.

He nodded. "Then there's Harmony. And Clara Kushiyama."

"But why?" I asked.

Wayne didn't answer. I expanded the concept in case he hadn't caught it the first time.

"We have to figure out *why* anyone would want to kill Vesta," I said. "Motive, that's the question." The real question, I thought, was why anyone *wouldn't* want to kill Vesta. But I kept that bit of spleen to myself.

"Okay," he agreed. "Why?"

"Harmony, for instance," I went on. "Vesta teased her cruelly. And she's . . ." I tried to think of a word that described Harmony's combination of confusion, obsession, frantic fear and bruised innocence.

"Crazy," Wayne finished for me. Well, at least he was succinct.

"How about Clara?" I tried.

"Not sure," he responded in a voice as heavy as my overfed

stomach. "Nearly the same age as Mom, though. Could have known each other before. It's possible."

"Uh-huh," I murmured, but I didn't really buy it. "I talked to Gail in the rest room tonight," I told him. "She's one helluva disturbed psychotherapist. Was she always so unhappy?"

"Don't really know," Wayne replied thoughtfully. "Didn't see much of her growing up. She was a lot younger than me. I must have been thirteen or fourteen when she was born. Saw her a few times when Dru visited, but after Mom went to Shady Willows . . ." He shrugged his shoulders as his words trailed off. I guessed that Dru hadn't visited much after Vesta was locked up.

"How about Dru's first husband?" I asked quickly.

"I met Raoul once, maybe twice," Wayne said. "He was polite, but . . . oh, distracted."

"Distracted like he was thinking of killing himself?"

"Maybe." Wayne shrugged again. "Didn't seem like a very happy guy."

"Remember how your mother accused Dru of murdering him?" I asked, sitting a little straighter in my seat. Had Vesta's accusation been a serious one? Pieces of Friday night's events flipped through my mind as I searched for Vesta's exact words. But all I could remember was the general content of her tirade.

"You know Mom," Wayne muttered.

I nodded. I did know. Vesta had referred to me as "the adulteress" for most of the time I had known her, despite my repeated assurances that I was divorced. Still, an accusation of murder—

"Bill's the really strange one," Wayne said, interrupting my thoughts. "Never understood why Aunt Dru married him. Alcoholic. Never talks. Doubt that he actually earns a living in real estate." He paused for a moment as he eased the car toward the Mill Valley turnoff. "Guess I just don't want it to be a blood relative," he muttered a moment later.

I looked at him in the dim light of the car. Misery was all that I could see in the lines of his face.

"Who exactly don't you want it to be?" I asked softly, pretty sure I knew the answer already.

"Uncle Ace," he admitted. His voice got higher and louder as he went on. "He's a great guy, Kate. Just hasn't had a chance to show it this trip. He's got two great kids, Eileen and Earl. Eileen's a doctor. Earl is Eric's father, works as an actor and a stuntman. And Ace . . . I can't exactly explain." Wayne sighed. "He's just a great guy."

I had a feeling I knew what Wayne was trying to tell me by talking about Ace's children. He was telling me that Ace had been the closest thing to a father that *he* had ever known.

"Is there any particular reason why you're worried about Uncle Ace?" I asked carefully. I felt like I was playing Twenty Questions . . . with dynamite.

"He's not telling me something," Wayne answered, his voice low. "I can tell by the way he's acting. There's something he wants to say and can't."

"Oh," I said. I had a bad feeling in my chest, something beyond indigestion even. What if the murderer was the man who had worked so hard to keep Wayne's childhood intact? I wriggled in my seat uncomfortably, telling myself it just couldn't be. But still . . .

Neither of us said another word until Wayne pulled the Jaguar into the driveway and stopped.

"I keep hoping it's not Uncle Ace," he said softly. "Would I turn him in if it was?" He pulled the key from the ignition. "I don't know the answer to that question."

I put my hand on his thigh as he turned to stare through the windshield.

"You know what I used to wish for when I blew out the candles on my birthday cake?" he asked a few moments later.

"No, what?" I prompted, expecting more about Ace. But he surprised me.

"I wished for Mom to be happy," he said. My heart contracted. What a thing for a little kid to wish for. "I carried a lucky penny too. Rubbed it every day, asking God to make her happy." He shook his head slowly back and forth, never taking his eyes from the windshield. "And then I went to college and left her . . ."

And then she slit her wrists and ended up in Shady Willows for the next twenty-odd years, I finished for him silently. My cheeks began to burn. Suddenly, I felt angry with Vesta, very angry. Wasn't it enough to have abused her son for eighteen years? Did she have to destroy him completely? I told myself to calm down. Vesta was dead. And Wayne hadn't been completely destroyed. He was here now with me.

"It wasn't your fault," I told him, slowly and carefully. "You did the very best that anyone could have done."

"Thank you," he said solemnly and turned to kiss me on the forehead.

But I knew that he didn't really believe me.

Monday morning, I did paperwork and listened as Wayne talked to someone at the funeral home about text, music and ministers. Finally, he hung up and turned to me.

"Have to go look at caskets—" he began.

The phone rang, interrupting him.

Wayne snatched up the receiver before the answering machine could kick in, his face tensing as he said "Hello."

"Judy from Jest Gifts," he told me, his face softening. "For you." This was one of the benefits of having him home during the week. He was a great secretary.

"Kate," Judy said breathlessly when I picked up the phone. "The pound wasn't open yesterday—"

"The pound?" I repeated. This time I wasn't playing therapist.

"Yeah, you know," she told me. Then she lowered her voice to a very loud whisper. "To go pick up the ringer dog to fool Jerry, so he'll take it away instead of Daisy or Poppy."

"Oh . . . yeah," I said unenthusiastically.

"So anyway, I thought I'd go today," she went on. "Patty—you know Patty, my friend from softball—she said she saw a little dachshund that looked just like mine at a shelter in San Jose. So, is it okay if I take an extra long lunch? Jean said she'd watch the phones and—"

"It's fine to take a long lunch," I told her, "but maybe you ought to rethink this dog business. What if you get the dog and Jerry doesn't take it? Then you'll have three dogs—"

"Oh, I can handle that," she assured me. Or at least, she tried to assure me. "It's a great idea. I'm glad you came up with it—"

"But I didn't come up with it—"

Wayne bent over me, depositing a soft kiss on the top of my head.

"See you later," he whispered.

"Wait a minute," I ordered. "Where are you going?"

"To the pound like I said," Judy answered promptly.

"Funeral home," Wayne said a beat later. "Over to the condo to check on Harmony first."

"Wait for me," I called out, only thinking cover the receiver after I'd finished.

"You wanna come with me?" Judy said. "Jeez, that'd be great, Kate. We could meet over here—"

"No, no," I told her hastily. "I'm sure you'll be fine by yourself. I'll talk to you later, all right?"

". . . go alone," Wayne was saying as he headed out the front door.

I hung up and ran to catch him. There was no way I was going to let him face the caskets alone. Or Harmony.

We talked about Harmony on the way up the highway to the condo, trying to figure out what we could do for her. Halfway there, I was stunned by a single thought. Wayne was talking again. He wasn't chattering by a long shot, but he was answering my questions and even asking his own.

"Are you okay?" he asked me now, looking at me with concern. My revelation must have shown on my face. I felt my mouth gaping open and closed it.

"I'm fine," I told him. I smiled. "Wonderful, in fact."

He frowned at me for a moment, then shrugged away his confusion and went on.

"Maybe if we talk to Harmony, she'll be able to tell us who her family is," he said. "Her friends." He shook his head. "Can't keep her in the condo forever."

"Not at fifteen hundred a month, that's for sure," I agreed.

"Don't think Mom would have wanted it this way," he added quietly.

I resisted a groan. Wayne was the one paying the mortgage

on the condo. Vesta had never paid a cent. As far as I was concerned, she didn't deserve a vote, alive or dead. But I didn't say any of that.

"Listen, sweetie," I said instead. "Clara thinks Harmony might need hospitalization. What do you think?"

Wayne's frown went deeper, pulling his brows down over his eyes. He didn't answer me. Damn. I'd obviously hit a mine field. Wayne felt responsible for Vesta's long sojourn in the mental hospital. And now he was probably worried about being responsible for Harmony's.

I was still trying to think of a way to rephrase my question when we pulled up to the curb in front of La Risa Green. We walked up the too familiar path to the front door in renewed silence.

I rang the bell. Then we waited. And waited. I rang the bell again, and we waited some more.

"Maybe she's gone out," I said hopefully. Or maybe, I thought, she's refusing to answer because we might be from a UFO. Or maybe she's committed suicide. Or maybe—

"I've got my key," Wayne said before I could think up any other theories.

He bent over and unlocked the door. Always the gentleman, he motioned me in first.

I stepped through the doorway. The crystal-and-cross-drawings were still taped to the living room wall. But now there was rust-red paint splashed on the carpet, even sprayed in arcs across its beige surface and onto the furniture. Harmony lay in a heap in the center of the paint. I took a step toward her. That was when I realized that the splashes of color weren't paint after all.

- Fifteen -

THE RUST-RED SPLASHES on the beige carpet were blood, Harmony's blood.

My mouth went dry. My mind kept saying *No*, over and over again. I wanted Harmony to stand up and say it was all a joke. But it wasn't. My head buzzed with adrenaline. And I couldn't seem to think clearly. Had she really killed herself? Was that what I was seeing?

Harmony lay crumpled on her side, still wearing her favorite crystal-and-cross-studded jacket over Vesta's black dress. Her head and neck were twisted so that her pale eyes peered up through a crust of dried blood to the ceiling above. I could hardly make out the rest of her face. There was just too much blood. And the features were all wrong. I caught a glimpse of something sticking through the flesh of her cheek. I realized it was bone, and shivered, wondering why the room had suddenly gone so cold. Then I noticed the broken teeth that had spilled from her open mouth. And the room began to shimmer.

No, not suicide. Murder. Or maybe I'm just dreaming, I thought as my legs went weak beneath me. I closed my eyes. Maybe it would all go away.

Someone moaned from behind me. I opened my eyes and turned. Wayne. I had forgotten Wayne.

He stood with one big hand covering his face.

"How could this happen?" he whispered, as if to himself, then repeated it again more loudly. "How could this happen?"

"Someone killed her." I answered him literally, too stunned to deal with the existential aspect of his question. I was surprised I could speak at all. I rubbed my cold hands together and tried to think.

Murder, not suicide. Both Harmony and Vesta. There was no possibility remaining in my mind that Vesta had swallowed poison voluntarily. Because Harmony—

I shuddered violently and tried not to think of her crumpled body behind me. A surge of bile burned my throat.

"I'm so sorry," Wayne said in a whisper. "I should have kept this from happening." He had taken his hand from his face and was now staring out over my head.

"Stop that!" I snapped. "Just stop that! How the hell do you think you could have stopped this? Precognition and an army? Because, without them, there's not a damn thing you could have done."

Wayne looked down at me, surprise evident in the upward curves of his brows. At least he'd heard me. Maybe my outburst had done us both some good. My head was beginning to clear now. And I could feel a few, faint prickles of warmth in my cold hands.

"Sorry," whispered Wayne. He looked down at his feet.

I heard a snort of laughter and then realized that it was my own. I couldn't believe I had laughed. But it just seemed so terribly funny that Wayne had apologized for apologizing.

"Oh, sweetie," I said and reached for him.

He put his arms around me and held on tight. I could feel the trembling in his body as well as my own as we embraced each other for several minutes. Finally, I broke away.

"We have to call the police," I said softly.

"I know," he replied.

We went together to the phone in the kitchen.

Someone at the La Risa Police Department told us to stay put and not touch anything until they got there. So we did, sitting on kitchen chairs next to each other, holding hands.

"Something's missing," Wayne muttered after a few minutes of silence.

"What do you mean?" I asked.

"Something's missing in the living room," he replied, and sighed. "Can't remember what, but something." He shook his head as if to clear it.

I got up and walked to the kitchen doorway to peek into the living room. It looked about the same to me as the last time we had visited. Except for Harmony's body of course. I kept my eyes away from her as I scanned the scene. The black leather furniture looked the same. The crystal-and-cross-drawings were in place. There was still food on the coffee table, apparently the same food that had been there the morning before. And Vesta's water gun was on the floor near the door.

"What's missing?" asked Wayne from behind me.

"I don't know," I answered slowly. *Was* there something missing?

Then we heard the sirens.

We hurried back to our chairs and were sitting quietly when we heard the police officers tromping through the still open front doorway. Neither Wayne nor I had ever thought to close the door.

"Police!" someone shouted.

"We're in here!" I shouted back.

The officer who came through the kitchen door was one we'd met earlier. A well-muscled man with a well-trimmed mustache and buzz-cut hair. I couldn't remember his name.

He stared at us coolly for a moment, resting his hand on his gun butt. Did he think we were going to make a break for it after calling them in the first place? I felt Wayne stiffen at my side. A quick glance told me that his face had gone expressionless again.

"Hey," I said defensively. "*We* called *you* to report the body." I regretted my tone instantly. But oddly enough, it seemed to work.

"Excuse me, ma'am," the officer said with a little jerk of a bow. The only thing he didn't do was click his heels together. Yoder, I remembered—his name was Yoder. "I'm afraid you'll have to wait here until Detectives Upton and Amador arrive," he told us.

"Hey, Stan," came a voice from the other room.

Yoder did his little bow again, then left the kitchen.

We could hear bits and pieces of the conversation from the next room. "No weapon," was one of the more interesting bits. Was that what Wayne had thought was missing? "Those two in there," was a more disconcerting bit, especially because I couldn't hear the end of the sentence.

I kept listening, though, because every time I stopped I thought of Harmony. Poor crazy Harmony. My eyes teared up. I didn't know why, but I felt as though it had been a child who had died, not a middle-aged woman. Maybe that was because Harmony had never grown up. At least not properly. I took a deep breath, trying to dispel the sadness.

Then I heard the rumble of new voices. "Ask them where Jasper and Caruso are," someone said.

Damn. Was that Detective Sergeant Upton talking to Detective Amador?

A tall, cadaverously thin man and an equally tall black woman with a round, freckled face walked in. That was them all right.

"Hello, sir. Ma'am," I said as politely as possible. My mother had always told me "courtesy counts." It was worth a shot.

Detective Amador smiled and returned my greeting. Upton, on the other hand, directed a fierce glare somewhere over my right shoulder, popped a few of his knuckles and brusquely told Amador to get some chairs. In a few moments, they were both sitting across from Wayne and me.

"Amador, tell them they're going to have to answer a lot of questions," Upton said angrily.

Uh-oh. The man wasn't in a good mood today. I told myself to calm down and pretended to listen to Detective Amador's good-natured relay of Upton's instructions. I wasn't about to answer the man directly. Nor was Wayne. We had both learned our lesson the first time around.

"Ask them why the hell they came here in the first place," Upton ordered, tapping his foot impatiently.

"Why did you come here today?" Amador asked.

"Needed to check on Harmony," Wayne growled, sounding none too friendly himself.

"Huh!" barked Upton.

I waited to see if Amador would attempt a translation. When she didn't, I tried to explain.

"Harmony had been acting pretty strange lately," I said. "Clara Kushiyama told us she might need hospitalization. And since Harmony had been living with Wayne's mother, we felt some responsibility, so we—"

"I thought the Kushiyama woman was Mrs. Caruso's nurse," Upton interrupted. He rotated his head slowly. I could hear the tight tendons in his neck crackle with the movement. "Ask them why she was so interested in Harmony Fitch."

I waited impatiently for the relay. "We asked Mrs. Kushiyama to help with Harmony," I clarified, once it came. "Harmony was in bad shape and we didn't know what to do. We couldn't just kick her out of the condo—"

"Ask her why not," Upton ordered.

It went on like that for a while. And then some.

By the time Upton let us go, Wayne and I had shared every morsel of information we had ever gleaned about Harmony, a half-hour description of her party the morning before, an even longer description of our own movements after that party, and more. Much more. I began to suspect that Upton's method of interrogation was indeed a very effective method, and not madness at all, about the time he told Amador to tell us that they were going to seal the condo.

"And tell them not to leave town," were Upton's final words. Or Amador's maybe. I wasn't sure whose words were whose by that time. I had passed from the state of shock I had been in after finding Harmony's body to a state of extreme mental and physical fatigue. I was almost grateful. It kept me from thinking too much.

"Well, at least the police will investigate now," I told Wayne as we got into the Jaguar.

"So will I," he promised, his voice a rough whisper. "So will I."

Apparently, he wasn't as tired as I was.

I never did escort Wayne to the funeral home to select a casket. Once he had parked out front, he insisted on going in by himself. And when I began to argue, he turned and silenced me with a glare.

"Know you're trying to help, Kate," he said. "But this is between me and Mom."

"Oh," I answered, feeling my cheeks flush with embarrassment. Embarrassment and a hint of resentment, actually. "I guess I'll go pick up a picnic."

He nodded, got out of the car and strode off to the funeral home. I sighed and shuffled across the street to the health food store. The image of Harmony's body flashed into my mind as I came to the automatic doors. I swallowed hard and hurried inside, glad I had a task to do. Someone had to pick up food for the picnic that Wayne insisted we were going to have with the Skeritts, even though he hadn't bothered to tell them about it yet.

The deli section had Thai rice, Greek dolmas, Japanese noodle salad, Lebanese tabouli, Russian cabbage rolls, Guatemalan black bean enchiladas and a variety of breads. All vegetarian. That added to the bag of apples I had at home ought to be enough for eleven, I decided. I wasn't going to get anything with mystery meat in it, not this close to the funeral home. And it was certainly enough for the two of us who were probably going to be faced with eating the whole international feast when Wayne couldn't convince the Skeritts to come.

But Wayne did convince them. He called Ace's room at the Redwood Grove Inn when we got home. The Skeritts arrived within a half hour. Every last one of them.

"Wow," breathed Eric as he came through the door. "This is totally, totally cool. Can I play a pinball machine?"

I nodded and flipped the switch on Hayburners. He hit the reset button and the machine came to life, clunking, humming and flashing lights.

Mandy lowered herself gracefully into one of the swinging chairs and pronounced it "simply splendid."

Her grandparents just stared, letting their eyes travel from the swinging chairs to the overflowing bookshelves, the pinball machines and the framed pinball backglasses on the wall, and back again. But Dru was equal to the occasion.

"Oh my," she trilled. "This is such a *fun* house. Don't you think so, Bill?"

Bill's face twitched in a hint of a nod that didn't disturb his usual vague smile.

"Oh, this room is so healing, Kate," Lori chimed in. She was wearing a plum-colored batik blouse over jeans and a hot-pink turtleneck today. And plenty of thin metal bracelets that jingled as her arms opened wide as if to embrace the entire living room. "The plants are really happy, I can tell. And the people too. Oh, it's just wonderful." She threw her arms around me and hugged.

I returned her hug. If nothing else, Lori seemed sincere. I wasn't so sure about Dru. "Fun" sounded like a euphemism to me. Whether it was a euphemism for messy or badly decorated or something else altogether, I wasn't sure.

"So, kid," Ace said, putting a meaty hand on Wayne's shoulder. "Where're we going for this here picnic?"

"Around the corner," Wayne answered briefly, not mentioning that the "corner" was almost a mile long. Maybe he wanted to wear them all out so they'd be more likely to confess. Actually, he probably hadn't even noticed how long the walk was. He was a strong walker.

So were all the Skeritts as it turned out. Maybe it was because they all had such long legs, but no one complained as we marched along, each of us carrying a blanket or a piece of the picnic lunch. Dru exclaimed over some of the more picturesque houses and better-tended gardens that we passed. Eric tried to engage Mandy in a discussion about martial arts, but she just giggled. True love at last? And Lori sang the theme from *Oklahoma* for some undisclosed reason. But mostly we just walked. It felt good. There weren't many cars on the street on a weekday, and the October air smelled crisp and clean.

The park we came to was really a mini-park, a sloping section of lawn about half the size of a baseball field, complete with a couple of big oak trees and a pocket-sized playground in one corner. We were the only ones there. Wayne and Ace laid out the blankets on the grass and we arranged ourselves in a rough circle, Dru giggling about her "old bones" as she lowered herself carefully. The thin blankets didn't do much to disguise the fact that the ground was hard, cold and lumpy. Still, nobody complained. The Skeritt clan was a hardy lot.

Once we were all settled in, I passed out paper plates and wondered if anyone here had heard about Harmony's death yet. No one had mentioned it. And no one's appetite seemed impaired, I noted a few moments later as everyone scooped, prodded and speared food from the passing deli containers. Everyone but Wayne. And myself. I took a little Thai rice so I wouldn't look out of place. And then I wondered if someone else here was only pretending to have an appetite. Because one of these people had probably killed Harmony, had probably beaten her to death. I felt a sudden sting of angry tears.

"Allergies," I murmured hastily, wiping my eyes.

"You know what, Aunt Kate?" Eric said through a mouthful of food.

I shook my head, trying to smile.

"There's medicine you can take for allergies."

"Is that a fact?" I said, my tears subsiding. Eric was such an earnest know-it-all, he made me smile for real.

"Uh-huh," he told me, then took another bite of something that might have been a cabbage roll or a dolma.

"Wayne and I have been worried about Harmony," I said, with no attempt at a more graceful segue. "Anyone have any ideas?"

"Ideas about what exactly?" Trent asked. At first I thought he was teasing me, but his eyes were serious. And intent.

"Oh, what to do with her now that Vesta's gone," I answered casually.

"I shouldn't think that would be your problem," he advised me.

I opened my mouth to argue with him, then remembered why I was asking these questions.

"I think Harmony must be here as an irritant," Lori offered.

"What do you mean, 'an irritant'?" I asked, turning to her.

"Well, we're all here for a purpose," she began. She tilted her head at me as if inviting confirmation of this basic proposition.

I nodded. I wasn't about to air my own spiritual ambivalence.

"But some of our purposes aren't so obvious, or so

pleasant," she continued, shaking her plastic fork for emphasis. "For instance, there are people who are here in this lifetime to understand what it means to oppress others. Like Saddam Hussein. Or those guys in the CIA."

"Oh, dear," Ingrid interjected. "I don't really think Hussein could be here for that purpose. I think he must be rebelling against God's purpose, if anything." I wondered briefly what she thought of the CIA.

"But see, Mom," Lori said excitedly, her plastic fork really wiggling now. "That's the point. Everyone thinks that they know what a *good* or a *bad* purpose is. But it's not that simple. It someone is reincarnated for the purpose of suffering oppression, someone has to oppress them, right?"

"Well," Ingrid whispered, shaking her head, "I don't know about that—"

"So some people come into this life to experience being the oppressor," Lori finished triumphantly.

"Are you saying Harmony was supposed to be an oppressor?" I asked, completely confused now.

"No, that was just an example," Lori answered, shaking her head. Her earrings jingled merrily. "Harmony's an irritant. She's in this life to annoy other people. To shake up their thinking. It's a very important purpose."

"A hard job, but someone's got to do it?" Gail said mockingly.

"That's it!" Lori cried, pointing her fork happily at Gail. Apparently Lori hadn't heard the mockery in Gail's voice. Or maybe she had but didn't choose to acknowledge it.

A dog barked somewhere in the silence that followed Lori's cry. No one seemed to be eating anymore.

"Oh dear," murmured Ingrid.

"Hey, can I be an irritant?" demanded Ace. He stuck his thumbs in his ears and wiggled his fingers. Then he crossed his eyes and stuck his tongue out.

Eric and Mandy doubled over laughing.

It wasn't that funny. But Dru was laughing too. And Lori. So much for my discussion of Harmony.

"Well, if there is such a thing as an irritant," Trent commented dryly, "Ace must indeed be one."

"Oh, Dad," Lori said, spooning tabouli into her mouth. "You're such a card sometimes. But anyway, Harmony is an obvious irritant—"

"That's enough, Lori," Trent broke in. "Harmony is a behavior problem, nothing more and nothing less."

Lori stopped short. I could see the struggle in her eyes. Was it worth it to challenge her father? Finally, she shrugged her shoulders and went back to her tabouli. Why did she let him do that to her?

"Poor troubled soul," Ingrid murmured sadly. For a moment I thought she was talking about Lori, but then I realized she had probably meant Harmony.

"You know what?" Eric asked. Heads turned his way. "You can do all these totally cool things with the punctuation on computers. You can make smiley faces and sad faces and . . ."

Ten minutes later, I was trying to figure out how to get the subject back to Harmony.

"So, Gail," I said finally. "You're a psychotherapist. What do you think about Harmony?"

"What do you really mean by that question?" she asked back.

"Well . . ." I temporized. Damn, she was cold. Was she still mad at me for playing therapist the night before? I reworded my question. "Do you think Harmony was crazy enough to need institutionalization?"

Gail just stared at me. She didn't even say "hmm."

"She was obviously pretty screwed up," I persisted. "All the things she said about UFO's—"

Gail interrupted me quietly. "Why are you using the past tense?" she asked.

- Sixteen -

I SAT THERE on the cold lumpy ground, mesmerized by Gail's cool stare. Why *had* I used the past tense? Had I subconsciously meant to tell the murderer that I too knew Harmony was dead? That I had seen what was left of her battered face? I looked into Gail's unblinking brown eyes and thought of Harmony's pale blue ones staring upward. Goose bumps sprang up on my arms. I rubbed them as I tried to think, then decided to tell the truth.

"We found—" I began.

"Oh Gail, honey," Dru bubbled gaily. "Why are you always so critical? Past tense, present tense, what does it matter? You're not an English teacher, for heaven's sake." Dru's playful tone should have taken the sting from her words. But somehow, it didn't seem to.

Gail shifted her unblinking gaze to her mother without a smile.

"Here we are in this nice little park and you're all gloomy," her mother finished up. "Have some fun!"

"Mother," Gail answered, her cool tone edged with a hint of heat. "Not having your infinite capacity for denial and repression, I find it difficult to have 'fun' while wondering if my aunt has been murdered."

Dru let out a high-pitched giggle, as if Gail had just said something witty. A whole new set of goose bumps raised the hair on the back of my neck.

"You know what—" Eric put in.

"What?" said Ace and then wrestled the boy to the ground before he could answer.

"Wheee!" Lori shouted and launched herself on top of Ace, knocking over the nearest deli containers as she did.

I didn't bring Harmony up again.

The walk home was more leisurely than the one to the park. I placed myself in the middle of the pack so I could listen in on the various conversations.

". . . this totally awesome psychologist named B.F. Skinner," Eric was saying to Ace and Wayne at the front. "He taught these pigeons how to drop the bombs in World War II by pecking at the targets. They were totally good at it, but these dweebs wouldn't let them . . ."

I switched my attention to Dru and Gail, striding along a few feet behind the men.

". . . just because one boy doesn't like you anymore. It doesn't mean anything," Dru said. Now, this was interesting. "Remember, honey, there are plenty of other fish in the sea."

"Mother, how many times do I have to tell . . ." Gail began, and then she lowered her voice. Damn.

". . . how Grandpa treats Mom," I heard from behind me. It was Mandy's voice and it sounded angry.

"I know he gets grouchy," a penetrating whisper replied. Ingrid's, I was pretty sure. "But he really loves you and your mother, dear. He just, oh . . ." Ingrid's voice faltered.

"It's okay, Grandma," Mandy said, her tone softened. "He isn't completely hideous."

Then I heard the jingle of bracelets. I turned in time to see Lori striding up beside me.

"I just had a wonderful inspiration, Kate," she told me, laying her taloned hand on my arm. "Since you and Wayne have shared so much with us, I thought I could give you both massages." I looked down at her long red fingernails and shuddered. "I can do shiatsu or Swedish or deep tissue," she went on blithely. "Even acupressure. And I just took a seminar in foot reflexology."

I tried to think of a way to signal Wayne that I needed help here. But all I could see was the back of his head.

". . . so then they put the rat in this totally cool box, see, and . . ." Eric was saying.

I turned back to Lori, who smiled widely.

"Doesn't this beautiful day just make you want to sing?" she demanded, and without waiting for an answer, she leaned her head back and burst into song. "Amazing Grace, how sweet the sound . . ."

I bolted into a near run, wondering how opera singers could stand it. Did it hurt their eardrums as much as mine to be sung to at top volume by someone so close by?

My ears were still ringing by the time we reached home.

We all trooped up the steps and into the house again. Dru flung herself onto the couch gracefully and let out a long theatrical sigh. Eric headed straight for the pinball machines. Lori followed behind him, humming a new tune. Everyone else stood around with varying degrees of uncertainty on their faces. What were we supposed to do now? I snuck a peek at Wayne. *His* face was set in stone. No help there. I took a deep breath, readying myself to play hostess.

"Would anyone like a hot tub?" I asked, glad I had thought to turn up the heat earlier.

"Oh my," Ingrid quavered, twisting her wedding ring around her finger. "Well, I just don't know—"

"Go ahead, Mama," Lori encouraged her. "It'll do you good."

"Well, I—" Ingrid began again.

"Do we get to wear bathing suits?" Dru asked, tilting her head coquettishly. "Or do we soak *au naturel*?"

Ingrid's face reddened under her white hair. So that was what was bothering her.

"Of course you can wear suits," I said hastily, counting spares in my mind.

I had quite a collection, the living legacy from a friend who had lost eighty pounds over the course of one year (and unfortunately gained most of it back the following year). The extra-large ought to fit Ingrid, I thought. She was broad as well as tall. And Gail would be about right for the large. Dru and Lori were tall but slender. Mediums? And Mandy might be okay in a bikini. I knew Wayne had extra trunks for the men. I looked at him again.

"Only room for five or six in the tub," he muttered, barely loud enough to be heard. But Ingrid heard him.

"Oh my," she said again, visibly brightening. "I wouldn't want to take anyone else's place."

Lori laughed and crossed the room to kiss her mother's cheek. Ingrid smiled back at her daughter sheepishly.

"Well, I'm game," Ace said heartily. He turned to Wayne. "What about you, kid?"

Wayne shook his head. I resisted the urge to scream. It was his idea to invite his family over. And one of us should sit in the hot tub with the others, not just in the name of hospitality but to listen for any stray confessions of murder. Wasn't that the point of this visit? I stifled a sigh. It looked like I was elected for hot-tub duty.

"Grampy, can I just play pinball?" Eric asked, feeling for the switch on the bottom of Hayburners as he did. The machine lights came on and he pushed the reset button, returning the metal horses in the recessed backglass to their starting positions before Ace even had a chance to tell him yes. Or no, for that matter.

Mandy didn't even bother to ask for permission. She just powered up the other machine, an old wood-railed Gottlieb model by the name of Texan, and shot a ball.

"Dad," Lori said. "You should go soak in the tub with Ace. You need to relax more."

I thought Trent would argue, but he didn't. He just nodded his well-groomed head ponderously. Then Dru said she'd "just love" a hot tub. And pretty soon she had convinced Gail too.

I passed out bathing suits before anyone could change their minds.

After fifteen minutes of taking turns dressing—boys in the guest bathroom and girls in the bedroom—we were all in the hot tub on my back deck, soaking. And I was glad I had been elected. The hot, churning waters were doing a good job of massaging my shoulders, better I was sure than Lori could have done. I closed my eyes and leaned back into the jet of hot water, feeling my muscles loosening. Over the hum of the tub, I could hear the sound of bells ringing from the living room. Someone was racking up a good score on a pinball machine.

"Wow, this is the life," Ace moaned appreciatively from where he sat on my right. I opened my eyes as I turned to gaze at him through the steam. Sweat was trickling down his homely face. But his body wasn't homely, I'd noticed. It was trim and muscular, even more muscular than Wayne's. All that weight-lifting, I supposed. "I'll bet Vessie sure enjoyed this hot tub," he added.

I shrugged, embarrassed. Vesta had never used the hot tub in the months that she'd lived here, not because she was modest or wouldn't have enjoyed it, I suspected, but because it was mine and she had hated anything that was mine.

"Vesta wasn't always so hard," said Dru quietly, as if in answer to my thought. Her mascara was running a little in the steam, but her eyes still sparkled. "She was a good sister to me when I was little." Dru straightened up abruptly, causing a small tidal wave to move across the tub and splash next to me. "Remember the fairy costume she made for me the year Ma was sick?" she asked Trent.

"Yes," Trent answered with a slow nod. "I do remember." Then he sighed. As I watched him, I realized that he looked pretty damn good in swimming trunks himself, not as muscular as Ace, but more muscular than I would have thought from seeing him fully clothed. And just as trim. If Wayne's body looked as good as either of his uncles' when he reached their ages, I was going to be one happy woman.

"Hey, how about the puppet theatre Vesta made for us that summer?" Ace remembered aloud. He laughed and the water reacted, splashing over the side. "Now that was really grand!"

"Old cardboard boxes and tape and paint," Trent said dismissively. But then a smile gentled his face. "Vesta was an artist, all right. She made it all shine."

"And the puppets," Dru put in. "All different animals from socks. I had a gray rabbit—"

"I had a lion," said Ace.

"What was yours?" Dru asked Trent. "I remember Nola had a cat and Camille's was a dog, but I can't remember yours."

"A horse," he answered briefly.

"That's right," Dru trilled. She leaned back against the tub's edge with a smile.

I leaned back too and tried to imagine Vesta making cute little puppets out of socks. I wiped the perspiration from my face with a wet hand. No, I decided, I just couldn't imagine it.

"What happened to Aunt Vesta?" Gail asked from my left. Her tone was softer now, almost dreamy. I turned and saw that her face had softened, too. Her eyes looked large and vulnerable without her glasses. Maybe that was one reason she usually wore them. "Why do you think Aunt Vesta changed?" she pressed.

Trent frowned across the tub at her. Dru looked at him for a moment and then at Ace. Ace shrugged massively. The water rippled and splashed with his movement.

"Well, honey," Dru said, her voice deeper now than usual, "it was real hard on your Aunt Vesta when Pa . . . well, when he threw her out of the house."

"But why did he throw her out?" Gail asked softly.

"She was pregnant, honey," Dru answered. "And she wasn't married. That meant a lot more back then."

"Oh," said Gail, nodding her head. She didn't say anything else.

In the silence that followed, I could hear someone from the house laughing. Was that Lori? And the sound of an unseen airplane overhead.

"Hey, remember," Ace said, filling the silence. "Remember when . . ."

And then the three siblings were talking again, recalling growing up in Hayward. They'd all had part-time jobs when they were in high school. And they'd worked hard. Ace made everyone laugh telling us how he'd always managed to drop one watermelon from each shipment when he'd worked at a grocery store. That way, the employees had been forced to eat it, since they couldn't very well sell it cracked open.

"And that was the best watermelon I ever tasted," he finished up.

"What were my grandparents like?" Gail asked.

The tub went silent again. Gail sure knew how to kill a conversation.

"Well, honey," Dru answered finally, "they were hard-working people, religious. Your grandfather worked at the local cannery. Your grandmother was a housewife."

Nobody bothered to restart the conversation after that. We just sat in the tub, soaking and sweating. And thinking our own private thoughts.

I closed my eyes and sank down even deeper into the hot water, listening to the sounds of pinballs from the house and the sounds of dogs and kids and cars from the surrounding neighborhood. This is so peaceful, I thought, I could almost forget about Harmony.

But as soon as I thought it, I found I couldn't forget Harmony. It was like trying not to think of a white elephant. My mind kept showing me pictures of Harmony both as she had been alive and as she had been that morning, battered and bloody on the floor. A slide show by Stephen King.

I popped my eyes open. Dru was gazing at me, her head tilted to one side, and Trent was frowning down at the tub water as if it had offended him. I tipped my head back to look out over their heads, focusing on my neighbor's shingled rooftop for a moment and then on Mount Tamalpais in the distance. Still, I shivered, cold even in the hot water of the tub. And then I began to think about Vesta—

"Are you okay?" Gail asked from my left, perceptive as ever, even without her glasses.

"Just a chill," I answered quickly, then realized how stupid that sounded from someone sitting in a hot tub.

"Maybe we should go in now," said Dru.

"All right," I agreed, suddenly tired of both the hot tub and its occupants.

I was even more chilled when we all stood up, wet in the cool October air. I shepherded everyone back into the house quickly and pulled out towels to rub away our goose bumps. Then we took turns changing back into our clothes.

Eric was still playing Hayburners when I made it back to the living room, the last person to have dressed.

"Just one more game, Grampy," he was begging Ace. I

wasn't surprised. I'd heard the same plea from pinball addicts of all ages.

"Hooboy, you've been here playing for long enough already," grumbled Ace, but he gave in. "One more game," he said. "Just one."

But Eric managed to sneak in at least three more games under Ace's not so watchful eyes. And then, at last, the Skeritts filed out the door, saying their goodbyes.

Lori gave me a departing hug as well, and whispered, "Don't forget, you've got a free massage coming."

"I won't," I assured her uneasily.

And then they were all gone, except for Ace, who stood in the doorway staring back at Wayne.

"Wayne," he said softly. "I . . ."

"What?" asked Wayne, his voice deep and brusque.

Ace stared for a moment longer, then shook his head. "Nothing," he said. Then he put on his goofy clown grin again. "Hey, you've got a great house here!" he boomed. "Not to mention a gorgeous woman. I'm happy for you, kid."

And then he turned and left, clattering noisily across the front deck and down the stairs.

Wayne and I followed Ace out as far as the deck and watched as his Volkswagen van and Trent's Volvo station wagon pulled out of the driveway, popping gravel.

Wayne turned to me, once they were gone from sight, his face stiff and cold. "Well?" he asked.

"Well, what?" I shot back in annoyance. "Are you asking me if anyone confessed in the hot tub?"

He didn't answer me, but I saw the flash of hurt that widened his eyes for an instant.

"Oh, I'm sorry, sweetie," I told him, feeling instantly guilty. "I guess I'm just sick of Skeritts. And I don't think I know anything more this afternoon than I did this morning."

"I do," he said quietly.

"You do?" I asked in surprise.

"Lori wants to marry her acupuncturist, but her father would stop sending her monthly checks if she got married," he began, holding up one finger. "Gail's boyfriend just left her," he continued, raising another finger. "He was a law student. He just passed the bar *and* moved in with his bar review instructor. Uncle Trent wants to retire and Aunt Ingrid wants to go back to work as a teacher, but he doesn't want her to. Eric's mother abandoned him when he was four. Now Uncle Ace and Eric's father, Earl, take care of the boy. And Bill Norton is an alcoholic," he finished up, raising his thumb.

"Now, that I *had* guessed," I replied dryly and was rewarded with a hint of a smile on Wayne's stony face.

"Like to sit down?" he asked.

When I nodded, he pulled up a couple of sagging porch chairs for us and faced them out toward the garden.

So we sat and talked about the Skeritts. I told him all I could remember of the hot-tub conversations. We threw around some character analysis for a while and concluded nothing. But at least we were sitting together and holding hands as we concluded nothing. Then we just sat in silence for a while, looking out at the garden. The summer impatiens were still blooming around the apple tree, and the electric-blue lobelia. Pretty soon I'd be putting in winter primroses—

"Been thinking about the funeral," Wayne said.

I turned to him, gardening plans abandoned. His face was grave, his brows low enough to cover all but the bottoms of his eyes.

"Uncle Ace is right. Mom wasn't religious," he murmured, his voice almost inaudible. "Ceremony shouldn't be religious either."

I nodded my understanding.

"Gotta call her friends," he went on. "Not sure who they are, though."

Did Vesta even *have* friends? The question was too sad to ask out loud. Harmony was the only friend that I knew of. And Clara had been her nurse. But beyond them—

"Paul Paulson," Wayne said.

"Who?" I asked.

"Mom's nosy next-door neighbor," he clarified. "The one who tried to sell us real estate—"

"Oh yeah," I said, remembering the obnoxious man with the chubby tan face and booming voice. "I have his business

card somewhere. He'll know who Vesta knew at the condo."
I stood up, glad of a task to do. "I'll call him."

I went back indoors to do just that, with Wayne following
behind me. But when I got to the phone, I noticed that the
light was blinking on the answering machine. Someone had
called while we were out on the deck talking.

I rewound the tape and pushed the playback button.

There was a pause and then a whispered message.

"Stop asking questions," it said. "Don't make me kill you
too."

– Seventeen –

I STARED DOWN at the answering machine, stunned for a moment. Then my heart began to pound. *Don't make me kill you too.*

"This is good," growled Wayne from behind me. "I've spooked Mom's murderer. Now I know for sure."

"Just what do you know for sure?" I demanded, whirling around to face him. My mouth felt too dry to speak properly. I swallowed hard before going on. "That the killer wants to kill *me* now? Or *you*? Or both of us?"

Wayne's face paled as I spoke. "Not you!" he cried, his eyebrows rising to reveal brown irises encircled by the white of panic. "I never thought the murderer was talking to you. Thought it was me." He reached out for my hand and grasped it hard. "Kate, you have to be careful. Don't go anywhere alone. Stay here—no, no, not here." He shook his head frantically. "I know, go on a trip while I settle this thing—"

"Are you kidding!" I snapped. "You want me to leave you alone to face him? How do you think I would feel if you were killed? Better than you would if I was killed?"

"But—"

"We're together on this, Wayne," I told him, keeping my voice as deep and steady as I could. He tried to pull his hand back, but now I was the one grasping tightly. "I won't go anywhere without you. And you won't go anywhere without me. Not till—"

"But it was *my* mother—"

"I don't care whose mother it was!" I shouted. And then abruptly, as if I had just awakened from a dream, I thought, Is that me shouting?

Wayne's face seemed to sober too. His brows settled back down and he pressed his lips into a tight line.

"Okay," he said quietly. "What's next?"

I set the answering machine to play back the message. "Stop asking questions," we heard again. And, "Don't make me kill you too." Damn. The caller's whispers was not only low, but muffled, as if something had been placed over the mouthpiece. And there were long gaps between each uninflected word. Whoever it was, he or she had been very careful.

"Do you recognize the voice?" I asked Wayne, not really hoping for a positive identification. The voice could belong to one of the Skeritts. But it could also belong to Donald Duck. Or Barbara Walters. Or Bullwinkle the Moose, for that matter. Personally, I couldn't have recognized *any* of their voices, this well-disguised.

Nor could Wayne. He just shook his head and muttered, "Call the police?"

"I doubt if they'll know who it is either," I answered unhappily. "But I suppose we'd better call them, just in case."

The officer at the La Risa Police Department didn't seem very interested in our threatening call at first. But then I explained that the call might be related to the murders of Vesta Caruso and Harmony Fitch. After a flurry of telephone transfers, Detective Amador came on the line. I told my story again and she promised me that someone would be out for the tape within the next half hour. Then she paused. I had a feeling Detective Sergeant Upton was telling her to tell us something.

"Stay put," she ordered a moment later. "We'll want to talk to you both."

I was already regretting the decision to call the police by the time she hung up. And fifteen minutes of silent brooding over the death threat didn't make me feel any better.

"I might as well call Paul Paulson while we wait," I told Wayne. He nodded glumly.

I found Paulson's business card in my purse and punched in his number.

"Action Investments," a male voice answered.

As soon as I gave my name and asked to speak to Mr. Paulson, I was put on hold. Moments later, Paul Paulson came on the line, sounding suspiciously like the first voice I had heard. Was he pretending to be his own receptionist? I shook off the thought. I'd already worried enough about disguised voices for one day.

". . . Ms. Jasper, I'm so glad to hear that you've been thinking about this unique investment opportunity," Paulson was saying. "You know, predeveloped land is—"

"I'm not interested in investing," I cut in hastily.

"You're not?" he said, a dash of sincere hurt flavoring his usual pitchman's cheer. But I didn't have time to sympathize.

"No," I told him firmly. "I'm calling about Vesta Caruso's funeral."

The phone was quiet for a few beats, and then I realized he probably didn't have a clue as to who I was.

"You know Vesta Caruso, your next-door neighbor," I said. "Well, her son and I met you the day she was kill—the day she died."

"Of course," he boomed. "Poor Mrs. Caruso, an extraordinary woman—"

"I wonder if you happen to know if she had any special friends at the condo?" I interrupted. I had a feeling he could go on at length about Vesta's shining qualities, and I wasn't in the mood to listen. "Friends that might want to attend her funeral."

"Well, I for one would be happy to attend," he assured me. I just hoped he wouldn't try to sell any real estate at the funeral. "And old Mr. Quaneri, of course—"

"Mr. Quaneri?" I asked, curious at a name I'd never heard Vesta mention.

"Oh, Mr. Quaneri was quite an admirer of Mrs. Caruso's," Paulson told me. "He's very upset by her death. In fact he . . ."

The doorbell rang and I lost the end of his sentence. I put my hand over the receiver.

"Wayne," I hissed. "Can you give Paulson the funeral details?"

He nodded and took the receiver. I ran to the door.

There were two uniformed officers waiting there for me. One was a tall man with blow-dried hair. I remembered him. He had come to the condo on the day of Vesta's murder. The other was an Asian woman with a long ponytail.

"Officers Lee and Zappetini," the Asian woman said. "Where's the tape?"

I led them to the answering machine, still connected to the phone that Wayne was now using. I realized from the glares on the officers' faces that they didn't count talking on that phone as staying put.

"Can I get you some tea?" I asked. "Or something—"

"Just the tape, ma'am," the Asian woman said, consciously or unconsciously doing a credible Jack Webb imitation.

I wondered if she was old enough to have watched *Dragnet,* but resisted the urge to ask. Her grim expression was enough to forestall any more questions on my part anyway, especially foolish ones. I felt a little better when Wayne hung up the phone and gave them the tape. But not for long.

Officer Lee requested that Wayne and I accompany her and Officer Zappetini to the police station without further delay. At least they didn't make us ride in the police car. We followed in the Jaguar. Wayne didn't say a word on the way. And once we arrived, we were immediately ushered into Upton and Amador's office to listen to the tape a third time.

". . . kill you too," it finished up on full volume. Amador clicked off the tape player.

"Ask them if they recognize the voice," Upton ordered angrily.

It went downhill from there.

At the end of another twenty minutes of inquisition by relay, I asked Detective Amador if it was possible to either trace the phone call or use some of their technical whiz-bang to identify the speaker.

"Tell her we'll work on it," Upton snapped. He glared over my shoulder. "But if it's a local call—" He threw his hands up in the air.

"One chance in a thousand," Amador translated. "If we're lucky."

Wayne didn't say much on the way home, except to comment that Upton probably thought *we* had engineered the tape to divert suspicion from ourselves. Somehow, I wished he could have just talked about the weather.

I was heating up a can of mushroom-barley soup for an early dinner, and Wayne was sitting, staring, on the living room couch when the doorbell rang again.

I turned the soup down and walked to the door cautiously. But Wayne got there first. He took one big hand and shoved me behind him before opening up. I bristled. I didn't need his protection. And anyway, he shouldn't have bothered. It was only Felix at the door. Felix smiled widely as he stroked his mustache, a journalistic pit bull ready for action. On the other hand, I decided, just this once it was kind of nice here behind Wayne.

"Howdy-hi," Felix said, his tone dripping with camaraderie. "Heard you guys found another stiff. Care to share the gory tidbits with your good old reporter amigo—"

"No," Wayne growled and shut the door.

"Hey!" Felix shouted. Then we heard the sound of his fists pounding on wood. I wondered how long he would keep it up.

But Wayne jerked the door back open before I could find out. Felix fell more than walked through the doorway, his face mashing into Wayne's chest for an instant. He straightened quickly however and began to speak again.

"Didn't mean to ruffle your feathers, big guy," he offered. "Just wanted a little chat, you know, a little heart-to-heart—"

The sound of another car popping gravel in the driveway distracted him from his solicitation. I looked out and saw a Volkswagen bug screech to a halt behind Felix's old Chevy. It was my friend, and Felix's sweetie, Barbara Chu. Then I remembered that they'd been fighting since he'd moved in with her. Maybe she wasn't his sweetie anymore.

She got out of her Volkswagen and glared at the Chevy. Then she drew herself up to her full five feet and smiled serenely, looking like a slender, extremely beautiful, female Buddha. She walked by the Chevy and up the stairs without ever acknowledging Felix's presence.

"Hi, kiddo," she called to me when she reached the deck.

."I thought you might need a little emotional support." Then she held her arms open. "And a hug," she added softly.

I walked around Wayne and Felix to redeem my hug. Once I was wrapped in Barbara's embrace, I realized just how much I had been needing the comfort and affection she was offering. First, Vesta's body and then Harmony's, not to mention Wayne's silence and staring and— Tears of self-pity formed in my eyes.

"So, big guy," Felix said from behind me. "The porkers aren't figuring suicide on your old lady any longer. Not after that friggin' looney-tunes bought it. It's murder now. And they want to wrap it up quick and tight, if you know what I mean."

I was pretty sure *I* knew what Felix meant. And it wasn't good. *Quick and tight*. Barbara and I dropped our arms simultaneously.

I turned to look at Wayne, who loomed over Felix like a stone vulture. Who could be quicker and tighter than the victim's son? My limbs went cold. Could Wayne defend himself from suspicion in his current state? He could barely talk. And the way he was acting, I might have thought he was a homicidal maniac myself if I didn't know him better. Fear shut down my lungs.

"Keep breathing," Barbara ordered instantly. "And ignore Felix. He's just walking all over people as usual, trying to get a story."

I started breathing again, but I couldn't ignore what Felix had just said. For all of his insensitivity, he was usually honest with the information he shared. And for all of Barbara's claim to psychic power, I didn't think she was privy to the thoughts of the police department.

"I see more than you think," she said as if she'd heard my thought. And maybe she had. I took an even deeper breath, feeling a little warmer. "And one of the things I see is Felix leaving now," she added.

"Hey!" Felix protested as he turned to her.

"You're bugging these people," she snapped. "It's time to leave."

"Holy Moly, sweetcakes—" he began.

"Now," she ordered, the word emanating from somewhere deep in her throat.

Felix looked up at Wayne. Wayne glared back down. Felix opened his mouth and closed it again, then finally shrugged and started back down the stairs.

"Call me if you need to talk," Barbara sang out over her shoulder. "And don't worry. Everything will turn out fine." And then Felix and Barbara both got in their cars and drove away.

I stared after her fondly. "Barbara's incredible, isn't she?" I said to Wayne.

But he didn't answer me. He just shuffled back to the couch to resume staring. I sighed and went back to my burnt soup.

It didn't take me long to eat. Afterwards, I simultaneously did Jest Gifts paperwork and worried for a couple of hours. I had just checked off one batch of invoices and was working myself up to a full-scale anxiety attack when the phone rang. Wayne leapt from the couch and picked up the receiver before I even had a chance to push back my chair.

"Yes," I heard him say a few times, then "no," then "yes" again, and then finally, "probably fifteen minutes."

"Who was that?" I demanded when he hung up.

"Lori," he answered briefly, his eyes still on the phone.

"And what did Lori want?" I pressed, feeling like the mother of a sullen teenager.

"Talk," he answered. "Timber Lounge at the Redwood Grove Inn." He paused for a moment, then added, "They know about Harmony."

I insisted on going with him to meet Lori. He didn't bother to argue. That worried me even more.

The Timber Lounge was a small bar adjoining the Old Burl Cafe. It was decorated in hanging ferns like the cafe, but it was much darker. Once my eyes adjusted to the light, I saw Lori at the bar, sitting next to her mother. Ingrid didn't look well. Even in the dim light, I could see that she was crying again, her face buried in a handkerchief. There were a few other, scattered drinkers in the bar, mostly strangers, except for Bill Norton who sat drinking quietly a few stools down from Lori and her mother. Lori wasn't quiet, though.

"Hi, you two!" she called out happily. Heads turned at the bar as she swung her long legs from her stool and trotted over to us, her arms outstretched.

Lori's hug didn't feel anywhere near as good to me as Barbara's had. But then, I didn't suspect Barbara of murder. And Barbara didn't wear a ton of perfume either.

"The police came and talked to each of us about Harmony," Lori told us eagerly. I wished she'd lower her voice. "You knew all about it, didn't you?" she went on, grinning.

"Not all," I answered softly, hoping she'd follow my less audible example. "We found Harmony's body . . ." I faltered, replaying the scene once more in my mind.

"Have you figured out who killed her yet?" Lori demanded.

I looked up into her face. She was grinning and bouncing on her heels in excitement. She was having . . . fun.

"No," I answered shortly, wondering if hers was the cheerful face of a psychopath.

Something in my attitude must have registered. Her grin disappeared and she furrowed her Skeritt brow. "I know Harmony is dead," she assured me. "But she's probably passing on to a more joyous incarnation right now." She tilted her head as if asking me to agree.

"Maybe," I muttered, and for a moment I really considered the proposition. Maybe Harmony was happier now. She hadn't had much joy in this life—

"But what *we* have to do is to figure out who did it," Lori told me, her voice gaining speed and excitement again. "All three of us are intuitive people. All we have to do is approach this holistically—"

"Who do you think killed her?" asked Wayne from behind me, his voice low and grave. I started. I had almost forgotten he was there.

"Well . . ." Lori said. She sighed and ran her hand down her long blond braid, her eyes unfocused. "I don't know." But then she straightened up and grinned again. "Not yet anyway. I'm sure we can figure it out—"

"You can go ahead and take a seat," a waitress said from behind Lori, reminding me that we were all still standing in the doorway of the bar. "I'll be with you in a second."

We sat down at the closest table, a small round one under a hanging fern. Then Lori launched into her plan. It had something to do with personality analysis and hypnosis. At least I think it did. I lost track about five minutes into her monologue.

"See, under the Enneagram model, type three is a status seeker," she was saying. "An unhealthy three is narcissistic, even arrogant. Ted Bundy was a type three. So if we can analyze the personalities involved and find our three, then all we have to do is use Ericksonian hypnosis to lull him into—"

"May I join you?" a new voice interrupted.

I looked up, relieved at the interruption, to see Gail standing over us. I wondered briefly if Gail was a three.

"Have a seat," Lori said. Then as Gail sat down, "We've been talking about Enneagram theory. You must have read about Enneagrams, as a psychotherapist—"

"I've heard the theory," Gail said dismissively and turned her eyes to me. "Why didn't you tell us Harmony was dead?" she demanded abruptly.

"Interesting you should ask that," I replied, unable to resist playing therapist again. "Why do you think I didn't tell you?"

Lori giggled loudly. Gail didn't.

Wayne and I left not long after that. We rode home in silence. I turned on the radio. But instead of music, we were blasted with an ad for a new brand of organic clothing.

"Do you think anyone in any other state but California wears organic clothing?" I asked.

Wayne didn't answer.

I turned the radio off.

"Kate," Wayne said softly.

"What?" I replied, startled and not sure if I had actually heard him for a moment.

"Wanted to say I love you," he muttered, never taking his eyes from the road. His hands gripped the steering wheel even more tightly. "Can't show you right now. It's just too . . . too hard. But I do care. Know you do too. Know you're trying." He paused, then added, "Okay?"

"Okay, sweetie," I whispered. "Okay."

Maybe we would have talked more when we got home, but Uncle Ace was waiting for us on the deck, standing alone in the dark. Or waiting for me, anyway. He asked Wayne if he could speak to me in private. Wayne glowered in response.

"Your uncle isn't going to kill me on my front deck, for God's sake," I whispered into his ear. "Let me talk to the man."

Even in the moonlight, I could see the struggle in Wayne's face, his brows rising in objection, then lowering again in defeat. "Be in the kitchen," he growled finally. "Call if you need me."

Then he stomped into the house and slammed the door behind him. The deck lights came on an instant later.

I turned back to Ace. "Well?" I demanded impatiently. Wayne's favorite uncle was no favorite of mine right then.

Ace looked down at his feet for a moment, in a gesture reminiscent of Wayne's. I felt myself soften toward him. Then he lifted his homely face again. For once, he wasn't smiling.

"Wayne is my son," he said.

– Eighteen –

"WHAT!" I YELPED, then lowered my voice. I didn't want Wayne rushing out here. Not now. "What do you mean, Wayne is your son?" I hissed. "Vesta was his mother, wasn't she?"

Uncle Ace nodded solemnly under the deck light.

"But Vesta was your sister," I told him, hoping for a correction. Could Wayne be the product of incest?

Ace looked back down at his feet.

"Maybe we'd better sit down," I said weakly. I pointed to the sagging porch chairs where Wayne and I had rested earlier.

Ace took a seat obediently. I pulled my chair across from him and flopped into it. I couldn't seem to feel it under me, though. Maybe I was numb.

"Are you sure Wayne is your son?" I asked.

Ace sighed and looked down at his knees for a moment. Then he lifted his head again to face me. "No, not really," he admitted.

I felt an instant warm wave of relief.

"But I'm pretty sure he is," Ace went on. The wave receded, leaving me cold again. "Can I explain?" he asked softly.

I nodded, then wondered if I really wanted to hear his explanation. Brother and sister? It doesn't matter, a voice inside me said. Wayne is Wayne. But incest. If Wayne ever found out—

"I was fourteen," Ace began, leaning back in his chair, his eyes losing focus. "Vessie was sixteen. And beautiful. Not beautiful the way some girls were beautiful—Vessie had the family eyebrows and a long nose to boot—but beautiful all the same. Big, vibrant and alive. She put those girls with their little turned-up noses to shame, Vessie did. And she was funny. Jeez, she was funny. She did imitations. Birds, frogs, horses. And Pa, you shoulda heard her do Pa." He shook his head slowly and smiled gently. But then his smile disappeared.

"I knew it was wrong when she first kissed me," he said, his voice hard for a moment. "But she was so beautiful. I adored her. And pretty soon it went further. I should have said no, but I just couldn't."

He looked at me now. Did he want forgiveness? Absolution? I shrugged my shoulders. Whatever he wanted, I wasn't ready to give it to him.

"Anyway," he said brusquely, dropping his gaze, "it didn't go on very long. A few months at most. And then she seemed to get tired of me. Met someone else at school, I think. Must have been near a year later, she had a baby." He paused and smiled. "That was Wayne." he said softly, dreamily. "Vessie said I gave her the baby and I believed her. Oh, the timing seemed a little off, but not all women are the same, I guess. And I loved the little guy. I loved him from the minute I saw him."

He stared out over my head for a few heartbeats, then resumed. "Pa had thrown Vessie out by the time she had the baby. She got a job cleaning up at a local motel. Free room and board. And I was working as many hours as I could after school, giving her the money I earned. And visiting whenever I had time. Ma and Pa never knew that."

He looked into my eyes now. "Should I tell him, Kate?" he asked softly.

"Tell Wayne?"

He nodded, leaning forward eagerly. "Listen," he said, "Vessie tried to blackmail me for years. Asking for money. Asking me to visit. Telling me she'd tell Ma and Pa that Wayne was mine if I didn't. But she didn't understand. I *wanted* to give her the money. I *wanted* to visit. I loved that kid!" He sighed and slumped back in his chair. "I was just afraid of what it would do to him to realize . . ." He faltered.

"That he was the son of incest?" I finished for him.

Ace nodded. I thought I saw tears glistening in his eyes. "Should I tell him?" he asked again, his voice hoarse. "I'm proud of him. I love him just as much as my other two kids, maybe more. Should I tell him?"

I thought for a moment, but only a moment. If Ace told Wayne he was his father, Wayne would blame himself for the incest. I knew he would. He had blamed himself for everything else his mother had done. And then there was the shame. He'd haul that around as well as the guilt.

I felt myself shaking my head. "No," I answered. "Don't tell him."

"No?" Ace repeated sadly.

"You don't need to," I said, suddenly wanting to comfort the man. He had been fourteen. And Vesta had been two years older. I didn't need to blame Ace for what he'd done forty years ago anyway. He already blamed himself. "Wayne knows you love him. It doesn't matter if you're his father or his uncle."

I took his hand. It was rough and callused, its shape familiar. A lot like Wayne's, I realized with a start. But even a nephew's hand can be like his uncle's, I told myself quickly. Everyone had always told *me* that I looked more like my aunt than my mother.

"Really," I told Ace. "It's all right."

Ace was openly weeping now. He squeezed my hand and mumbled something that might have been "thank you," and then rushed back down the stairs.

I stood and watched his van take off before I went inside.

I found Wayne in the kitchen. I was relieved to see him finishing what looked like the last bite of a sandwich. I hadn't seen him eat anything else all day. He swallowed, then looked up at me.

"Well?" he said.

"Ace just wanted to talk," I told him, filling my voice with nonchalance.

Wayne's answering look conveyed anger, hurt and frustration all at the same time. I stepped around the back of his chair, avoiding his eyes, and began to massage his shoulder muscles. They had the resiliency of concrete under my fingers. I pushed in harder with the heel of my hand.

"What did Ace say?" he asked without turning.

"He just wanted to talk about you when you were a boy," I said. I felt Wayne's shoulders get even stiffer. "He really cares about you," I added, assuring myself that an omission was not the same as lying. But Wayne wasn't fooled.

"Stop it, Kate," he said, turning in his chair. "Tell me or don't tell me."

"I can't," I said weakly.

I watched his face stiffen till it looked as hard as his shoulders felt.

"Ace talked to me in confidence," I added. "It wouldn't be right to share."

"Does it have to do with Mom's murder?" Wayne asked me, his eyes fixed on my face unblinkingly. I shifted my gaze above his head.

I should have just said no and thought it out later. But my mind considered the question. Did Ace's confession have to do with the murders? We've been looking for a specific motive and here it is, my mind informed me. Vesta gets out of the hospital and threatens to tell . . . Threatens to tell whom? Ace wanted to tell Wayne himself. And I didn't think he'd care if anyone else knew, not enough to kill over, anyway—

"Well, does it?" Wayne pressed.

"It doesn't have to do with the murders," I told him, trying to keep the doubt I felt out of my voice. Then I wondered if Harmony had known. Hadn't she said something about inheriting Vesta's secrets?

"Kate, look at me," Wayne ordered.

I looked down uneasily. His eyes were stern under lowered brows. "Both Mom and Harmony have been murdered," he said, his voice as stern as his eyes. "What if they were killed because they were keeping family secrets? And now you're keeping a secret. Don't do this to me, Kate." His voice cracked.

I almost told him then. But I couldn't. What would he do if he knew? Would he kill himself? No, I told myself. Wayne was a very strong man in his own way. But still, I wasn't sure. A familiar nausea rose in me. I had known a boy who killed himself in high school. He had been filled with guilt and shame. And despair. For years afterwards, I had asked myself what I could have done to prevent his suicide. Even though his brother had come to me and told me that there was nothing I could have done, nothing short of giving him a new childhood. But this situation was different. I wasn't powerless this time.

"No, Wayne," I said. Suddenly I felt stronger, my body more substantial. "I'm not going to tell you what else we talked about. It had nothing to do with Vesta's murder. You'll just have to trust me."

Anger widened his eyes again. I pretended not to see it. Better that he was angry with me than confronted with Ace's revelations. Wayne didn't need any more guilt and shame, suicidal type or not.

"Turn around," I told him brusquely. "Your shoulders need a massage."

He glared at me for another moment, then moved to get up. I pushed his shoulders down hard. He landed back on his chair with an "oof." I began pounding his shoulders with the side of my hand, then the heel of my hand and then my knuckles. Finally, I started using my elbows, a trick a deep-tissue massage therapist had taught me. And slowly the stiffness in his muscles began to give.

When I couldn't pound any longer, he turned to me, his eyes downcast.

"You have to do what you think is right," he muttered. "Shouldn't have pushed you. Sorry."

I could have kissed him. I did kiss him. And he kissed me back, standing as he did and pulling me to him. And finally, all the fear and anxiety of the days before turned into passion.

It was about time.

I woke up happy on Tuesday morning. Even Wayne seemed happy. Actually, that might be putting it too strongly. But at least he didn't seem as unhappy. He ate breakfast with me, then walked to the living room. But instead of sitting on the couch and staring, he began to pace. For two hours I processed Jest Gifts mail orders and listened to the sound of his feet. *Clomp, clomp, clomp,* turn, *clomp, clomp, clomp,* turn, *clomp, clomp* . . . Finally, I put down my pencil and joined him in the living room.

"What's up?" I asked, catching him mid-turn.

"Gotta get specific," he announced. Then he finished his turn and clomped over to the far wall again.

I waited for his return trip and asked, "Specific about what?"

"Motive," he answered.

I caught his arm before he could turn again. "Talk to me," I ordered.

"Okay," he agreed with a sigh. He focused his eyes on mine. "Both of them were killed for a reason, but what reason? Why do people kill each other?"

"Could be a lot of things," I answered. "Money, anger—"

"Not money," he interrupted, shaking his head. "Neither of them had any."

"But someone could have *thought* that Vesta had money if they thought she owned the condo. And Harmony said Vesta willed it to her."

Wayne just shook his head again.

"All right," I agreed. "Money's unlikely. But anger isn't. Your mother was tweaking everyone's tails last Friday. Remember how she taunted Dru about her first husband? And it made Gail as angry as her mother," I added, thinking of Gail's bitter words that evening as we left the condo. "And Harmony seemed to be stepping into Vesta's shoes on Sunday. Who knows what she said to people before we got there?"

He nodded thoughtfully for a moment, but then started shaking his head again. "Maybe Harmony was killed in anger. The way she was beaten . . ." The color in his face faded and I knew he was thinking of Harmony's corpse. I put my arm around his waist, to comfort us both. "But Mom was poisoned," he went on. "You don't poison someone in a moment of anger."

"Not necessarily in a moment," I suggested. "Maybe

someone's been angry for a long time. A remembered wrong from childhood can grow as time goes on."

He stood silent, considering.

"Then there's always the possibility of blackmail," I said quietly, not sure if Wayne was ready to think his mother capable of blackmail. "Or just plain lunacy, or unrequited love or—"

"Unrequited love?" he interrupted again, raising his eyebrows.

"Paulson said a man named Quaneri was an admirer of your mother's," I told him.

"But was this man in love with Harmony too? Or—"

The phone rang, cutting off the end of his sentence, but I knew what he meant. Unrequited love wouldn't really work as a motive. I watched as Wayne answered the phone. But blackmail might work, I thought. Ace had told me how Vesta had tried to blackmail him. She might have tried it on someone else, someone less easygoing than Ace. And I could think of a number of Skeritts who were less easygoing. Gail, for instance. Or Trent. Or Ingrid—

"That was the coroner's office," Wayne said, putting the receiver down a few seconds after he had lifted it. "They want me to come up to the morgue at the Civic Center."

"Did they say why?" I asked.

"No, just that they had information for me." He was turning already and getting his keys. "You want to come?" he offered.

"No," I said slowly, deciding as I spoke. "I guess not." Assuming there were no Skeritts lurking at the coroner's office, he didn't really need my company. And I had work to do.

He gave me a kiss goodbye and left.

I was at my desk again, trying to decide which stack of paperwork to attack when I heard a rattling sound coming from the back deck. Was that someone at my back door?

"C.C.!" I called out.

She was usually the one responsible for strange sounds. But then I heard her sleepy meow from beneath my desk. It wasn't C.C. at the back door.

I heard another rattle and then what sounded like footsteps. I walked cautiously through the kitchen and looked out through the glass in the door, but I couldn't see anyone, only the covered hot tub. Maybe I had a hot tub poltergeist, I told myself as I walked back to my office.

By this time, C.C. had emerged from beneath the desk. She stood arched like a Halloween cat on my chair and stared in the direction of the back door. Then her ears went back, flattening against her skull. I hate it when she does that. I never know if she's seeing a bug or a ghost . . . or an intruder.

I rubbed my arms, trying to rub away the disquiet I felt. I could almost feel my own ears flattening. Finally, I dialed Jest Gifts, telling myself I needed to call in sometime and it might as well be now.

Judy answered the phone.

"Oh, Kate," she said without so much as a hello. "I got the cutest little dog at the pound! Her name is Rosy. But Jerry came over and he wasn't fooled for a minute. Maybe he really does know the dogs. He says he loves them as much as I do. . . ."

I listened to the flow of her words over the telephone line, still waiting for another rattle of the back door. But I never heard one.

". . . another awfully cute dog, but she's so thin. Do you think I should get her too?"

"What?" I asked absently.

"At the pound, Kate," Judy said, her voice raised in annoyance. "Aren't you listening? This other little dachshund—"

And then I heard the sound of footsteps on my front stairs. Loud, clattering footsteps.

"I gotta go," I told Judy.

But she was still talking as the footsteps pounded up to the front door.

My heart gave one answering thud and the door burst open.

- Nineteen -

I DROPPED THE telephone receiver, readying myself to face the intruder. Readying myself to fight. Or maybe to run. But before I could even take a breath, I saw who was galloping through the doorway. It was Wayne.

I felt all the little adrenaline couriers that had been speeding through my body execute simultaneous U-turns in relief.

"Marin County doesn't have a morgue!" Wayne shouted.

And then he was throwing his arms around me. He was wet with perspiration. "The phone call was fake, Kate," he told me. "Fake! Someone wanted you alone here."

"Hic," I said. I had meant to tell him about the knocking I'd heard, but something—maybe it was all of those little U-turns—had given me the hiccups. "Hic," I said again. Then, "Hic—damn."

I heard a sound like an insect trying to sing opera, and looked down. The telephone receiver was still dangling inches from the floor.

"Hic-Judy," I said, pointing.

Wayne released me, but stood hovering less than a yard away as I painfully extricated myself from Judy's telephone soliloquy. Apparently she hadn't even noticed I'd dropped the phone, she had been so engrossed in the story she was now finishing up about a Santa Cruz Superior Court judge who had given a divorcing couple custody of their two German shepherds on alternate months.

"I don't really think that's fair to the dogs," she said finally. "Do you, Kate?"

I murmured a "No" between hiccups and struggled to get out a final spasmodic "goodbye," before hanging up.

Then I turned back to Wayne, glad to have had time to think before telling him about the knocking. He was already scared enough. That was made clear as he began to speak again.

"Was halfway to the Civic Center when I remembered someone from the coroner's office telling me that they didn't have a morgue," he said. His voice was high and shaking, even now. "No morgue, that's why Mom's body was held at the mortuary. So I stopped the car and called from a phone booth. Coroner's office said they hadn't called me. I turned around and came back as fast as the car would go."

He threw his arms around me again. "Was so afraid I'd be too late," he groaned into my hair.

Had someone really been here to kill me? I thought of Harmony's corpse and shivered in Wayne's arms.

"Did you see anyone near the house?" I asked his chest. My hiccups were gone now, frightened away. "Any of your relatives' cars in the driveway or on the street?"

He drew back from me and shook his head. His eyes were still round with panic.

"Should we tell the police?" I asked slowly. "Or will they just think we made it up?"

His mouth opened, then closed again. Finally, he let loose a big sigh and seemed to deflate. His eyes returned to their normal shape. "You're right," he admitted. "Wouldn't do any good."

His brows descended like curtains. "Gotta find the murderer," he growled. Then he turned back to the living room and resumed pacing.

I never got a chance to tell him about the rattling. It was just as well. His spell of total panic seemed to be over. And I was scared enough for the two of us anyway.

I went back to my desk and tried to lose my fear in work. But my mind paced along with Wayne as I checked off orders. Two dozen Santas in gilded cages. Check. Had the person who called Wayne tried to open my back door? Six hollow-tooth cups. Check. And if so, why were they interested in me and not Wayne? Because I was the one asking questions, I supposed. Thirteen shrunken-head ornaments, eight "uh-huh" ties and three sets of chiro-crackers. Check. If we told the police everything, would they give us police protection? No, I was sure they wouldn't. They didn't have the personnel. Thirty-three shark mugs. Check. Wayne was right. We had to figure out who the murderer was ourselves. But how?

A few hours later, I still didn't have an answer. But Wayne seemed to think he did.

"Dinner tonight with all of them," he announced and picked up the telephone receiver. Then he turned to me, frowning. "Where?" he asked.

"Do we really have to feed them to get answers?" I asked back. My stomach churned out a nonverbal equivalent of a whine.

"Yes," he replied succinctly.

I took a deep breath and thought for a moment. "How about the Laughing Mango Cafe?" I suggested finally. "It's fun."

"Fun," Wayne repeated in a monotone and then started to punch in numbers.

It took him a while to get anyone. I listened as he tried Ace's room and Dru's room without success. Then he asked for Trent's room. Five minutes later he was off the phone.

"Talked to Aunt Ingrid," he told me. "Everyone else is out for a walk on the Golden Gate Bridge, but she says they'll probably be happy to meet us at the Laughing Mango." He paused. "Aunt Ingrid didn't sound very happy."

"Aunt Ingrid never sounds happy," I assured him.

He shrugged.

"What about Clara?" I asked, thinking she might be of help in evaluating Wayne's relatives, having worked with psychotics most of her life.

"Of course," Wayne murmured. "Shouldn't have forgotten Clara. She's a suspect too."

"I didn't mean—" I began, but Wayne had already picked up the phone again to talk to Clara.

"Wayne Caruso," he said. Then, "Wanted to know if you'd like to go to dinner . . ."

I wandered through the kitchen to the back door and peered through the glass. Was there evidence of an uninvited visitor out there? I listened for a moment. Wayne was still talking. I opened the door and stepped outside. I couldn't see any footprints on the deck or beyond it on the hard ground. There were no carelessly dropped business cards or cigarette butts or gum wrappers. Or clubs or vials of poisons, for that matter. Should I call the police over, just in case? It wouldn't prove much if they found evidence of the presence of any of the suspects. Most of the Skeritts had been on the deck the day before—

"Where are you, Kate?" Wayne shouted, panic in his voice again.

"In here," I called back, hastily stepping into the kitchen and shutting the door behind me.

Wayne told me that Clara Kushiyama had accepted our dinner invitation. We would pick her up on the way. And Ace called later that afternoon to say that the whole family would be at the Laughing Mango Cafe at six. Wayne made reservations for twelve people. The stage was set. Now all that was needed was for one of the actors to confess. I didn't have the heart to tell Wayne just how unlikely I thought that would be.

"So, how did you get into psychiatric work?" I asked Clara. She was sitting in the front seat of the Jaguar next to Wayne. We had picked her up at her apartment a few minutes earlier, on our way to the Laughing Mango Cafe.

She turned to look at me in the back seat. "I guess I've always been curious about people," she answered, her words slow and soothing. "Especially people in institutions. I was interned at the Manzinar camp in Southern California during World War II."

"Terrible thing," Wayne growled.

"I wasn't happy about it at the time," Clara admitted. But there was no bitterness in her tone or her serene face. Her fingertips slowly brushed her dark hair back from her forehead. "It was pretty scary, with all of those armed soldiers determined to guard us 'potential enemies of the United States.' Being of Japanese ancestry was enough back then to count as a 'potential enemy.' And even after it stopped being quite so scary, it was still dreary. Especially for a teenager. I was fourteen when we were first interned."

"I'm sorry," Wayne said. "It should have never happened."

"Well now, *you* don't need to apologize," Clara said kindly. "You probably weren't even born at the time."

"But still—" he began. Then he stopped. As he turned to her, I saw the edge of his sheepish grin. The expression warmed me, reminding me of the Wayne in waiting, the man I had known before his mother was killed. "Guess I was having delusions of grandeur," he murmured. "Wanted to apologize on behalf of the United States."

"Okey-dokey," Clara answered with a soft chuckle. "Apology accepted." Then she turned to face me again. "Anyway, as to your question, Kate. I was always interested in institutions. And in outsiders, especially the insane. The logic of the insane fascinates me because it always makes sense of their behavior. But first, one must understand the context from which it springs."

I nodded eagerly, remembering. "I worked in a mental hospital too, about twenty years ago," I told her. "There was this one woman who would begin screaming every time we tried to get her out of bed. Finally, I asked her why. It turned out that she thought the floors were electrified and would electrocute her. So I brought her some rubber-soled shoes. It was really exciting when she got out of bed and walked."

"A perfect solution, my dear," Clara said, smiling. "So few people even bother to figure out the motivation."

"How about the motivation for murder?" Wayne asked. "Does that make sense if you know the context?"

Clara's smile made way for a more serious expression. "I imagine most murderers have reasons for murder that make sense to them," she replied slowly. "The reasons just don't make sense to us."

"But are reasons justifications for behavior?" Wayne went on. "Or just excuses?"

Clara didn't have an answer for that one. At least, not one

she was willing to share. Neither did I. The Jaguar purred along in silence until we got to the restaurant a few minutes later.

The Laughing Mango Cafe tried very hard to be a fun kind of place. It certainly had fun decor. Its white plaster walls were covered with Bugs Bunny and Porky Pig posters as well as various colorful representations of mangoes. And most of the mangoes were complete with cartoon arms, legs and laughing faces.

The Skeritts were all gathered in the bar under a pink neon version of a dancing mango, this one sporting bulging eyes and a top hat. But somehow the Skeritts didn't look as if they really appreciated the fun decor. Bill and Dru sat silently frowning with drinks in hand at a table they shared with Gail. Trent, Lori and Ingrid sat at another table, without the drinks but with similar frowns. Trent looked up as we entered the bar and gave us a strained, polite smile. Ace was at yet another table with the two kids. No one was talking. Except for Eric, of course.

"You know what?" he was saying to Mandy. He didn't wait for her answer. "In New York they're training these totally cool seals to retrieve stuff from the ocean for the police. Like guns and drugs and stuff—"

"That's really hideous," Mandy drawled. "What if a gun goes off?"

"But they're only seals," Eric objected. "That's why it's so totally cool."

Mandy's chocolate-brown eyes narrowed. I felt an animal rights lecture approaching.

"Hi, everyone," I called out quickly. "They have a place set up for us outside."

It was supposed to be fun outside, too, on the whitewashed cement patio. We sat at a long table made up of a series of smaller tables covered in blue-checked linen. We had a sideways view of the bay over a fence made of metal pylons and thick brown rope. It was all very nautical. There were gulls galore, flying around and screeching over the sound of waves and wind. And the wind was cold, much colder than I expected. I wondered if they could move us to a table inside. But before I could propose the idea, Eric started up again.

"So these seals can even take pictures," he told Clara. She had made the tactical error of sitting next to the boy. "Really. It's totally incredible! And they can unbuckle seat belts too. . . ."

I looked down at my menu. There were plenty of burgers under the dancing mango logo: tofu burgers, bean burgers, turkey burgers and beef burgers. And lots of fish, including tequila prawns and blackened red fish with mango chutney. And tostadas, and tacos—

"These are such cute little menus," Dru said. She and Bill were at the other end of the table. I could just hear her high, tinkling voice over the wind. "And the food looks so fun. Don't you think so, Bill?"

In reply, Bill took a sip from his glass.

A busboy tossed a few baskets of bread and mini crocks of butter on our table and then retreated. Lori passed a basket to me, exclaiming over the corn and molasses breads. I took a piece of each kind and passed the rest along to Gail. I bit into the molasses bread gratefully. It was as good as I remembered, and warm besides.

"Do you know what else?" Eric asked Clara, his eyes eager under his thick glasses. I could hear *his* voice just fine.

"What?" she answered, looking at him with apparent interest. I had thought Clara was a saint before, the way she'd put up with Vesta. Now I was certain.

"I read this totally audacious article about DNA profiling last night," he told her. He crammed bread into his mouth and went on, spitting crumbs. "If they get a trace of your blood, it's practically like a fingerprint. Or sperm. Or . . ."

He was still lecturing when the waiter came for our order. And Clara was still listening. Actually, everyone seemed to be. It was easier than talking, I guessed.

"Bean burger with mango relish," I ordered when my turn came.

Eric looked over at Mandy before he placed his order, then muttered something inaudible into the wind.

"What was that?" the waiter asked.

"Beef burger," he said in a normal tone.

Mandy turned to him and mouthed one word, "Hideous," then turned away. It looked as if that budding relationship was doomed. But Eric was irrepressible. Once the waiter was gone, he started in about genetics again.

"This really smart dude named Mendel figured it out," he told Clara. He looked over at Mandy. Was he still hoping to impress her? "There's like recessive genes and dominant genes and they control all sorts of things like . . . like . . ." He faltered as Mandy glared back at him.

"Like eye color," Clara put in gently. She smiled encouragingly. "Blue is—"

"Yeah, oh sure," he said. "Like eye color. Blue's recessive and brown's dominant, so two blues make—" He broke off again. This time he seemed to be staring at Gail, sitting beside me. "Hey, why are Gail's eyes brown? Both of her parents' eyes are blue!"

You could almost hear the whoosh as heads turned simultaneously to look at Gail.

"Because Bill Norton is not my real father," she answered brusquely. "My *real* father had brown eyes."

"So," Clara said. "Father with brown eyes and a mother with blue eyes could make a child with brown—"

"Oh, yeah," Eric said quickly. "I knew that."

"I'll bet you did," Mandy drawled, rolling her eyes to the cloudy sky above.

"Now, sweetie," Lori said reprovingly to her daughter, but I could hear the laughter in her voice.

I buried my own laughter in a cough. Poor Eric. I wondered if he had stayed up late last night studying genetics to impress Mandy.

"And you know what else?" he said a few moments later. Fortunately, the kid knew how to bounce back. Fortunately for him anyway.

"What?" Clara replied. Her eyes were creased into an affectionate smile.

"I read that male sperm count is down to half of what it was fifty years ago—"

"Uh-oh!" Ace interrupted. He opened his eyes wide and rolled them slowly toward his lap.

Everyone laughed at that one. Well, not everyone, actually. Gail didn't laugh. Or Trent. Or Wayne, for that matter. But a lot of us did. Even Eric.

"Hey," the boy followed up, "does anyone know what an entomologist studies?" He gave us approximately three seconds to come up with an answer, then answered himself. "Bugs!" he announced gleefully. "These dudes are totally awesome. They can tell all sorts of things about a dead body by the bugs. See, first there's flies, then eggs, and then maggots—"

"Whoa, boy!" Ace interrupted. "Enough is enough."

"But Grampy!" Eric objected. "I was just—"

"Why don't you tell everyone about your sports career," Ace suggested quickly.

"Ah, I'm not that good," Eric said. He lowered his eyes for a moment. Was he being modest? Or was he really terrible? "But I did hit a totally awesome home run for our baseball team. You see, I figured it out . . ."

But I didn't hear the rest of his sentence. The minute Eric had said "baseball," I'd stopped breathing. I blinked my eyes and saw the living room of Vesta's condo as it had been yesterday morning when we'd found Harmony's body. And finally, I knew what was missing. It was Harmony's baseball bat.

– Twenty –

I FIGURED I'D just close my eyes until I could breathe better, but the all too familiar vision of Harmony's battered body appeared the instant my eyelids came down. I pulled them back up and looked over at Wayne, hoping for a little visual relief. He sat silent and still between his Uncle Ace and Aunt Ingrid, his gaze straight ahead and unreadable. Had he thought of the baseball bat too, the baseball bat that Harmony had carried for protection? Had he wondered if it had been turned on her and used to beat her into— No, I told myself. I wasn't going to think about that anymore.

The wind raised the hair on my forearms. It was too damn cold out here, I decided, shifting in my chair impatiently. I surveyed the faces around the table. No one else looked cold. No one was shivering but me. Ingrid was smiling vaguely at Eric as he continued his monologue. Trent was smiling at the boy too, but the effect was marred by the muscle that twitched in his jaw. Ace leaned back in his chair, looking comfortable as he listened to his grandson. And Mandy was still glaring in Eric's direction.

". . . and I'm, like, way taller than the other kids on the basketball team," he was saying. "It's totally cool . . ."

When I finally got around to looking at Gail sitting beside me, I realized she wasn't watching Eric like the rest of the table. She was watching me. Her stare seemed to intensify as my eyes met hers. I resisted the urge to look away, and clamped my teeth into a smile. She didn't return the smile. She just stared. God, she was a spooky woman, I thought. Then I wondered if she knew what I was thinking.

"I played basketball in high school too," Lori announced

loudly from my other side. My heart jumped in my chest like a startled deer. Gail didn't even blink. I turned slowly to face Lori, my heart beating double time.

"It's a wonderful way to get in touch with your body," Lori went on enthusiastically, waving a piece of cornbread in the air to make her point. "Sports can be a true meditation. . . ."

I had just managed to get my pulse back to normal, when our meal came.

Dru tasted one of her tequila prawns and pronounced it "delicious." Ace grunted his appreciation of the grilled salmon with mango chutney. Wayne poked at his tostada. And I stared at my bean burger, wondering if I could eat it. I snuck a look at Gail. She shoved a forkful of fettucini in her mouth and looked back at me. I picked up the burger and bit into it.

"Yum," I mumbled through my mouthful, banishing all thoughts of Harmony. Or at least trying to. "The mango relish is great."

I swallowed hard and wondered why it seemed so important to eat the damn burger. A duel of nerves with Gail, with fettucini and bean burgers as our chosen weapons? But why duel with Gail in the first place? Because she was the murderer? I snuck another glance at her. She was still watching me out of the corner of her eye as she ate. I forced myself to take another bite and suddenly my viewpoint shifted. What if Gail thought *I* was the murderer?

"So, Kate," she said to me quietly. "How do you feel about your mother?"

After I had finished choking on my bean burger, I told her I felt "just fine" about my mother. She didn't ask me any more questions.

It was deep into twilight by the time everyone had finished eating. The patio lights buzzed on as the waiter came back with dessert menus.

"None for me, thank you," Clara said and stood. Then she murmured, "ladies' room," and turned away from the table.

"Me too," I announced, popping out of my seat like a jack-in-the-box.

The rest room had a Looney Tunes poster, a painted plaster of Paris laughing mango and two stalls. Clara was washing her hands when I came out of my stall. I couldn't wait any longer.

"Do any of these guys act like murderers to you?" I blurted out.

She sighed and suddenly I saw the age in her serene face. It was in the wrinkles around her eyes and the hollows beneath them. I even thought I could see more gray hairs than before in her black pageboy. Maybe it was the lighting in the bathroom.

"I wish I could tell you that I recognized the murderer among them," she said slowly. "But I just can't. Oh, they're an odd bunch. Bill Norton seems very depressed as well as alcoholic. And Mrs. Norton appears to be in complete denial about his condition. I'd guess that Trent Skeritt is quite distressed beneath his smile. And Ingrid Skeritt is certainly upset, but that would seem to me to be a normal reaction to these circumstances."

She turned to the mirror above the sink and stared, apparently lost in thought.

"What about Gail?" I asked.

Clara smiled gently. "I would guess that Gail is a very emotional woman trying very hard to be unemotional," she replied. "A common malady among psychotherapists, I can assure you."

"But not necessarily a murderer," I finished for her.

"No," she agreed, the smile leaving her face. "I've known a few murderers in the course of my work. A man who killed his wife. A much younger man who killed his mother. And a mother who killed her own child." She shook her head sadly. "Each of them was quite clearly psychotic. The mother heard voices telling her to kill her child and then herself, but—" She broke off suddenly. "I didn't mean to go on like this, my dear," she apologized. "Sometimes the despair weighs on me."

"I understand," I told her. And I did. That's why I had left psychiatric work twenty years ago.

"Anyway," she said more cheerfully, "the only murderers I've known have been obvious in their insanity. If the murderer in this case is one of Mrs. Caruso's relatives, then he or she is not so obvious."

I nodded glumly. Clara wrapped an arm around me and hugged. For a moment, I felt absurdly childlike and protected. Then she removed her arm.

Neither Wayne nor I said anything more about the murder until we had dropped Clara off at her apartment and were cruising back down the highway.

"Remember Harmony's baseball bat?" I asked then.

Wayne nodded.

"Shouldn't it have been——" I began.

"By the door with the water gun," he finished for me. So, he *had* thought of it, too.

"Do you think it was gone because the murderer used it to . . ." I took a breath. "Because it was the weapon?" I finished.

"Maybe." He shrugged. "But maybe it's just somewhere else in the condo."

"Do we talk to the police about it?" I asked aloud. Not that I really wanted to be grilled by Detective Sergeant Upton another time if I could possibly avoid it.

"Not yet," Wayne answered softly. Then he turned toward me. I wished he'd keep his eyes on the road. The speedometer was pushing eighty. "We have to figure this thing out soon, Kate. Everyone's coming to the funeral tomorrow. But after that, I don't know how we can keep them here." Then, to my relief, he turned his eyes forward again.

I didn't bother to ask Wayne who he thought could have swung the baseball bat. They all could have. The Skeritts were damn sturdy people. Hell, between them they could have made up a whole baseball team. Or a basketball team, I thought. They were all tall enough.

Felix was waiting for us under the light on the deck when we got home.

"Howdy-hi, you guys," he called out, stroking his mustache predatorially as he came down the stairs to greet us.

Wayne stepped forward, holding up his hand like a stop sign. "Not talking about the murders," he growled.

"Hey man, no problemo," Felix assured him. He leaned his

head to the side to peer around Wayne in my direction. "Just wanted a little heart-to-heart with Kate here about my sweetie pie. Man, Barbara's gone totally bonkers on me since I moved in with her! Says *I* have weird habits. This from a woman who channels dead aliens from the planet Gonzo." He put his hands together as if in prayer and rolled his eyes up in his skull. "Ooglee Booglee, Squiglee Ooglee, speak to me, oh dear departed Gonzola." Then he dropped his hands in disgust. "Holy Moly, it's enough to—"

"Get to the point," Wayne ordered.

"I thought maybe Kate here would know why my old lady's so pissed at me, that's all," he said, looking at us with wide, soulful eyes. "I don't have a clue."

I thought for a moment. It seemed to me that Barbara had used the adjectives "gross" and "cheap" among other things. But before I could think of a gentle way to tell Felix this, he opened his mouth again.

"Speaking of clues," he said. "Word is the La Risa oinkers still don't have diddly on their top two murder cases. But I thought you guys might—"

"Out!" Wayne and I shouted at once.

"Poor Felix," I said as he steered his old Chevy out of the driveway. "He probably really doesn't have a clue why Barbara's mad at him."

Wayne just turned and stared at me, then slowly shook his head and walked up the stairs. Felix was clearly a taste he had never acquired.

Wayne was already pacing the living room by the time I came through the front door.

"Let's go for a walk," I suggested when he stopped at the opposite wall and turned.

"Okay," he said and stomped out the door and down the stairs without another word. After the minute it took me to figure out that our walk was already in progress, I raced out after him, only stopping to close the door behind me. I caught up to him on the street. It was dark there, lit only by the deck lights and glowing windows of the houses we were passing. And we were passing them mighty fast as Wayne marched ahead.

I had wanted to talk to him as we walked but I didn't have a chance. I was too busy panting with the effort to keep up with him. I felt like a dachshund following a German shepherd, doing double time to make up for my short legs.

After half an hour of jogging behind him, I managed to gasp, "stop, turn around," and "slow" before sitting down on the cold hard pavement.

He turned around and stared for a moment into the darkness, then bent his head down to look at me where I was sitting.

"Kate," he murmured. "What are you doing on the ground?"

"Resting," I panted.

It was only when he squatted in front of me and scooped me up in his arms that I realized he was crying. I felt the wet shock of his tears first and then heard the rasp of his breathing.

"I'm sorry," he sobbed. "I'm so damn sorry."

Somehow, I was pretty sure this wasn't just an apology for walking too fast.

Then he began to march again, carrying me in his arms as he did and weeping.

He probably would have carried me all the way home if I hadn't asked him to put me down. And even at that, I had to ask three separate times before he heard me.

By the time we got home I was tired and sore. And very worried.

I led Wayne straight to the bedroom. He didn't resist as I pulled him along by the hand, or as I helped him to undress and tucked him into bed. When I bent down to kiss his forehead, he stared up at me, his eyes blank.

"Are you all right?" I whispered.

"Fine," he said without blinking.

"Will you call me if you need me?" I asked.

"Yes," he answered.

"Close your eyes, sweetie," I ordered.

He closed them. I turned out the light.

I tiptoed out of the bedroom and shut the door softly behind me. Then I gave in to the luxury of a few moments of pure panic. Was Wayne insane with grief or just insane? Being carried in his arms as he wept had not been romantic. It had been scary. Damn scary. He was out of control. He was suffering terribly and I didn't know how to help him. Maybe he needed professional help.

And then I thought of Clara. She would know what to do. Wouldn't she?

Clara answered my phone call on the second ring.

"Kate, my dear," she said. "I was just thinking of phoning you."

"About what?" I asked quickly, impatient to talk to her about Wayne.

"My answering service has just given me a very strange message. It came in about a half hour after we all left the Laughing Mango." She paused.

"And . . ." I prompted.

"Someone called for me. The woman who took the message wasn't sure if the caller was a man or a woman. She said the voice sounded 'fuzzy.' In any case, this someone said he or she had a job offer for me, to care for a relative in Arizona, and promised to leave an airplane ticket and cash for me in my mailbox if I would leave a confirming note tonight on the community bulletin board at the laundromat across the street. And to top it all off, the caller said he or she would pay twice my usual rates as well as the airplane fare and lodging in Arizona. All very mysterious, I think."

"It sure is," I whispered. The telephone receiver felt cold against my face.

"Of course, I can't really consider the offer," Clara said slowly. "I have my regular clients to look in on. But it does seem strange. The caller apparently didn't even leave a phone number. I'm wondering if this has anything to do with the two deaths."

"Have you told the police yet?" I asked carefully.

"Told them what?" she asked back. I heard her chuckle over the phone line. "That someone offered me too much money?"

"This isn't funny," I argued. "The caller might be the murderer—" I stopped mid-sentence. Why would the murderer want her out of town? "Do you know something?" I demanded.

"Not that I'm aware of," she said slowly. "And believe me, I have asked myself that question over and over again."

"I think you should talk to the police," I told her. "Or come and stay with us where it's safe—"

"Listen, my dear," she put in, "I've worked with psychotic patients most of my adult life and none has harmed me seriously yet."

"But this could be the murderer," I protested. Why wouldn't she listen? "If you won't call the police, then leave the note and I'll watch who reads it—"

"Just forget I mentioned it, Kate," she interrupted firmly. "I didn't mean to trouble you—"

"But, you—"

"Now, now," she scolded me. "Don't make me feel bad. No one's going to sneak up on this old woman." She paused. "So why did you call me, my dear?" she asked calmly.

It was like arguing with a rock. She was worse than Wayne. Worse than me, even. I sighed and told her about Wayne. At length.

"All very natural under the circumstances," she assured me. "His grief will probably come and go in cycles for some time. Along with periods of numbness and renewed shock and anger. And guilt. But eventually it will all pass into acceptance. Don't forget, Wayne has a great deal of inner strength. He'll make it through. Just let him know it's okay for him to be having these feelings. And I would certainly be glad to talk to him again if you think it would help."

"Tomorrow morning," I suggested quickly. I could kill two birds with one stone this way. I could get Wayne some help and have another chance at talking Clara into going to the police.

"Okey-dokey," she agreed. "I'm free from nine to eleven."

"We'll come by at nine then," I said and hung up.

When I tiptoed back into the bedroom, Wayne was asleep and snoring softly. Maybe the walk had done him some good. I undressed and crawled in beside him, then willed myself to think only positive thoughts and dream sweet, nonviolent dreams. It didn't work any better than it usually did.

The next morning, I woke from a nightmare about an alien from another planet, probably the planet Gonzo. The alien had at least a dozen tentacled arms, and each one of them waved a separate baseball bat as it chased me down the darkened street Wayne and I had traveled the night before.

My eyes popped open and I saw with relief the sunlight floating in through the skylight. I lay there for a few minutes basking in the brightness before I noticed Wayne next to me. He lay on his side, propped up on one elbow. And he was smiling.

"Whatcha looking at?" I asked drowsily.

"You," he whispered. "You're beautiful."

"Do go on," I ordered.

He was quick to comply. "You're smart too," he told me. "And compassionate. And sexy——"

I rolled over on top of him.

"Oof," he said, and then quickly added, "And as light as a nightingale's wing." He almost got through it with a straight face, but not quite.

That walk had done him more good than I realized, I decided as I bent my head down to kiss his welcoming lips.

Later, as we lay together with our arms wrapped around each other, he whispered, "Don't let me forget the joy again, Kate."

"I won't," I promised. Then I remembered Clara's advice. "Or the sorrow, or the anger, or the love," I added. "It's all fine. All of it."

"Okay," he said solemnly and held me even closer.

I peeked over his head at the clock. It was almost eight.

"Hey, we gotta get going," I told him.

"Why?" he asked. "The funeral's not until this afternoon."

"I promised Clara we'd visit."

His brows lowered to half-mast. So much for joy. I had a feeling we might get into the anger portion of the feelings-that-were-fine-to-have soon.

"I wanted her to talk to you," I explained further.

He unwrapped his arms from around my torso. "I'm okay," he said impatiently. I kept my grip on him.

"I know," I said softly. "But do it for me, all right?"

"Okay, fine," he growled ungraciously. "But remember, she's a suspect. Could be dangerous."

"I'll drive," I added quickly.

His brows came down even further, but only for a moment. Then his homely face split into a grin.

"Forgot negotiation skills when I was describing your attributes earlier," he said.

I kissed him once more. Damn, it was good to have him back.

An hour or so later, we were traveling up Highway 101 on our way to Clara's. I was glad to be driving again. Not that my old brown Toyota was in the same class as Wayne's Jaguar. (Actually, it wasn't even in the same species.) I had just finished telling Wayne about Clara's mysterious message from her answering service when I saw the green sign announcing the turnoff to her La Risa apartment.

"Don't like the sound of it," Wayne commented quietly. "Did she call the police?"

"No," I told him uncomfortably. "I couldn't talk her into it."

Wayne frowned.

I pushed a little harder on the accelerator as I took the turnoff.

I had just parked by the curb in front of Clara's apartment building when I heard a siren in the near distance. As I opened my door, the sound grew closer.

– Twenty-one –

AND THEN I saw where the sound was coming from. There was an ambulance moving toward us. As we watched, it pulled to an abrupt stop in front of the apartment building, and two attendants, one male and one female, jumped out and ran into the entrance.

Clara? *No*, I told myself. Not necessarily. The ambulance could have come for anyone. This was a big apartment building, with a lot of occupants. Already, a few of them were emerging from the ground-floor units. And others peered out over their balconies from up above.

"I heard a cry and this big thud, so I went upstairs to look," someone was saying. I spotted the speaker, a gray-haired woman standing in a knot of people at the front of the building. "I thought maybe she had a heart attack. But her door was wide open. She was just lying there on the floor, bleeding. . . ." Her voice trailed off into what sounded like a sob.

Bleeding, but alive?

"Was she breathing?" someone asked.

"I think so," the gray-haired woman said. "But she didn't say anything when I talked to her. She looked so . . ." Her voice trailed off again.

The female attendant came jogging back out the entrance.

"How is she?" someone called out.

"She'll be fine," the attendant called back quickly. I had a feeling that would be her answer no matter what the condition of the patient. But the words still offered a small measure of relief. Whoever the injured woman was, she was apparently alive. "Now step back please," the attendant ordered and rolled a gurney out of the ambulance and into the building.

Then I heard another siren. I turned and saw a car with the La Risa Police Department insignia approaching. I looked at Wayne. He looked back at me, eyebrows raised. The car pulled in near the ambulance.

"Police," announced the uniformed man emerging from the vehicle. As if he could have been anything else. Then I realized the uniformed man was Officer Yoder. His buzz cut was a dead giveaway. "Who placed the call?" he asked.

The gray-haired woman raised her hand and stepped forward, but she didn't look very happy. Her shoulders were hunched as if anticipating a blow. Maybe she was afraid of the police. I wouldn't blame her.

"Well, ma'am, if you'll—" Officer Yoder began. But he stopped as the gurney came wheeling out of the apartment building.

I guess I hadn't really believed that Clara was the victim until I glimpsed her lying on that gurney. But it was her. Even at this distance I could see the serene moon of her face looking all the more serene because it wasn't moving. Her head was propped up on one side. As they wheeled her into position at the back of the ambulance, I saw the edge of a large white bandage outlined against the black of her hair. And then she was in the ambulance and gone from view. The doors closed and the siren wailed as the ambulance pulled away from the apartment.

"Oh, damn," I said and began to cry. Why hadn't I talked to her? Or called the police myself? Or— Wayne put his arms around me. I could feel his body trembling as I leaned into him.

I looked up into his face. His eyes were closed, but tears were still leaking out.

"Oh, sweetie—" I began.

"Hey, Stan," came a voice from behind me. "Look who's here."

I turned and saw Officer Zappetini, standing tall with one hand on his gun. He grinned widely at us.

My tears dried instantly. As did the inside of my mouth.

And in the same instant, all that leftover moisture transferred itself downward to settle in my armpits and in the palms of my hands.

"Excuse me for a moment, ma'am," Officer Yoder said politely to the gray-haired woman. Then he trotted over to us.

"What are you doing here?" he demanded, his tone not nearly so polite as it had been with the woman.

"We were supposed to see Clara," I told him.

"Clara Kushiyama?" he asked and I wondered if he had just now made the connection to the other murders.

"Uh-huh," I said. "We had an appointment for nine—"

"Wait," Zappetini interrupted gleefully. "Shouldn't we Mirandize them first?"

"Good thought," Yoder agreed. He marched to his car, brought out a clipboard and then marched back to us. This short march seemed to take an eternity.

"Let's get this over with," he said, looking at Wayne. His words sounded ominously like an order to me. "First, you, Mr. Caruso. You have the right to remain—"

"I know my rights," Wayne assured him brusquely.

"Okay, sign here," Yoder said and Wayne signed the form on the clipboard.

I let him read me my rights all the way through, trying to slow my beating heart as he did. A small crowd had gathered around us by the time he finished. As I signed at the bottom of the form, a second patrol car pulled up.

"Let's take them down to see the boss now," Zappetini suggested.

Wayne and I rode together in the back of the police car. At least they didn't handcuff us.

Once we arrived at La Risa police headquarters, we had to go through the whole Miranda routine a second time. Only this time we got the relay version.

"Tell her she has the right to remain silent," Detective Sergeant Upton said to Detective Amador. Amador told me and I said I understood.

"Tell her . . ." he went on.

And then they did the same thing to Wayne, despite his assurances that he knew his rights. All told, I heard those damn rights five separate times. By then, I could have recited them myself to the next suspect who came into the station.

Once they had both of our signatures on the second set of forms, they asked me to wait outside with Officer Zappetini. I tried to meditate during the half hour that I sat with him in the hallway, but instead of embracing stillness, I found myself contemplating Clara's injury, Harmony's battered corpse and what a jail cell would really be like. Would my cellmate be psychotic, sociopathic or drunk? And if drunk, would she be vomiting drunk, passed-out drunk or mean drunk? And what if I had more than one cellmate—? I almost missed it when Amador told me it was my turn.

The interrogation wasn't as bad as I expected, though. Maybe Upton and Amador appreciated the fact that neither Wayne nor I had called attorneys. I explained all about Clara and her answering service message. I did what I could to trace her involvement with the other Skeritts from the time of the buffet to last night's dinner. And I pointed out that Wayne and I had arrived at Clara's apartment about the same time the ambulance had, not before. (This small exculpatory point had occurred to me in between contemplating possible cellmates.) Upton glared over my shoulder and asked Amador to ask me if anyone saw us arrive.

"I'm not sure," was the only answer I could come up with.

In fact, that was the only answer I could come up with to most of their questions. I told them what I knew about Clara's relationship with Vesta (not much), and what I knew about Clara's background (even less). And I told them most emphatically that Wayne and I had been together all morning. I did not tell them in what positions, however.

And then, finally, Upton told Amador to tell me I could leave. I was so relieved, I had to restrain myself from whooping and hugging Wayne where he stood frowning in the hallway. But I sobered up during the police car ride back to the apartment building, where my Toyota was parked. We weren't in jail, but Clara was still hurt.

I decided to exercise my right to remain silent as I drove us home in the Toyota. Wayne didn't seem to mind. He wasn't doing much talking himself. The only really talkative one in the car was my conscience. It told me I should have done something to prevent Clara's injury. My eyes teared up again. I'd known the murderer was dangerous and I'd let Clara—

"Not your fault," Wayne commented.

"Thanks," I sniffled.

His absolution helped a little, but not much. Of *course* Wayne figured it wasn't my fault, I told myself. He probably thought it was his.

I called La Risa General Hospital the minute we walked into the house. I figured that's where they would have taken Clara. But the switchboard operator told me she didn't have any information on a patient by that name.

"But she is a patient there, isn't she?" I pressed.

"I'm afraid I don't have that information," the woman insisted.

"Well, who does?" I demanded.

"I'm afraid I don't know," she said.

And so on.

As I hung up the phone, I turned to Wayne. He looked down at me, a somber expression on his battered face.

"You get the runaround?" he asked.

I nodded and put my arms around him.

He held me for a moment before saying, "Time to get dressed." And only then did I remember that Vesta's funeral was that afternoon. I looked at my watch. We had less than a half hour. No wonder Wayne looked so somber.

It took me four minutes to change into a black sweater and a long black skirt. I couldn't find any pantyhose without runs in them, so I wore a tall pair of black boots over my knee socks and reminded myself to sit like a lady so no one would notice. Wayne had changed into a charcoal-gray suit by the time I finished.

I didn't insist on taking my car to the funeral. I didn't really feel like driving anymore. And driving the Jaguar gave Wayne something to do. He certainly wasn't talking as he sped up the highway.

"It'll be all right," I said.

He shrugged.

I sighed in return. If only each of us could believe even half of the other's assurances, we'd both be happy people. But of course we couldn't.

As Wayne took the turnoff to the funeral home, I offered up an agnostic but sincere prayer to whoever was in charge that Clara would heal quickly and completely. She was too good a woman to lose. Then I offered a more selfish addendum, that she would not only recover but would be able to tell the police who had assaulted her. Then the police would know it wasn't Wayne or me.

Apparently, the funeral immediately preceding Vesta's was still in progress when we arrived at the McLoughlin and Edwards Funeral Home. A man dressed in a well-cut black suit met me at the door and escorted us into a waiting room located off to the side of one of the two chapels. As he opened the door, strains of what sounded like organ music drifted by. I was still looking back over my shoulder, trying to locate the source of the sound when I heard a loud sniffle.

I swiveled my head around to look where I was going, and saw Ingrid, blowing her nose into a large handkerchief. Lori put her arm around her mother. Then I noticed that all the Skeritts were in the room, seated on padded black folding chairs.

"It's only a passage to another life, Mama," Lori insisted. But her voice was low and subdued. Her clothing was subdued too. She was wearing a navy blue jumpsuit today, no bracelets and only the smallest of gold rings in her ears.

In fact, everyone looked subdued as we entered. Even Eric sat without speaking, looking down at his feet. Dru managed a brief, wobbly smile in our direction. Trent and Lori nodded, and everyone else stared. Ace's homely face looked frozen. There were tears in his eyes.

"Wayne," he whispered.

As Wayne went to him, the older man stood and opened his arms. The two men embraced and our escort went out the door. Dru patted the seat next to her and I sat down dutifully.

By the time Wayne took his own seat next to Ace, our escort had brought in a new group of people. I wondered who they were, until I recognized Paul Paulson bringing up the rear. These had to be the other neighbors Paul had promised to bring. I stood to meet them.

"Ms. Jasper, right?" Paul greeted me. He kept his voice low, but his tone still had an undercurrent of exuberance. Apparently he alone remained unintimidated by the atmosphere of the funeral home.

A frail, stooped man with a gnarled brown face approached diffidently.

"This is Mr. Quaneri," Paul said. He patted the elderly man on the shoulder. "He was a great admirer of Mrs. Caruso's."

"Oh . . . how nice," I said and shook Mr. Quaneri's hand. I just couldn't think of anything better to say.

"She was a good woman," Mr. Quaneri told me, and tears flooded his eyes. I was shocked by the realization that this man had cared for Vesta enough to mourn her loss. What had Vesta been to him?

As I tried to think of something comforting to say, Paul introduced another neighbor, a Mrs. Somerville, and then another.

Not long after I had been introduced to each and every member of the small group, our escort returned.

"We are ready for you now," he announced in the resonant tone of a B-movie vampire hungry for a taste of blood.

I made my way over to Wayne and held out my hand. He took it without a word and together we followed an usher into the chapel.

The chapel was a modest, whitewashed room with windows set high into the walls above our heads. There were five or six rows of benches on either side of an aisle that led to the front of the room, where a slender woman stood behind a lectern. She had a lovely oval face, set off perfectly by the white lace collar on her black dress. I assumed she was our nondenominational minister.

Vesta's coffin was to the right of the lectern, on a marbleized dais. As I looked, I felt Wayne's hand begin to tremble in mine. I squeezed it hard, wishing I could do more to comfort him, but knowing he would be embarrassed by any further attention. At least the coffin was closed, and it was almost invisible under the sprays of yellow and white gladioli which covered it. Golden curtains were pulled back to either side of the coffin, as if just opened.

The usher cleared his throat.

Wayne and I walked down the center aisle to sit on a hard bench in the front row. I resisted peeking at Wayne's face, allowing him whatever privacy I could in this public place. From behind us came the rustling sounds of people seating themselves, a few whispers, and scattered coughs and throat clearings. And then the music began. It was Chopin.

"We meet here today to pay tribute to the life of Vesta Skeritt Caruso," the woman at the lectern declared as the music died away. Her voice was deep and carrying, surprising from such a small body. "And we meet here to express our love and admiration for her. And also to bring some comfort to her family and friends who are here and mourn her untimely death . . ."

I heard someone sob behind us. Probably Ingrid, I thought, and felt my own eyes blurring with moisture.

"The catastrophe of her death cannot be altered, but it can be transformed by love . . ."

But who would transform Vesta's death by love? Her son? Mr. Quaneri? I tried to think of her with love now, as I never had while she was alive. Poor, unloved, unlovable Vesta. I sniffled back a tear.

". . . her son Wayne tells me that his mother found life difficult at times, but that she was unique. Unique in her love of life, her vitality, her fearlessness, her sense of humor . . ."

It was all true. I felt for Wayne's hand again and held it, wondering why I had failed to notice these good qualities in Vesta when she was alive.

"Mrs. Caruso's unique nature is both a cause for grief and a cause for celebration. It seems that if you look through the whole universe you will not find anyone else like Vesta Skeritt Caruso . . ."

Amen to that, I thought.

". . . we will each remember her in our own way . . ."

Especially the murderer. I shifted uncomfortably on the hard bench. The murderer was probably sitting somewhere behind us.

"And now we have come to the end of our ceremony," the minister told us. "Will you please stand and observe a moment of silence for Vesta Skeritt Caruso?"

We all rose. I could hear Wayne's hoarse breathing beside me. I put my arm around his waist, my own crying finished as I leaned into him, ready to support his weight. He sagged against me for a few more ragged breaths, then straightened. Finally, I allowed myself to look into his face. His eyes were closed and his face was wet with tears. I closed my own eyes and said a quick goodbye to Vesta.

The moment of silence seemed awfully long. I could hear more than one person crying behind me as I waited for it to end. And then I heard the sound of something electric. I opened my eyes and watched as the golden curtains closed around Vesta's coffin as if by magic.

"In a little while you will leave this chapel," the minister resumed, her voice softer now. "You will go to your homes, gathering places or places of work. As you go, remember Vesta Skeritt Caruso in your own way. And in the days to come, share your thoughts and feelings with others. There is no burden so large that it cannot be shared." She paused for a moment. "And now let us be seated and listen to Chopin."

We sat. The music came on again, softly in the background.

The minister stepped down from behind the lectern and put a hand on Wayne's shoulder, then bowed her head at the rest of us and left.

When the music ended, we all rose.

Ingrid came to Wayne first and kissed him softly on the cheek. Trent shook his hand. Ace engulfed him in a bear hug. Somehow, Wayne had become a receiving line. He endured it all stoically, his face stiff and set. Mr. Quaneri was next.

"For your mama," he said to Wayne, and pulled a bouquet of roses from behind his back and thrust it into Wayne's outstretched hand. He stood on his tiptoes, gave Wayne a peck on the cheek and then retreated as if embarrassed by his own audacity.

Wayne's eyebrows rose, then came down again as Lori approached him with arms open wide.

A couple of Vesta's other neighbors shook Wayne's left

hand, the one without any roses. Dru offered her own variety of cheek-kissing. And finally, Paul Paulson came over and patted Wayne on the back.

"Your mom was one great lady!" he boomed and pressed a business card into Wayne's empty hand.

Wayne looked over at me, a plea in the curve of his eyebrows.

"Time to go?" I whispered.

He nodded.

I could hear Paulson on our way out.

"Have you ever considered an investment in predeveloped land?" he was asking someone.

I resisted the urge to look and see who that someone was, and led Wayne out of the McLoughlin and Edwards Funeral Home just as fast as I could without running.

On the way home in the Jaguar, I thought of Harmony suddenly. Who would arrange her funeral? I turned to ask Wayne, but his scowling profile told me this was not the time. Did Harmony have relatives? Had they been notified? And what about Clara? My hands went cold as the question hit me. No, I reminded myself. Clara was going to be fine. She wouldn't need a funeral.

I still hadn't convinced myself by the time we pulled into the driveway, but I tried to smile anyway. Someone had to. I turned to Wayne.

"How are you doing, sweetie?" I whispered.

Before he could answer, a car pulled in behind us, a blue Ford that I had never seen before. And a second car pulled in behind the Ford. I recognized the second car by the familiar insignia on its door, which read "La Risa Police Department." Uh-oh, I thought as a van pulled in behind the police car.

Then a woman stepped out of the driver's side of the Ford. It was Detective Amador. Detective Sergeant Upton hopped out of the passenger's side and turned to Amador.

"Tell them we have a search warrant," he bellowed.

– Twenty-two –

"WE HAVE A search warrant," Detective Amador told us as we climbed out of the Jaguar.

"But what for?" I asked in confusion, slamming the door behind me. I couldn't seem to get my mind around what was happening.

"For your house and for both of your cars," she answered without consulting her boss. I thought I saw sympathy in her gentle smile. Or maybe it was just pity.

"Like to see the warrant," Wayne requested quietly as he walked up behind me.

Amador handed it over. Wayne scanned the document and handed it back to her.

"Looks fine," he said.

I was glad it looked fine to him. I had no idea what a search warrant was supposed to look like. I still couldn't believe this was happening.

"Tell them to get going," Detective Sergeant Upton ordered.

At first I thought he meant for her to tell *us* to get going, but Amador turned and delivered the order to Yoder and Zappetini, who had popped out of the police car like eager genies. I wasn't sure if the cheerful-looking blond woman emerging from the van behind them was included in the order too. The blonde wore a baseball cap with the La Risa police insignia, but no uniform.

I was about to ask who she was when she turned and slid open the rear door of her van. The back of her blue windbreaker read EVIDENCE TECHNICIAN in white block letters.

She pulled out a pair of latex gloves, shut the door and walked up the crowded driveway, smiling pleasantly.

"Do you have a key for the front door?" she asked.

"Oh, I'll let you in," I assured her. I started toward the stairs.

"Tell her and her boyfriend to wait out here," Upton snapped. At least he didn't bellow this time.

As Amador transmitted the message, Zappetini pushed by me and stood in my path. Did he think I was going to make a run for the house? My hands were trembling when I gave the technician my house key, with anger as much as fear. She and Yoder marched up the front stairs and into the house. Zappetini followed them and stationed himself at the front door with his arms crossed.

I looked over my shoulder at Wayne. His face was a study in impassivity, but I could see the tension in his stiff shoulders and in his clenched hands. He needed comfort now. He had been through enough at his mother's funeral. Then I wondered if Upton knew about the funeral and had timed this search accordingly, hoping to rattle us.

"So, do we all just stand around waiting in the driveway?" I demanded angrily.

When no one answered my question, I took a deep breath and tried to make my face as wooden as Wayne's. I doubt if I succeeded. But I must have made some impression, because Detective Amador let out a little sigh and whispered in her boss's ear, then climbed the front stairs and started nosing around the deck. She poked at the potted plants sitting near the door and hanging from the deck railing. She picked up each of the sagging porch chairs and looked under them. She kicked at the mounds of leaves from the walnut tree. Then she came back down and whispered in her boss's ear again.

"Tell them we can all wait on the deck," he said.

Once the message was duly transmitted, the four of us trooped up the stairs, passed Officer Zappetini on guard at the front door and took seats on the sagging porch chairs, which Amador had rearranged. I heard voices coming from the living room as I sat down.

". . . some really nice pinball machines." That sounded like Yoder.

"Anything inside them?" A woman's voice. The evidence technician's.

"Nothing yet."

"Keep looking."

I turned to Amador. I didn't want to think about the two people searching my house. If they were searching my house, that meant the police thought we had something to hide. Something like poison or a weapon. Or bloodstained clothing. And that meant they thought either Wayne or I was a murderer. My skin tightened. I shook my head. How could they think that? Then I remembered Clara.

"Is Clara all right?" I demanded.

Amador turned to Upton for an answer.

"Tell her we don't have any information about Clara Kushiyama at this time," he said. Then he rotated his head and began to drum his fingers on the porch chair.

"But she is alive and functioning, isn't she?" I pushed, not waiting for the delay of Upton's words. "She knows that neither Wayne nor I attacked her. All you have to do is ask her who did."

When Upton didn't say anything, Amador gave a little shrug. I knew it was hopeless. But why hadn't Clara spoken up yet?

I didn't like my own answers to that question very much.

"Tell her we know she's been involved in murder before," Upton said, interrupting my grim train of thought.

"We know you've—" Amador began.

"Kate's only 'involvement' was as a witness," Wayne interrupted. He sat up straight in his chair, 200 watts of glare radiating from his eyes. "Each of those cases was solved. The murderers confessed. Kate can't be blamed for those murders or for any others."

Upton looked over Wayne's shoulder, apparently unimpressed, and popped a knuckle.

"Tell him we know he inherited from a man who was murdered."

"We know—"

"Now stop that!" I snapped. "You know damn well Wayne didn't murder that man."

Upton shrugged and looked up at the October sky.

"Wayne is not murderer material," I insisted. I lowered my voice. "He couldn't hurt anyone, much less his mother. He loved her. You ought to be looking at the rest of the relatives. They're the ones who hated her. You should have heard the things she said to her sister and her brothers—"

I stopped when I noticed that Upton hadn't bothered to interrupt me. He wanted me to jabber on like this. I was sure of it. I closed my mouth and joined him in staring up at the October sky. The view through the limbs of the walnut tree was especially nice.

Upton's further attempts to prod us into unguarded speech seemed painfully obvious. He instructed Amador to tell me that he had signed statements from witnesses who said I disliked Wayne's mother intensely. Wayne didn't bite. Instead, he moved his own gaze upwards. That made three of us. If anyone walked by, they'd probably look up too, wondering what we were all watching so intently. Upton went on. Then there were the statements that Wayne had endured a dysfunctional childhood, that Wayne was a deeply conflicted and potentially violent man. I had a feeling we had Gail to thank for that assessment.

Upton took a couple more jabs at us, then got up and stomped to the other side of the deck. Amador followed him. I moved my chair closer to Wayne's and took his hand in mine, then closed my eyes and leaned nonchalantly back in my seat.

Time moved excruciatingly slowly after that. Sometime during the next couple of hours, the evidence technician exited the house. She went to her van and got a roll of brown wrapping paper and some paper bags, then went back inside. That was pretty exciting.

A while later she and Yoder brought out three wrapped packages, each slender enough to be held in one hand but at least four feet long. It felt like Christmas in hell as I tried to guess what was in the wrapped packages. Yardsticks? I had only one that I knew of. Rolled up posters? Broom handles?

What? Then she went back in and brought out a bunch of paper bags. I wouldn't even try to guess what was in those. I looked at Wayne. He shrugged his shoulders.

Then they started their search of the yard, taking cuttings of various plants and putting them in plastic bags. They searched the cars. They searched the backyard. They searched the deck. And finally, they were done. The technician handed me my keys and a written receipt. It listed "3 wooden rods, approx. 4 feet long and 1½ inches in diameter; misc. herbs, teas and spices; misc. plant cuttings."

Upton told Amador to tell us not to leave town, Amador told us and then the whole lot of them pulled out of the driveway in reverse order.

"Three wooden rods?" I murmured to Wayne as we watched them go. "Where did they find three wooden rods?"

"Curtain rods?" he guessed.

I shook my head. As far as I knew, all my curtain rods were brass not wooden. And they certainly weren't an inch and a half in diameter. Unfortunately, I'd have to go inside the house to find out what was.

"After you," I said to Wayne.

We walked through the front door. I suppose it could have been a worse mess inside. At least the furniture in the living room was still standing. But the pillows were all piled on the wrong side of the room and the books were in a series of piles near the empty shelves. I started to feel sick when I peeked into my office. My stacks of paper were no longer in stacks. One desk had been pulled out from the wall along with the crates of old paperwork I had stored underneath it. Another—

"I'll help you clean it up," Wayne offered softly.

"Thank you," I whispered back without really hearing him. I couldn't understand the mess. Why didn't they put things back after they were finished? We might as well have been burglarized. Except that burglars might have been neater.

"Sorry," Wayne said even more softly.

I came back to earth with a thump. So my house was a mess. Wayne's mother was dead. That couldn't be cleaned up. And Harmony was dead. And Clara? I turned to Wayne.

Maybe I turned too fast. The room began to shimmer in front of my eyes.

"You okay?" Wayne asked.

I took a deep breath and tried to remember when I had last eaten. Not since the night before, I was pretty sure.

"I'm just hungry," I told him, relieved to have found a physical cause for my distress. "How about you?"

"I'll make you something to eat," was all he said.

I followed him into the kitchen. All my herbs were gone. Not just the healing herbs and the teas but the Schilling and Spice Islands jars too. They must have been looking for whatever had been in Vesta's herbal tea, I realized. Some deadly dill or bloodstained basil. Or—

"Guess I can't make you that spaghetti sauce from scratch tonight," Wayne commented, jerking his head at the nearly empty spice cabinet.

I looked up into his face, confused. What spaghetti sauce? His eyebrows were raised, the corners of his mouth curved upwards. It took me a while to interpret this data. Then I realized he was making a joke. Hallelujah! Shaking my head at that weak joke felt as good as eating the peanut butter-and-banana sandwiches he made for us. Even better.

After we finished stuffing our faces, we went to the bedroom to change our clothes. I opened the closet door. All the clothes that had been hung up were now piled on the floor. I picked up a blouse and tried to rehang it. But there was nothing to hang it from.

"What the hell?" I whispered.

"Four-foot wooden rods," Wayne answered. "That's what the hangers were hanging from."

"But why—" I began.

"Long, rounded, varnished wooden objects—" he said.

"Like Harmony's baseball bat," I finished for him.

Fifteen minutes later, we had changed our clothes and were heading for the Redwood Grove Inn in the Jaguar. When I'd asked Wayne if he thought we needed a lawyer, he told me that we needed to solve the murders. Period. And inevitably, he had arranged another social outing with the Skeritts. They would be waiting for us in the Timber Lounge for cocktails before dinner at the Old Burl Cafe. How lovely. Before leaving the house, I had called the hospital to ask about Clara, but once again I had been told nothing.

"You don't have to be here," Wayne said once he had parked in the motel parking lot. It was twilight now and peaceful. It would be so easy to go somewhere else, to drift away—

"I want to be here," I told him, shaking off any dissenting thoughts.

We walked into the Timber Lounge together. It was dark in there under the hanging ferns. I heard the Skeritts before I saw them.

". . . must decide if we leave tomorrow or not," a resonant voice was insisting. As my eyes adjusted to the light, I saw that it was Trent who was speaking. He was standing with the rest of the Skeritts near the bar, his hands clasped behind him, his trim body erect and dignified.

"But, Dad," Lori objected loudly. She waved a hand in his face as if to get his attention, jangling bracelets as she did. He glowered at her, making full use of his heavy Skeritt brows, but she went on anyway. "How will we know who killed Aunt Vesta if we leave? I don't think we'll really heal until—"

"I'm sure the proper authorities will notify us once they uncover the perpetrator's identity," he said crisply. "It's simply a matter of time."

"Two people dead," Ingrid whispered hoarsely. She shook her white head slowly. As tall as she was, she looked shrunken now. But then again, that was comparatively easy in the land of the giants.

"It's all part of the karmic plan, Mama," Lori explained enthusiastically. "We'll heal. We'll find out who did it ourselves—"

"But that's totally bogus," Eric interrupted shrilly. "How can we find out anything ourselves if we leave?"

Lori waved her hands in the air. "That's exactly what I mean!" she exclaimed.

"Grampy and I will stay," Eric offered eagerly. "Won't we, Grampy?"

Ace shrugged his massive shoulders, reminding me of Wayne once again.

"You know what?" the boy continued, bouncing on the balls of his feet. "I've been reading all these totally cool books about investigation techniques. All we have to do is like work as a team—"

"What if one of our team is the murderer?" Gail asked quietly.

No one seemed to have an answer to that one. Everyone just stood, stunned, as Gail and Eric stared at each other nose to nose, glasses to glasses.

"Hi, you guys!" I called out as if I hadn't heard any of the conversation.

Dru came out of her trance first.

"Well, hello there!" she called back, her voice high and taut. "Fancy meeting you here." She giggled at her own little joke. Bill toasted us silently with his everpresent glass.

I forced an answering smile onto my face as we walked over to the group.

Ace put his arm around Wayne's shoulders when we got there.

"Hey, kid," he greeted him. "Been trying to figure out how much longer we're staying." He looked down at the floor, then added, "If you don't mind a goofy old guy like me hanging around, I'd like some more time with the two of you."

Wayne didn't say anything. Ace pulled his arm away from Wayne's shoulders slowly.

"We'd love it," I said hastily.

Ace reached for my hand and pulled it to his lips, smacking loudly as he kissed it.

"Hooboy, forget Wayne," he suggested with a quick grin. "Just the two of us. Whaddaya say?"

I winked at him, conspiring to ignore his hurt feelings. I knew that it was Wayne he wanted to see, Wayne he loved. I stared at his homely clown's face. Was he really Wayne's father?

"Hey, Kate," Lori whispered in my ear. "Can I talk to you a minute?"

"Sure," I answered, turning away from Ace.

She jerked her head to indicate the other end of the dimly lit room. Her beaded earrings dangled musically as her head moved. She had changed into a new outfit since the funeral, pink stirrup pants and a paisley dashiki.

I followed her across the room obediently, past a harassed-looking waitress who was pushing tables together for our family group. I took a quick look around me. There didn't seem to be anybody else in the bar but the waitress and the Skeritts.

Lori waited until we had reached the safety of the furthest corner from the rest of the family before she spoke. And even then, she peered back over my head first.

"We had a visit today from your friend Felix," she whispered. Her brown eyes were wide as she gazed down at me.

"Oh, no," I muttered, shaking my head. "Did he talk to everyone?"

Lori nodded.

I groaned.

"Is he hideous or something?" Mandy asked from where she stood next to me. I started. I hadn't heard her footsteps.

"He *is* hideous," I answered gravely. "Worse than hideous."

Mandy giggled. Oh well, let her think I was kidding.

"Felix said you were very, very intuitive," Lori told me. "That you'd solved murders before." She lowered her voice again. "He said you'd probably solved these murders too, and just weren't telling. Is that true, Kate?"

I shook my head vehemently, inwardly damning Felix. What if he had told the murderer that?

Lori put her face very close to mine and looked into my eyes. I held my breath to keep from drowning in the scent of her sweet and spicy perfume.

"Really?" she asked.

"Really," I whispered back.

Lori was the first but not the last of the Skeritts who wished to speak with me privately. Gail shanghaied me as I walked back to the main group, whispering that she would be over later tonight to discuss suspects with me. I nodded agreeably. What fun. I'd make sure I was armed for the meeting.

Then Trent took my arm and led me in the opposite direction, asking if he could speak to me alone sometime before dinner. I resisted the urge to tell him to take a number, and accepted his invitation.

Dru was next. Only she didn't need any privacy.

"Your friend Felix told us you were quite the detective," she gushed. "So when are you going to solve our little murders for us?"

I took a leaf from Wayne's book and shrugged my shoulders enigmatically. I was even able to smile at her as I thought about throttling Felix the next time I saw him.

Bill leaned toward me, wafting alcohol.

"Death turns you on, huh?" he asked.

I was stunned. The man had finally spoken. Considering his words, I was just as glad he didn't do it more often.

I shrugged again, leaving off the smile this time.

Trent tapped me on the shoulder. I turned away from Bill and Dru gladly.

"Can we talk?" Trent asked quietly.

"Sure," I said. At least he didn't smell of alcohol.

"Perhaps it would be better if we went outside for a moment," Trent suggested.

I looked for Wayne and saw him with Ace, listening to the older man with a solemn expression on his face. I wouldn't interrupt them.

I nodded and followed Trent as he led the way out of the bar. It was dark outside now, even darker than it had been in the bar.

"I thought we could talk by the pool," Trent explained as he led me down the concrete stairs. For a moment, I thought I heard footsteps behind us, but I couldn't hear them when I stopped to listen. The hair prickled on the back of my neck. Maybe I shouldn't have come out here without Wayne. Especially alone with one of the suspects. But that was silly, I told myself. I was still within shouting distance. As least I thought so. And besides, everyone had seen me leave with Trent, hadn't they?

I felt cheered by the squat garden lamps sticking out of the concrete around the pool. They illuminated the whole area. There were three stone statues of dolphins poolside, and plants in cement containers between the lounge chairs. The Redwood Grove Inn probably wanted to discourage anyone from carrying the plants home. The pool water undulated, catching the light and reflecting it in hypnotic patterns. The sound of the water gently lapping against concrete echoed into the silence.

"So, what's up?" I asked Trent brusquely. It was too cold out here. I wanted to go back to the warmth of the bar.

"I have something to show you," he answered quietly.

He reached under one of the lounge chairs and pulled something out. It took me a moment to recognize that what he was holding in the lamplight was Harmony's wooden baseball bat.

"Where did you find it?" I breathed.

– Twenty-three –

But Trent didn't answer me. Instead he drew the bat back shoulder-high, like a batter at home plate ready to swing.

"No!" someone screamed.

Trent hesitated a second before following through.

I didn't stop to wonder who had screamed. I stepped backwards as fast as I could until I was at the edge of the swimming pool.

His swing was a good one. It would have knocked my head into the outfield if my head had stayed put.

"Damn you," he said quietly and strode forward, winding up to swing again.

I didn't wait for his follow-through. I turned and dived into the pool. God, it was cold! I just hoped I'd come up again. As I struggled silently upwards toward the surface, I could feel my clothes absorbing liquid, weighing me down like concrete. My Reeboks must have weighed at least ten pounds now. I was relieved to feel them touch ground. I was in the shallow end! I popped my head out of the water and sucked in air.

"No, Trent!" I heard over the echoes of my own breathing.

I looked up in time to see Trent throw the bat at me. I ducked. I didn't need to. The bat landed harmlessly beside me, disappearing in the water. Fingerprints, I thought. That bat was evidence! I turned to find it. It bobbed up obligingly, touching my shoulder. I reached out to grab it. Did water wash off fingerprints? Did it wash off blood?

Then I heard the sound of running footsteps. And the voice again, "You mustn't do this!"

I turned to the sound and saw Ingrid jogging toward Trent,

her white hair luminous in the lamplight. Trent picked up a dolphin statue and lifted it above his head.

"Mustn't I?" he hissed. "I have! And she knows. Her reporter friend told me. She knows!"

I abandoned the bat as I dove deep into the cold water. An instant later, I felt the shockwaves of the statue splashing down behind me. Damn. Trent must have believed Felix's claim that I knew who the murderer was. I cursed my ex-friend and swam blindly along the rim of the pool, bobbing up when I couldn't hold my breath anymore. My head was just above water, my wet clothing dragging me down. I grabbed at the concrete edge of the pool and held on tight.

". . . I killed my very own sister," Trent was saying. His voice was deep and steady, even calm. Only his face betrayed his feelings. His eyes were round, the whites gleaming around the brown irises as he scanned the water. His face didn't look like a college dean's anymore. It looked like a madman's.

"I carried the dried oleander leaves with me," he said softly. "Organically grown in my own garden." He giggled for a moment, then went on in an even, measured tone. "She was planning to blackmail me again. She wasn't just after money this time, she wanted to torture me. My sister was riddled with envy, of course. She hated my success. Initially, I thought I'd kill myself with the oleander, make her sorry. But why should I? She was the criminal. And when she drank her herbal tea the evening we arrived, I realized how easy it would be to slip the dried oleander into the mixture of herbs. No one else would drink that tea. Only she would die."

"Oh, Trent," Ingrid sobbed. "It *was* you."

He didn't seem to hear her as he went on.

"It took me until Friday to work up my resolve. When she said she was going to tell, it was as if she were asking me to kill her. She was going to tear down the very structure of my life. A man in my position has enemies, of course. Enemies who would destroy my success." He turned away and strode in the other direction, his delivery still clear but distracted. The absent-minded professor. "I've worked hard for my position. And of course, I couldn't allow her to tell Wayne."

I wanted to ask what it was he couldn't allow Vesta to tell Wayne, but I didn't have a chance. Trent picked up another statue and lifted it above his head. I dove once more as he threw it. I reversed course underwater, aiming for the far end of the pool where the ladder was. But I ran out of air before I could get that far.

". . . she was trying to drag me back down," Trent was saying as I surfaced again.

I stroked as hard as I could toward the other side of the pool. But my sodden clothes made the strokes a struggle. It was like swimming in quicksand. With audio.

"I pulled myself out of hell the hard way," Trent's voice continued behind me. "Years of working and smiling. A million smiles." He paused. Was he smiling there in the lamplight? "God, I hate to smile. And Vesta wanted to drag me back down into hell. No, I couldn't allow that."

The muscles in my arms and legs were burning with the effort when I finally made it to the other side of the pool. I clutched the concrete edge triumphantly and let myself breathe for a few moments. I could hear my gasps echo around the pool. But I was still a few yards away from the metal ladder. And Trent's voice was still pouring out behind me.

"I simply couldn't allow her to drag me back into hell," he said. "Surely, you must see that."

I wondered if he was talking to Ingrid or me as I pulled myself along the side of the pool, hand over hand. Or was he talking to himself?

"But why, Trent?" Ingrid cried, her voice filled with the emotion that was absent in his. "Why?"

"Wayne is my son," he answered quietly.

I lost my grip and sank beneath the surface. I struggled back up frantically, coughing up chlorinated water as I surfaced. I grabbed the concrete edge once more. Was Wayne Trent's son? I looked over my shoulder. Trent had turned to Ingrid. He was tall and muscular in the lamplight. He would be as muscular as Ace if he worked out. As muscular as Wayne. Was it true, then?

Ingrid stared at her husband, wide-eyed. Did she believe

him? I turned away and began pulling myself toward the ladder again, keeping my mind on the present.

"I was the eldest of the family," Trent explained. "My father beat me daily. My mother knit and read *Mein Kampf*. A charming woman." A bark of laughter punctuated his words. "There was no love, only cold hard discipline. They wouldn't even allow me to grow flowers in the garden. Their concept of gardening was to cut everything down to the ground and then poison it if it had the effrontery to grow again."

"But Vesta . . ." Ingrid faltered. "Wayne?"

"I didn't grow up!" Trent hissed. I was almost relieved to hear the momentary spurt of feeling in that hiss. But his voice was even again as he went on. "I survived my childhood. My love for Vesta was the only bright spot in an otherwise bleak landscape. I was seventeen. She was feminine then, almost beautiful. And she was sweet. Our love was a refuge for us both."

I touched the metal rail of the ladder gratefully.

"How old was Vesta?" Ingrid asked in a hoarse whisper.

"Fifteen, but she was a woman, I can assure you, she *chose* to be with me."

Poor Vesta. Only fifteen years old, and her innocence abused by the brother she must have loved and trusted. No wonder she had been so bitter. I felt a simultaneous surge of pity and forgiveness for Wayne's mother as I gripped the first rung on the ladder. Then I strained to haul myself up to the next rung. My water-logged clothes felt like a two-hundred-pound anchor, dragging me back down.

"I know there are those who would see our love as tawdry, who would label it 'incest,' but they would miss the beauty and sweetness." Trent paused. "My enemies would use it against me."

The wind hit me, chilling me to the bone as my shoulders came out of the water. Suddenly, I couldn't hear Trent speaking anymore. I swiveled my head around and saw him watching me from across the pool.

"I have to kill her," he said quietly.

He turned away from me to look behind him. Was he

looking for another weapon? I scrambled up the last rungs of the ladder clumsily. God. It was cold out here. But at least I was across the pool from Trent, safe for the time being. I stepped out onto the concrete and looked around me, dripping and shivering. The pool was surrounded by a tall fence. Could I climb that fence? The only other way out meant passing within yards of Trent.

"You told me *Ace* was Wayne's father," Ingrid accused, her voice loud and clear. Trent turned to her, momentarily distracted.

"Ace believed he was the father," Trent answered dismissively. "Good old Ace. He slept with her when I went away to college, but she dropped him the minute I came back that summer. She had only slept with Ace to make me jealous. She loved me! Me!" He pointed at himself like Tarzan as he raised his voice. Then he lowered it again. "Ace was always so gullible. Look at the eye color. Vesta and Ace both had blue eyes. How could their son have brown? And the timing: Ace didn't sleep with Vesta again after I got home. And the baby was born a year later. The fool. He never guessed I was the father."

He turned away from Ingrid, searching for me with his eyes again.

"Ace tells me he was foolish enough to tell Ms. Jasper that he was Wayne's father," he said just as his eyes found me.

"Was it you who sent Wayne on the wild-goose chase?" I asked him, keeping my tone as even as his. His eyes widened, showing whites again.

"Once Ace had told you he was Wayne's father, I knew it was only a matter of time before you thought of me," he said. "I had to protect myself. Only Wayne got back too soon—"

"Well, I *didn't* think of you," I interrupted him, incensed at the arrogance implicit in his paranoia. "Why should I? I only—"

I broke off when I saw he was no longer listening. He had turned and lifted a lounge chair above his head.

"It is far too late now," he told me and heaved the chair in my direction. It splashed down halfway across the pool.

"But why kill Vesta?" Ingrid asked from beside him.

"She was going to tell. She had threatened before, even while she was pregnant. But my money had kept her quiet. I was a father before I was twenty, going to college and working two part-time jobs to raise a son I could never acknowledge. She never stopped trying to drag me down. Never." He bent over one of the concrete planters and wrapped his arms around it, then tried to straighten up. But he couldn't. It was too heavy. He paused to catch his breath, then went on. "When Wayne went away to college, she finally cracked. I arranged for her to go to a mental hospital—"

"*You* put her in the hospital?" I demanded. True, I had heard Vesta accuse Trent of putting her away. But at the time I had thought it was just another one of her wild accusations.

"Yes, yes," he answered impatiently. "I had her committed and made sure she was on plenty of medication. . . ."

I shivered in the cold and thought of Wayne blaming himself for his mother's commitment and over-medication all these years.

". . . the minute she got out, she began with her demands again. We were to come to a family reunion, at her beck and call. I was to dance attendance or she would tell." He trotted toward the remaining stone statue. Ingrid followed him.

"Did you kill Vesta's friend too?" she asked.

"Of course," he replied, bending over the statue. "Harmony had stepped into Vesta's shoes as blackmailer. All of her talk about 'family secrets.' She knew." He paused as he lifted the statue. There was no way he could throw it far enough to hit me where I was. Didn't he realize that? Suddenly, I wasn't afraid of him anymore.

He set it back down again as if he'd heard my thoughts. He stared across the pool at me.

"I'm not a violent man, you know," he stated for the record.

"Well, you sure coulda fooled me," I muttered. It was easy to backtalk him while he was safely across the pool.

His brows lowered into a glare. Wayne's glare. He really was Wayne's father, I thought. A wave of nausea swept over me along with a spasm of renewed shivering.

"I kept the rest of the oleander. I mixed it with marijuana

from Lori's room and took it to Harmony as a house gift—"

"From Lori's—" Ingrid cried.

"Yes, Ingrid," he snapped at her. "Our daughter smokes marijuana. I will have to speak to her about it sometime."

He turned back to glare at me again. "Unfortunately, Harmony refused to smoke my little gift. But she put down her bat and turned her back to me. I took the opportunity she gave me. I took the bat and swung it." He closed his eyes and was quiet for a moment.

His voice was deep and trembling as he went on. "She began to turn toward me as I swung, and kept on turning even after the bat hit her head. Maybe she was already dead. I've heard that dead people keep on moving. I'm not a man accustomed to violence. I didn't know what to do. And then, she looked at me with those empty eyes." His shoulders slumped. "I lost control then. It was inexcusable, but I did. I swung the bat into her face. It hit her nose and blood spurted. She stumbled and I hit her again. Blood went everywhere as she spun around. I just kept swinging and hitting her. I couldn't seem to stop."

He opened his eyes again and pulled his shoulders back, clasping his hands behind him, in control once more. "But then she was no great loss, was she?" he added.

My eyes teared up in the cold. Harmony *was* a loss. I screamed inside. But I didn't scream aloud. I was afraid again. If not physically, then morally. This man was evil.

He kept his eyes on me as he began to walk clockwise around the pool. Ingrid reached for him. He batted her hand away impatiently.

"I have to kill her," he said again, his words as cold as my soggy clothes. "If you want to help me, Ingrid, I would appreciate it. But just don't hinder me."

"How about Clara?" Ingrid demanded.

She was trying to distract him, I realized. She had been all along. Trying to save my life.

"I kept the bat," he told her without turning. "Her door was unlocked. It was even ajar."

Had Clara left the door open for Wayne and me?

"I slipped in and hid behind a couch. When she came into

the room, I stepped behind her. She must have heard me. She cried out. I hit her with the bat before she could turn and see my face. But I didn't kill her."

"I know you tried to get her out of the state first," I said, keeping my tone as sympathetic as I could. "To Arizona—"

"Yes, yes," he interrupted. He kept walking around the pool. I began to circle clockwise too. He stopped for a moment.

"I had to do something about her. She knew. All her talk about genetics and eye color. She looked right at me and said a brown-eyed father and blue-eyed mother might give birth to a brown-eyed child. She knew I was Wayne's father. And she was going to tell everyone. She wanted me to lose respect. I'm a respected man, a dean. I couldn't risk it."

As we stared at each other across the pool, I remembered Lori telling me the murderer was a type three, a status seeker. Had she been thinking of her father then?

He began to circle the pool again. "Clara was whispering to you last night," he accused.

"But she didn't know!" I shouted angrily. God, what an ego this man had. An ego that had cost at least two lives. "She *told* me she didn't know who the murderer was. She was just making conversation with Eric."

He continued to circle. Had he even heard what I had said?

"Trent, stop this," Ingrid ordered, trailing behind him. Then she turned her head to look at me. "Can't you let it go, dear?" she begged. "No one else knows. Just us three."

I shook my head. Her body collapsed inward, as if I'd punched her. Damn. She had to know I couldn't let it go. Or was she as crazy as her husband?

"Trent, you have to stop this right now," she admonished him, using the voice you'd use with a child.

"So, you're against me now, too," he whispered.

"I'm not against you!" she shouted back. She stepped around in front of him. "I protected you. I was afraid it was you who killed Vesta, but I never said anything. I even tried to scare Kate off with a note in her purse."

I had forgotten about that note. What had it said? Something about letting sleeping dogs lie? Now I knew why the poor woman had been crying so much. Hard not to when you suspect your own husband of murder.

"But it's gone too far, Trent," Ingrid insisted, her voice stern. She straightened her spine. "You need help, professional help."

"I asked you to stay out of my way!" he hissed and slapped her with the back of his hand.

Ingrid went stumbling sideways as the sound of the slap echoed around the pool.

No, not a violent man.

He was walking faster around the pool now. He hadn't even glanced back at Ingrid where she sat crying on the concrete. I kept pace with him, keeping the pool between us. I sure hoped he wouldn't start running. I didn't know if I could outrun him in my sopping clothes. But did I need to outrun him? I looked at him again.

He was at least twenty years older than me. And he didn't have a weapon. Just rage. I shivered. Was I too water-logged for tai chi? In an instant, I knew I needed to shed the wet clothes. At least the shoes, if nothing else.

I bent down and quickly untied one shoe and kicked it off, then took a couple of uneven steps backward to make up for lost time. Trent was still stalking me and closer now. I bent over and untied the other shoe, keeping my eyes on him.

"Uncle Trent?" came a deep voice from the shadows.

I allowed myself a quick glance past Trent and saw Wayne come into the lamplight. But there was no time to acknowledge him. I kicked off my other shoe. Trent was almost to me, moving in long strides now, his eyes round and edged with white.

I was out of time.

I centered myself in a tai chi stance as Trent took a last stride toward me, his hands outstretched. When I felt his fingers touch my neck, I sank my weight into my back leg and turned away from him, raising my arm. When I turned back, my raised arm moved with me, sweeping away his hands. I sank back once more and then shifted my weight forward, bringing up both of my arms this time and pushing from my center. When my hands met his stiff torso, he toppled.

He toppled so easily that I thought it was a trick for a moment. But when I looked down I saw that Trent was just another crazy man, not unlike the patients I had cared for some twenty years ago in a mental health facility. He wasn't a dean anymore. He wasn't even someone who could scare me.

"Damn you," he cursed from the ground, but his voice had no more force. "Why couldn't you just leave me alone?" he whispered.

"Kate?" I heard.

I looked up and saw Wayne running toward us.

"It's all right!" I called out. "Everything's all right!"

But that didn't stop him from running. "Uncle Trent?" he asked as he reached us. I wasn't sure what he was asking. Or what he had heard. His brows were pulled too low over his eyes for me to see in.

Trent looked up at Wayne and began to sob.

"You were my son," he cried. "My son! And I couldn't tell you, couldn't touch you, couldn't even love you, because they might figure it out."

Wayne's face paled as Trent said the word "son."

But Trent kept on, unseeing. "They would have used it against me, you see. Everyone wants to drag me down——"

"Your son?" asked Wayne slowly. "You're saying you're my father?"

But Trent didn't seem to hear him. He put his head into his hands and whispered, "My enemies. You have no idea of the enemies I have!"

"You killed my mother," Wayne said, his voice low and trembling.

Trent looked back up at him. "I had to," he explained, sounding like the dean again. "I couldn't allow her——"

"You're no father of mine," Wayne told him.

I walked around Trent and put my hand into Wayne's. Together, we helped Ingrid up off the concrete and went inside to call the police.

– Twenty-four –

WAYNE KNELT TO lay a spray of white roses on his mother's grave. I pulled my eyes away from the roses and looked out over the cemetery, resisting the pressure of rising tears. Everything was so green here. I breathed in the scent of newly mowed grass. It smelled incongruously of life, of picnics and backyard parties and softball practice. I imagined Vesta having her birthday party here, her head thrown back laughing, happy and loved by her family. Why not? It was easier than imagining her at peace. Even in death, Vesta Caruso at peace just didn't seem credible.

Wayne closed his eyes and moved his lips silently as he stood again. Was he telling his mother that we'd found her murderer? That he loved her? That he understood and forgave her everything? This time I couldn't stop the flow of tears. I knuckled the moisture from my eyes and wondered how I could cry so much over a woman I had never even liked when she was alive.

Wayne turned to me, his eyes open again but barely visible. His lowered brows were visible, though, squeezed together into the same intense scowl he'd worn ever since we'd called the police the night before. He had stood guard over Trent wearing that scowl, talked with various members of La Risa's police department for hours wearing that scowl, and gotten up in the morning with that scowl. At least he didn't seem to be feeling suicidal. Not that I actually knew what he was feeling. I figured he was angry at the very minimum. But I wasn't sure of that. All I really knew was that he had stopped talking again.

"Would you like to be alone for a while, sweetie?" I asked him gently.

He shrugged his shoulders, scowling past me without blinking.

"Ingrid seems to be bearing up well," I said conversationally.

Wayne grunted.

He had grunted earlier this morning too when Ingrid had come to the house to offer a hoarse but abjectly sincere apology for Trent's behavior. How can you apologize for murder? Or for fatherhood? But I gave her points for trying. The gesture had obviously been hard for her. Lori had been there for support, her arm wrapped tightly around her mother's shoulders. And Mandy had been there too, wide-eyed and quiet, holding her grandmother's hand and stroking it. Three generations of Skeritt women, taking care of each other.

On the way out, Lori had whispered in my ear. A prominent criminal law attorney had been engaged to defend her father, one who specialized in the insanity plea. She was trying to forgive her father, she said. But she didn't know if she was ready. I didn't know if I was ready either.

I shook off the thought and brought my attention back to Wayne.

"At least Clara's going to be all right," I said, continuing my monologue. "All she had was a minor concussion. It was good to hear her voice on the phone—"

"He's my father," Wayne interrupted. I jumped in place, startled by his return to the land of the living and speaking. "He killed my mother," he added in a whisper.

"Oh, Wayne," I whispered back. I put my arms around him, but his body was stiff and unyielding. "It'll be better in time," I promised as I released him.

"No," he said. His head swayed back and forth in slow motion like a wounded bear's. "It won't be better. Glad now you refused to marry me. I'm tainted—"

"Stop that!" I exploded. His brows shot up and then he looked at me, really looked at me, his eyes in focus. I knew I should be kind now that I had his attention, gentle and understanding. But I couldn't seem to control myself. My ears were ringing with all the things I hadn't said in the last week.

"You are not tainted!" I shouted into his face. "I didn't want to marry you because I've been married before and it makes me nervous. It wasn't about *you*. It was about *me*! And I don't care who your parents were, you are not tainted. You are Wayne. And I love you, goddammit—"

"But look at the insanity, Kate," he insisted, his usually deep voice high now, almost shrill. "Both of my parents—"

"So what?" I interrupted. "It doesn't mean anything about *you*. *You* are still the same person, kind and loving and blaming yourself for every damn thing that goes wrong in the universe—" I paused mid-screed and lowered my voice, trying to remember what it was like to be reasonable. "It doesn't matter who your father is, Wayne. He was your father for forty-three years and you didn't know it. Are you any different now?"

"But Uncle Ace . . ." he began. He couldn't seem to finish. His gaze dropped again to the flowers on his mother's grave.

Trent Skeritt had told Wayne all about Ace's sexual relationship with Vesta the night before, as Wayne and I had stood guard over him, waiting for the police. Trent's tattling was a final act of betrayal I would find very hard to forgive. Because I was almost certain that Trent had poisoned Wayne's mind against Ace intentionally, jealous of Wayne's love for his younger brother. And I was even more certain that Wayne had been as hurt by the revelations about Ace as anything else he had heard from Trent last night. Trent hadn't been the surrogate father Wayne had loved and trusted through childhood. Ace had.

"Oh, sweetie," I murmured, my anger gone as fast as it had arrived, leaving me limp and tired. I heaved a long sigh, then made myself stand up straight. If I got depressed, where would that leave Wayne?

"Well, at least Judy and Jerry are reconciled," I told him with forced heartiness. "She got yet another dog at the pound yesterday. And Jerry has called off the divorce. So they're living together again, only now they have four dachshunds. Pretty funny, huh?"

Wayne didn't answer me. He was still staring down at his mother's grave. "Barbara and Felix are getting adjoining apartments," I added. Wayne lifted his head slowly, only to stare past me again.

"Listen," I said, knowing I was probably only talking to myself. "Maybe we could go on a little vacation—"

Wayne's head and shoulders jerked as if he'd received an electric shock. Was it something I said? He was still staring past me, but his eyes were focused again.

I looked over my shoulder. Ace Skeritt was a few yards away, walking toward us with an immense bunch of daisies in his hand and a tentative grin on his clown's face.

"Wayne," Ace called out softly.

Wayne didn't return his uncle's greeting. He only knit his brows together a little tighter.

"I'm sorry, kid," Ace whispered when he reached us. "Can you ever forgive—"

He turned his head away abruptly without finishing. I wondered why, until I heard the rasp of his sobs.

"I—" he began again, but he couldn't seem to finish.

Wayne's scowl loosened by a hair, the wrinkles between his brows softening ever so slightly as Ace sobbed. But still he didn't move to comfort his uncle. He didn't even speak.

After a little while, Ace coughed and cleared his throat.

"It's okay, kid," he growled, keeping his face averted. "You don't need any more of my crap to worry about. I just wanted to say goodbye is all."

He bent down and put his flowers next to Wayne's on Vesta's grave, then turned and walked away.

I peeked underneath Wayne's scowl and saw the glint of tears in his eyes.

"Uncle Ace!" I called out. Not that I had any idea what to say as a follow-up.

Ace turned back to us. He was no longer grinning. His wet face was a sad clown's now.

I looked at Wayne again, willing him to go to his uncle.

Wayne's hand rose slowly in front of him as if by levitation. I doubt if he even knew he was raising it.

But Ace didn't question the gesture. He strode forward and gripped that hand, then reeled Wayne into his arms. Now it was my turn to avert my eyes. The way they were hugging and crying and pounding each other's shoulders, I felt like an intruder peeking over the fence into a men's retreat.

I slunk off happily and found a stone bench to sit on. Wayne was going to be all right. When I closed my eyes, I could feel the warmth of the sun on my shoulders. I could even hear birds singing and the sound of distant traffic. Sleep tugged at me irresistibly, the sleep I hadn't had the night before. As I lay down flat on the stone bench, I told myself it wasn't a good idea to lie down in a graveyard. But I was asleep before I could remember exactly why it wasn't a good idea.

"I love you," someone whispered.

I opened my eyes and saw Wayne's battered face hovering above mine. His liquid brown eyes were visible and vulnerable under his heavy brows.

"Sorry I've been so distant," he said. "I know I wouldn't have found out what happened without you. And I'm sorry I didn't answer you before. Sorry I've been such a pain."

I opened my mouth to forgive him, but he wasn't finished yet.

"I *do* care about you," he went on earnestly. "And I *am* glad Clara is okay. And it *is* pretty funny about Judy and Jerry and the dachshunds. And I *would* love to go on a vacation with you. And . . ."

I lay there a few more moments letting the river of words wash over me. Then I sat bolt upright. Wayne was babbling! Wayne never babbled. Except when he was scared. Was he scared of losing me?

"Wayne?" I cut in when he stopped to take a breath. "Do you still want to marry me?"

His eyebrows rose in confusion. Then he nodded slowly. I reached for his hand.

"Will you marry me?" I asked formally.

"But . . . but why, Kate?" he asked back. "I'm not worth—"

"The answer is 'I do,' kid," came Ace's muttered prompt from behind.

"I do?" whispered Wayne.

Ace and I both groaned.

Wayne cleared his throat and tried again.

"I do!" he boomed, loud enough to wake the dead.

I took a quick look around me to make sure he hadn't. Then I stood to seal his acceptance with a kiss.